Praise for
Niobia Bryant
Books

"A well-crafted story with engaging secondary characters."
Affaire de Coeur, 4½ stars on *Admission of Love*

"*Heavenly Match* is a wonderfully romantic story with an air of mystery and suspense that draws the reader in, encouraging them to put aside everything and everyone until they have read the book in its entirety."
RAWSISTAZ Reviewers on *Heavenly Match*

"'Sexy as sin'" describes this provocative novel to a T."
Romantic Times, 4½ stars, TOP PICK on *Can't Get Next to You*

"Run to the bookstore and pick up this delightful read. This reunion story is touching, warm, sensuous, and at times, sad. But just try to put Bryant's book down."
Romantic Times, 4½ stars, TOP PICK on *Let's Do it Again*

"Niobia Bryant has penned an awe-inspiring tale of finding true love no matter the consequence. Thoroughly enjoyed and highly recommend, *Heated* is sure to please."
RAWSISTAZ Reviewers on *Heated*

"In Bryant's first mainstream fiction offering, she does a great job of bringing forth characters th_____ ____rse and interesting . . . _____ _____ar-acters. *Live and Le_____ ___ ___ ___e.*"
Romantic Times

"Bryant reintroduce_____ _____n her latest novel, whi____ _____arks: hot men, spicy women and a sexually captivating story."
Romantic Times on *Hot Like Fire*

BOOKS BY NIOBIA BRYANT

Romance
Admission of Love * +
Three Times a Lady #
Heavenly Match * +
Can't Get Next to You < >
Let's Do it Again
Count on This < >
Heated + §
Hot Like Fire + §
Make You Mine #

Mainstream/Women's Fiction (Trade)
Live and Learn ~
Show and Tell ~

Mainstream/Urban Fiction (as Meesha Mink)
Desperate Hoodwives
Shameless Hoodwives

Anthologies

You Never Know/*Could It Be?* (novella)
CARAMEL FLAVA/*Den of Pleasure* (short story)

KEY

* Connected books
# Connected books
+ Books set in Holtsville, SC (Hot Holtsville series)
< > Connected books (The Dutton Sisters series)
§ Connected books (The Strong Family series)
~ Connected books

Make You Mine

NIOBIA BRYANT

Kensington Publishing Corp.

http://www.kensingtonbooks.com

DAFINA BOOKS are published by

Kensington Publishing Corp.
119 West 40th Street
New York, NY 10018

All Kensington Titles, Imprints, and Distributed Lines are
available at special quantity discounts for bulk purchases for
sales promotions, premiums, fund-raising, and educational
or institutional use. Special book excerpts or customized
printings can also be created to fit specific needs. For details, write or phone the office of the Kensington special
sales manager: Kensington Publishing Corp., 119 West 40th
Street, New York, NY 10018, attn: Special Sales Department, Phone: 1-800-221-2647.

Dafina and the Dafina logo Reg. U.S. Pat. & TM Off.

ISBN-13: 978-0-7582-3141-3
ISBN-10: 0-7582-3141-5

First Dafina mass market printing: May 2009

10 9 8 7 6 5 4 3 2 1

Printed in the United States of America

For you, Mama.

I hope it lives up to everything you thought it could be.

Prologue

Tamara Lawson snuggled down deeper in the spot on the sofa where she lay cuddled against her husband's strong side. "This is nice," she sighed, resting her hand on his strong muscled thigh.

"Yeah," Kendrick answered, letting his own hand caress her hip as they watched their favorite movie, *Love Jones*, on the wide-screen television in their living room.

"Everyone should be this happy."

Kendrick stiffened; his internal alarms immediately rang like a fire drill.

Tamara slipped her hand beneath her husband's T-shirt, rubbing his muscled chest in the slow, circular motion that she knew he loved. "Caress and Julius should be this happy."

"Tam-Tam," he warned, knowing exactly which direction the conversation was headed. It was a road well traveled for them. "Baby, please. Let's not go there, like you tell me all the time."

"What?" she asked innocently, as she sat up to look at him. "Caress and Julius are both single. Caress isn't seeing anyone now, and Julius isn't in a serious relationship. I think they'd make a cute couple—"

Kendrick used his hand to pull his wife back toward him and lightly tapped her hand on his chest to remind her that she had stopped the massaging. "Problem is, Tam-Tam, you're the only one who thinks so. Caress has begged you, Julius has bribed you, and now I'm asking you: stop trying to hook them up."

Tamara sighed as she settled back against his warmth and continued her rubbing of his chest. "A'ight, Kendrick."

He moaned in pleasure at the feel of her hands, letting his head fall back on the couch. "Promise?"

Secretly, Tamara crossed her toes. "Of course I promise, baby."

Chapter One

"Six hundred and ten . . . twenty . . . thirty . . . fifty . . . and seventy. Damn."

Caress Coleman looked down at her life savings, frustrated that no matter how many times she counted the money that was pitifully stacked on her small dinette table the sum would remain the same: six hundred seventy dollars. Oh, and fifty-three cents.

Big damn deal.

Caress dropped her head in her hand and reassessed the scenario.

Yesterday had been her last day as the administrative assistant for Sanctuary, a non-profit drug abuse shelter. Last week her boss informed her that the organization's grant funding her administrative position would not be renewed. Without the grant money, the funds were not available to pay Caress's salary.

Well, since she was laid off she of course went to file for unemployment benefits. Well, surprise surprise. She qualified for benefits, but the weekly check amount wasn't going to be enough to cover her bills. Not nearly enough.

"Think, Caress . . . think," she ordered herself, eyeing

first the stack of money and then the notepad listing all of her bills for the month. Usually she would split the payments in two, but living check to check would soon catch up to her without the next check to rely on.

She was going to have to rob Peter to pay Paul.

"Damn it," Caress swore again. She had been counting on unemployment benefits to tide her over until she found another job.

Caress was definitely feeling the unrelenting pressure of being stuck between a rock and a hard place. "Why didn't I carry my butt to college?" she asked herself aloud, just as someone rang her doorbell.

Caress folded the money into the side pocket of her purse and scooped up the change to toss in as well.

"Coming," she yelled out, leaving the tiny kitchenette of her studio apartment to make her way to the front door.

"Who?" Caress lifted up on her toes to peer out the peephole with one slanted ebony eye.

"Girl, it's Tamara. Open up this door with your scary self."

Caress smiled at the sight of her best friend, Tamara, childishly sticking out her tongue. Dropping back down on the soles of her size six feet, she stepped back to open the metal door. "What's up, girl?"

"Nothing much." Tamara breezed into the small studio like sunshine. "What happened with your unemployment?"

Caress followed Tamara to the second-hand leather sofa bed in the middle of the studio. "What I'm supposed to get ain't nearly enough to keep me afloat."

"What?" Tamara shrieked, dropping her small leather purse on the coffee table.

Caress leaned her petite frame back against the sofa. "That's exactly what I said."

The two friends fell silent, both lost in their thoughts. Caress and Tamara had been good friends for the past few years. They met when Tamara moved into the studio apartment next door. Even though they were as different as night and day, they immediately clicked. If anything, their differences seemed to draw them closer. While Tamara was loud, carefree, and friendly, Caress was more reserved and quiet, preferring to be seen rather than heard. Even when Tamara met and married Kendrick, moving into his one-bedroom apartment across town, the two women had remained thick as thieves.

"Caress, you know I'd help . . ."

Caress waved away any attempts Tamara made at offering her money. "You and Kendrick have bills of your own. I'll be all right, so don't offer because I won't take it."

Tamara knew that Caress's independence was a positive and negative trait. Growing up alone within the foster care system since she was two, Caress had learned early to fend for herself and depend on no one. But Tamara was her friend, and although she couldn't afford to spare much, she would gladly give Caress something if she'd just take it.

Knowing the direct approach wouldn't work, Tamara wisely changed the subject. "Let's go to the movies or something," she offered, reaching for the folded newspaper atop the coffee table.

"Sorry, but I'm not in the mood to roll third wheel."

Tamara snapped the paper open, casting a slick glance in Caress's direction from the corner of her eye. "We could double."

Caress looked to the heavens. "Does this Julius have any idea how much of a fan he has in you?" she asked sarcastically, already knowing exactly who her friend wanted her to date. "Ever since I finally kicked Bobby to the curb a few months ago, you've been trying to hook me up with this mysterious Julius."

For two years Bobby whirled through Caress's life, leaving her fifteen thousand dollars in debt because she was foolish enough to co-sign for his car and credit cards. She had finally told his part-time-working, no-time bill-paying behind to get out of her life. That had been her last foolish attempt at love and she wasn't about to grab a flashlight and go out looking for more.

Tamara opened the newspaper. "All I'm saying is that you're both single with a lot in common."

"Like what?" Caress asked pointedly, fixing her piercing ebony eyes on Tamara.

Tamara feigned extra interest in the newspaper. "Like, uhm, uhm—"

"Yeah, I thought so."

"It's just a date, Caress, something to take your mind off your troubles for one night."

True, if she didn't occupy herself she would stress about her situation all night long. It was amazing just how much your eyes stayed glued to the ceiling at night when you were contemplating unpaid bills. Although she could definitely use a diversion, Caress looked doubtful. "I don't know, Tam-Tam."

"Come on, girl. It'll be just four friends hanging out." Tamara smiled and nudged Caress with her shoulder. "It's just one night. What's the worst that could happen?"

Caress shot her best friend a withering look.

"Smile for me, baby. Think of your man, your mama, or those shoes you saw at the mall."

The nude svelte model did just as Julius Jones commanded. If she supplied the look, he would supply top rate photos. He was one of the top photographers in the tri-state area. Between his freelance work for some of the most elite fashion and beauty magazines in the country, he had an impressive list of clientele clamoring to come to his Jersey City, New Jersey, studio for their head shots or family photos.

"One more, Karina," Julius said loudly, his eye gazing at her through the lens before he rapidly snapped several more shots. "Okay, that should do it."

Julius handed the camera to his assistant who liked to be called Boo. Julius would only address him by his given name of Dwayne. There was no way he was going to call a grown man Boo, especially one who was so openly gay that Julius wondered if Dwayne was a cross-dresser in his spare time. Either way Julius didn't care. The only thing that mattered to him was Dwayne's skill with a camera and his ability to do the job as his assistant, and the man was excellent at both. Julius had no complaints. They were cool.

Julius walked across the length of the converted warehouse he used as his office and studio. At his desk he picked up some proofs to sort through. Suddenly the hairs on the back of his neck stood on end.

"I can't wait to see the finished photos, Julius."

He turned his head to find Karina closing the chocolate leather curtain that blocked his office off from the rest of the lengthy studio. The up-and-coming supermodel looked willow and beautiful in a short silk kimono that did absolutely nothing to hide the fact that she was nude beneath it. Funny how the sight of taut nipples pressing against the thin silk was more erotic to him than seeing her completely nude.

With a warmth in his eyes that could rival a fire, Julius gave her a long, leisurely look that was filled with intent. "I just hope I do you justice."

Karina took a bold step toward him, lifting her hand to

caress the ever-present stubble on his cheek. "I just hope I'm able to do you."

"Hey, Jules," his assistant called through the curtain.

"Dwayne," he threatened at Dwayne's use of the nickname Tamara gave him. He never once looked away from Karina as she sucked leisurely on her index finger in a decidedly provocative move.

"Oops! 'Cuse me, *Julius*, telephone."

He just shook his head. "Hold that thought," Julius told her.

Karina laughed huskily, pulling her finger from her mouth to outline his full bottom lip. "That's not all I'll hold."

He leaned past her to pick up the cordless phone on his desk, the ringer of which had been shut off. "Julius Jones here."

"Hello there, Julius Jones. Tamara Lawson here."

"What's up Tam-Tam?" he asked, keeping his eyes on Karina as she draped herself across the top of his neatly organized desk.

"Favor."

"What?"

"Double date. Kendrick, you, me and—"

"Let me guess . . . Caress, right?" Julius drawled, as Karina began the foreplay without him.

"Yes. Look, she got laid off and I thought a night out with some friends would lift her spirits. You game?"

Julius pulled a chair over and sat down to watch Karina's show, automatically straightening the crease of his black slacks.

"Jules?"

"Huh . . . what?" he asked, distracted as Karina played in the soft, moist folds of her feminine core.

"Look, you owe me."

"Not tonight, Tamara," he told her sternly. "Besides,

I have to finish packing. You know I leave for Africa in the morning."

"As anal as you are?" Tamara mocked, with a laugh. "You've probably been packed since last week."

She was right. "Look, I just can't tonight. Trust me on this."

"Jules."

"No, definitely not tonight," he insisted, as Karina began to purr like a kitten being stroked.

"Jules."

"Tamara, not—"

"Julius," she finished softly.

He massaged his five o'clock shadow, which he kept neat and taped up with a weekly trip to his barber. He always rubbed his beard when he had a choice to make. A sure thing with Karina or a mercy date with Tamara's unemployed friend.

"Stop rubbing that sorry beard and say something, Jules."

He laughed softly at her astuteness. They'd been friends since college and she knew him well . . . too well. "This is one helluva favor you're calling in. You . . . just . . . don't . . . know."

Karina trembled and purred softly with her own climax, boldly looking him in his eyes as she did. Julius swallowed over a lump in his throat. "Oh, you owe me . . . *big* time."

Frustrated, Caress yanked the shirt over her head and threw it on the open sofa bed with the rest of her discarded garments. For the past thirty minutes she had struggled with what to wear. Not that she was trying to impress Mr. Julius Jones, photographer extraordinaire. She just liked to look her best at all times.

Clad only in a denim skirt and her lace bra, Caress surveyed her slim wardrobe. Even when she was working she didn't have much money to buy new clothes the way she wanted, but she tried to buy a few nice pieces that could be switched up.

Caress turned and studied her reflection in the full-length mirror hanging on the inside of the closet door. She absolutely hated the odd shape of her body. She wished her breasts were more the size of cantaloupes than plums. Some might say more than a mouthful was a waste, but Caress could only laugh at that. She definitely wanted to graduate out of the itty-bitty-titty committee, especially with her wide hips, shapely legs, and full bottom. She caught all kinds of hell trying to buy a two-piece outfit when her top was a size medium and her bottom a large.

Stepping closer to the mirror, Caress leaned in to study her face. A lot of people likened her to Jennifer Lopez, but she didn't see the resemblance. Sure, they both had classic Latin features and long straight dark hair, but Caress was only half Latina while J.Lo was a full-blooded Puerto Rican. Caress's skin tone was definitely darker, and her hair had to be permed to maintain its polished straightness, both testaments to the African-American part of her heritage.

And it was a heritage she wanted to know more about.

She let her eyes drift across the studio apartment to the picture frame holding all the history she had in the world. It was a shame.

If not for the faded photograph of a Latin man and a Black woman stuck in her meager belongings when she was carried to Child Protective Services as a toddler, Caress wouldn't even know she was mixed. Her mother died when she was two. With no other family available to take her in, she became a child of foster care. Unfortunately that's all she knew of her lineage. Was her Latin side

Cuban, Puerto Rican, Dominican, or maybe Mexican? Was her Black side Jamaican, African, or American?

Questions and more questions.

Growing up without a past does that for a person.

Brushing off her sadness, Caress turned and reached into the pile of clothes on the bed for the long-sleeved V-neck shirt she discarded earlier. She pulled on the fitted top and then reached into her small closet for her black knee-length boots—it was a cool October night and the boots should be fine. "Not bad for thirty bucks," Caress told herself, as she sat down on the sofa bed to pull them on. "Not bad at all."

The entire outfit, including the boots, came from K-Mart, and if she didn't tell, no one would know it. Caress was glad for discount chains because she couldn't afford much else.

She decided to let her hair hang freely around her shoulders and put on only some peach-tinted lip gloss with a little blush. A few precious drops of her DKNY perfume and Caress was ready to rock and roll.

Glancing at the clock, she saw that she had some time before Tamara and Kendrick were supposed to pick her up. She grabbed the newspaper and opened it to the classifieds. She circled those jobs she wanted to apply for; drew a square around the ones she would settle for; and placed a big X through the ads she wouldn't even dare consider—like "DANCERS WANTED FOR BIG $$$$."

Caress snorted. "Hell, my breasts aren't big enough anyway."

She was just going over the revisions to her resume when her doorbell rang. Her ebony eyes darted to the door. She didn't know why, but she suddenly felt nervous. As she gathered her purse and her house keys, Caress thought, *If he smells like onions or has breath like a pooch, I'm going to kill Tamara.*

* * *

Julius stepped out of his enclosed frosted glass tub shower and reached for one of the neatly folded ivory-and-gold towels on the wooden shelves above the toilet. The scent of his soap mingled with the steam as he used his hand to wipe the condensation from the oversized square mirror over the pedestal sink.

A past lady friend once told him that his house looked like either a photograph in a home-design magazine or a hotel suite. Julius took much pride in that fact. He couldn't be comfortable in his home unless it was neat and orderly. A lot of people thought he had a maid service come in, but Julius took on the task himself at least once a week.

It was all so different from the small, cramped two-bedroom apartment where he was raised. *Everything about my life is different from back then*, he thought, before purposefully pushing the sadness of his past away.

As he brushed his teeth he thought with some dread of the night ahead. Tamara was throwing her friend on him like a shady car salesman trying to push a lemon on a dupe. If she was such a perfect woman, why didn't she have a man or at least a friend with benefits? Lord knows, if he looked into Caress's face and she resembled the character Sheneneh from *Martin*, he was going to freak out.

Turning around he looked down at the three-tiered metal shelf holding all of his colognes: nearly twenty different varieties. He splashed on the Joop!, rolled on his deodorant, and then let the plush Egyptian towel fall from his slender waist. Immediately, he bent to scoop it from the floor to place in the linen hamper. He took one last glance around the bathroom to make sure everything was in order before he strode nude into his bedroom. Passing his king-sized mahogany sleigh bed, Julius entered his walk-in closet. He flipped the switch to flood it with light.

When he first bought his home, he had the bedroom nearest the master suite converted to a walk-in closet. That left him with just one additional bedroom, but Julius thought it was well worth the sacrifice.

Here—like everywhere else in his home—was the same neat, organized, and polished decor. Everything had a place, and as far he was concerned everything belonged in its place. Tamara teased him all the time because it resembled a retail store.

Pulling open a drawer in the island located in the center of the closet, Julius extracted a folded pair of silk boxers from his selection of nearly fifty. He loved the feel of the cool material against his skin as he went throughout his day. He could never adjust to the tight, restraining feel of briefs, especially after he read they could reduce sperm production.

Not that he wanted kids anytime soon. One day . . . just definitely not right now. Without the entanglements of a wife, steady girlfriend, or children, he could travel on a whim for work or play. Tomorrow he was leaving for a three-month trip to Africa where he would take pictures for his first photography book, *My Africa*.

He enjoyed his freedom.

Julius surveyed his slacks all hung on wooden hangers and organized by color and season. He eventually selected a pair made of charcoal linen. Next he opened his sock drawer in the island and selected one of the thirty folded pairs before moving to the cedar shelves where he kept all of his sweaters neatly folded. He chose a black V-neck. Lastly, he turned to the opposite wall where all his shoes sat neatly aligned on shelves and selected his newest pair of black Kenneth Coles.

Within minutes he was dressed and checking out his

appearance in the mirror lining the west wall of the closet. He looked good, and he knew it. His appearance was very important to him. He liked to be polished and well-groomed at all times.

Before leaving his bedroom he effortlessly smoothed a dimple in his plush mocha comforter. He caught sight of his two extra large hard suitcases sitting on a pair of luggage caddies by the door. "This date better wrap up early," he said, just as his doorbell rang.

"Caress, this is Julius. Julius . . . Caress."

Caress's eyebrows raised an inch in surprise and pleasure at the man who stood before her in his living room. Mister Julius Jones was fine. His jet black fade and a trimmed beard made his amazing eyes appear even more vibrant and alive in his lean handsome face. His features were keen and attractive. His tall-and-slender build was to Caress's liking because she definitely wasn't into beefcake. And the clothes he wore fit his frame nicely, with ease and lots of style.

When she looked up into his eyes, her heart double pumped so hard in her chest that she was sure it could be seen through her shirt. Then he smiled down at her and she actually lost her breath.

Julius did a double take when he first laid eyes on Caress. The woman was stunningly beautiful and so obviously sexy that he wanted her stretched naked across his bed right then. She was as stylish as he and her petite size made him want to pick her up and cuddle her to his chest.

"Damn," he mumbled, rubbing his hand over his beard to wipe away the smile of pure, unadulterated pleasure.

* * *

Tamara took it all in with gleeful eyes. It would be hard to miss how pleased they both were . . . so far. Nudging her husband, Tamara's voice was filled with satisfaction when she said, "See, I told you so."

Chapter Two

They all left the movie theater, laughing and talking comfortably. The romantic comedy had put them all at ease, and it was a wonderful start to their double date.

"All right y'all, I'm hungry," Tamara offered first, interrupting the group's laughter about a funny scene in the movie.

"Food sounds good to me," Caress chimed in, hoping no one could hear her stomach growling.

Kendrick used his muscular arm to pull his wife to his side. "How 'bout Mahogany's?"

Julius, who towered over the petite beauty by nearly a foot, looked down at her. "That's cool with me. You?" he asked.

Caress nodded, feeling heated by the look in Julius's eyes and she felt her cheeks and nape warm. *Damn, this man makes me breathless*, she thought in amazement.

As they all walked to the parking lot of the movie theater, Caress liked being by Julius's side as she inhaled the faint scent of his cologne and enjoyed the warmth of their arms casually brushing. Even with the slightly cool winds of the fall evening she immediately felt heat infuse her body. Her nipples hardened into tight aching buds and Caress crossed her arms over her chest to hide that fact.

"Cold?" Julius asked, his voice deep and warm like a hot toddy. "I have a jacket in my car that you can use."

Cold? Hell, I'm hot! she thought. "No, I'm fine, but thanks."

"I still don't understand the need for different cars," Kendrick said to Tamara, as he used his remote to deactivate the alarm on their silver Honda Accord.

Tamara shot her husband an exasperated look. "Just get in the car, Kendrick."

Julius laughed low in his throat as he also deactivated his vehicle alarm. He moved with ease to open the passenger door of his green Range Rover for Caress.

Caress smiled her thanks to him as he waited until she was comfortably seated to close the door behind her. As he jogged back around to the driver's door, she followed him with her eyes—absorbing him.

"Buckle up," Julius said, smiling over at her as the car started with a purr. Soon he followed Kendrick and Tamara's Honda out onto the street.

"So you're a photographer?" Caress asked, as she crossed the three-point harness belt over her chest and lap.

He nodded. "Ever since I was a kid. I've always been fascinated by what moments in time you can capture—and keep forever—with a photo. Especially a well-taken one."

"Tamara says you've photographed some really beautiful women, some even in the nude. Must be a lot of . . . fun."

"I'd like to photograph you actually," he said, pulling behind Kendrick at the red light.

"Not in the nude," Caress quickly balked, even as she pictured herself so easily stripping down to nothing in front of him.

Julius turned his head to give her a leisurely once over. "Pity."

Caress flushed and the bud between her legs jumped to attention. Her heart raced.

"Please, if you've seen one set of T & A, you've seen them all," she teased, squirming a little in her seat under his direct and piercing gaze.

"I doubt that."

As the foursome walked into the restaurant's renovated brick building, Julius placed his hand at the small of Caress's back wanting to touch her. "Have you eaten here before?" he asked, as the hostess led them to the bar to await a table in the dining area.

Caress shook her head side to side to indicate she hadn't as she took in the interior of the two-level structure for the first time.

The contemporary décor was in hues of deep mahogany with rich blue-and-gold accents that were perfectly accentuated by the bright African sculptures and artwork adorning the brick walls.

"I've heard about it, of course, but I've never been," she told him, as she swayed on the barstool to the soft, sultry music filling the air from the live band playing on the stage at the front of the restaurant.

"Welcome everyone. Julius."

The foursome all turned to find a stunningly beautiful woman standing behind them with a beguiling and warm smile.

Julius didn't miss Caress's eyes darting between him and the woman. "Hello, Mahogany. What's special on the menu tonight?" he asked, before taking a sip of his Crown Royal and Coke.

"Roast lamb, grilled salmon, and of course, the jambalaya."

Tamara cleared her throat.

"Oh, I'm sorry. Caress, Tamara, and Kendrick this is Mahogany Woods, the owner of this fine establishment. Mahogany, this is Caress, my date, Kendrick, one of my best friends, and Tamara, my headache."

That earned him a pinch from Tam-Tam.

Mahogany smiled. "It's wonderful to meet you all. Julius, a pleasure as always. Enjoy your meal."

With that she was gone.

"She's gorgeous!" Tamara exclaimed, turning in her seat to face the bar.

"You got that right. Damn, she's—" Kendrick began.

Tamara's right eyebrow shot up and the rest of her husband's words evaporated like steam.

"So I guess you're a regular here, huh?" Caress asked, as she picked up her glass of white wine from the napkin embossed with the word Mahogany.

Julius looked over at her and felt a desire to push aside her long and fine hair to suckle the long line of her elegant neck. "I've never slept with Mahogany, Caress," he told her, surprised by his candor since he owed her no explanations on his life—past or present.

Caress took a deep sip of the liquid. "I never asked if you did."

He just laughed low into his drink, not believing for a second that the thought hadn't crossed her mind.

Their hostess appeared with menus in her hand. "Your table's ready. Right this way."

Caress and Julius picked up their drinks and followed the hostess across the hardwood dance floor to the wrought iron staircase leading to the stylish and hip dining area upstairs.

Julius smiled devilishly at the delectable sight of Caress's curvaceous bottom as he climbed the stairs behind her. Although he too thought she favored J.Lo, Ms. Lopez had nothing on Caress. *I really need to thank Tamara.*

Julius slid into the booth next to Caress. "I'm starving," he said, letting his thigh brush intimately against hers. He picked up the leather-bound menu in front of him.

Caress leaned in close to point at his menu. "I'll have the Caesar salad with grilled chicken and pine nuts. Right . . . here."

Her sweet scent wafted up to him, clouding his senses, as the touch of her breasts against his arm aroused him with an intensity. Clearing his throat, Julius signaled for their waitress. "I feel like steak myself."

When the waitress promptly appeared at the table, Julius ordered Caress's meal the way she requested and then ordered a T-bone well-done with mushrooms and shallots. He also requested a Heineken with his meal.

"I'll have a margarita," Caress said.

"Me too," Tamara added.

Kendrick smiled cockily at his wife. "You know what alcohol does to you."

Tamara rubbed her hand up his strong thigh to lightly stroke his member. "Problem?"

Julius winked at Kendrick, before turning to Caress with a questioning look in his eyes.

"Don't even go there," she said, blushing.

They all just laughed.

Caress was feeling the effects of the tequila in her drink by the end of her delicious meal. "I want to dance," she said suddenly, following yet another impulse.

Julius was in the restroom. Tamara and Kendrick were

so deep into each other that neither noticed when Caress left the table. Her feet guided her down the stairs and onto the crowded dance floor as the band began a jazz rendition of Mary J. Blige's classic rendition of "I'm Going Down." She found her own little space on the dance floor, closed her eyes, and let the rhythm of the music instinctively move her hips and feet.

Julius wanted Caress. She was beautiful, sexy, vibrant, and funny. Her touch gave him goose bumps. Her smile made his heart skip a beat.

At that moment, as he stood on a mini-balcony and looked down at her move with such abandon on the dance floor, he knew he wanted to bury himself inside her moist warmth. He wanted her grinding with him in the same fashion as she danced until their bodies were drenched with sweat and then spent.

Not once taking his eyes off of her, Julius descended the stairs slowly and crossed the dance floor to stand behind her. He grasped her wide hips with eager hands and began to rock his body with hers, enjoying the feel of her bottom cushioned against him.

Caress knew it was Julius as soon as his hands touched her. She already recognized his heat and his scent. With a soft smile she turned to face him, reaching up to wrap her arms around his neck and press her body close enough to feel the heat of his loins.

"Damn, I want you," he whispered in her ear as he nuzzled her neck with his lips.

Caress laughed softly and grinded close to his

lengthening erection. "I want you too," she whispered back with honesty.

"Oh, you do?" he moaned deep in his throat.

Tilting her head back, she looked up into his eyes with want and wild abandon. "Kiss me, Julius," she demanded softly.

He lowered his head to honor her request right there in the middle of the dance floor.

Caress sucked deeply on Julius's tongue with a lazy, satisfied moan, before ending the kiss with another touch of her lips to his. "You got me so hot."

"Do you feel how hard I am?" Julius countered, pressing the full length of his erection into her stomach with a wicked grin.

"Ahem."

They both turned their heads to see Tamara and Kendrick standing beside them. They had been so caught up in their heat that they hadn't even noticed them walk up.

"I hate to interrupt when y'all are having such a . . . ahem, good time, but it's getting late," Tamara told them with a knowing and satisfied smile.

Both Julius and Caress waved them good-bye in an animated fashion.

Tamara pretended to look offended.

Kendrick stepped forward, obviously taking control. "Good night, Caress. Julius, you take care on your trip man."

Trip? Caress thought, as Julius released her to shake hands with Kendrick.

"Caress—" Tamara began.

Kendrick grabbed his wife's hand and pulled her behind him. "Say good night, Tam-Tam," he called over his shoulder even as he continued to pull her toward the door.

"Safe trip, Jules. Call me, girl," Tamara shouted over the music, before she disappeared into the crowd.

Julius pulled Caress's petite frame back into his arms. "Where were we?" he asked, tasting her lips.

Caress forgot everything but his heated kisses.

Julius pulled the Range Rover to a stop in front of the brick duplex Caress pointed out. His fingers were entwined with hers in her lap, and he liked how it felt. "You're home, safe and sound."

"Yeah," she said softly, her body relaxed against the leather seat.

They both sat, not moving. He wondered if she was as reluctant as he was for the night to end. The seconds ticked into minutes as time sped by too quickly.

"Guess I better go in," Caress said in a reluctant voice barely above a whisper.

Julius raised her hand to kiss the back before he climbed out of the vehicle and came around to open the passenger door. Holding out his hand, he smiled down at her beauty. "I'll walk you to your door."

Accepting his hand, she looked up into his handsome bearded face and gave him a smile that was meant to beguile. "Thanks."

Together they walked up the brick path. She led him down the stairs to her basement studio apartment. "This is me," she told him softly, as she dug in her purse for her keys.

Julius took them from her and unlocked the door. "Here you go," he said, placing them back in her hand.

"Thanks."

"It was nice to finally meet you, Caress."

She smiled, licking suddenly dry lips, as he stepped closer to her and lowered his head. "And it was nice finally meeting you," she whispered, just before his lips pressed sweetly but firmly against hers.

They both moaned at the pure pleasure of it.

She caressed his low beard, wanting more . . . much more as she looked into those beautiful eyes of his. But she said, "Bye."

"Good-bye, Caress," Julius murmured against her lips. He turned with reluctance and climbed the steps with a final wave back at her.

"Julius!" she called out suddenly, following an impulse she couldn't fight off for the life of her.

He turned back, moving down one step to look at her. "Yes?"

Taking a deep breath, she said, "Don't go."

Their trail of clothing led a path straight to the sofa. Caress straddled Julius's narrow hips in nothing but her matching peach lace bra and panties. His hands massaged her full bottom, pressing her heated flesh closer to his erection bulging through his silk boxers.

They couldn't keep their hands off of one another.

His coal black eyes feasted on her breasts as her hardened nipples strained against the flimsy lace. His mouth watered. Nearly growling, Julius lowered his head to suck deeply on the tempting bud through the material.

Sparks of electricity shot through every inch of her body. "Suck harder," Caress demanded hotly, her back arching for more, as she flung her head back.

"Like this?" he asked huskily, nearly sucking all of her plum-sized breast into his eager mouth.

Caress gasped.

Not wanting the lacy barrier, Julius's hands rose, caressing her soft skin as he easily unlatched her bra and flung it away. "God, they're beautiful," he whispered hoarsely with truth, drinking in the sight of her small round breasts peeking through the soft strands of her hair.

Caress leaned forward to outline his lips with her tongue, the short hairs of his beard tickling her mouth as she did. He groaned in sweet pleasure. "You like?" she teased saucily, before slowly rising from his lap.

Smiling wickedly, Caress lowered her panties over her hips and shapely legs as Julius freed his long and hard member from its silk confines to massage it deeply with long strokes.

Naked and unashamed, she lay back on her large wooden coffee table, her head bent back toward the floor as she propped her feet on the edge and opened her legs to offer him a welcoming sight of her shaved womanhood and moist core.

Heated by her boldness, Julius rose from the couch to kneel between her quivering thighs with his member still hard and throbbing in his hand. The sweet scent of perfume mingled with her womanly scent, driving him nearly insane for a moment. He had to shake his head for clarity.

Caress reached blindly with her fingers into the silken folds of her own moist intimate treasure. Finding it slick and wet to her touch, she moaned wantonly.

Enjoying the show, Julius watched closely as she teased her own swollen bud until the desire to make her come filled him. With a swift lick of his lips he lowered his head to dip his tongue deep inside her core. His shaft hardened in his hands from the feel and taste of her as Caress bucked up from the table. He felt her body shiver as he suckled her bud like he was thirsty. It pulsed against his tongue matching the steady beat of his heart.

"Oh, Julius," she cried hoarsely, her chest light with emotions as white hot spasms pushed her to be lost to time or place. Blindly she reached for his head and pressed his swift-moving tongue closer.

"Give it to me," Caress demanded hotly, unable to think of anything but having his sizeable tool deep inside of her.

"What?" he asked thickly, rising to position himself so that the thick dark tip of his erection slid inside of her.

He clenched his jaw as his body jolted. "This?"

Caress bucked her hips up off the table again, driven with want for him. "Yes," she begged unashamedly.

Julius tensed for control, flinging his head back as her walls created a spasmodic rhythm against his tip. Feeling her climax finally ease, he gave her another thick inch. "Say please," he ordered, his own voice strained as he shifted his head to look down at her.

Caress pulled her upper body up, bracing her arms on the table's edge to look him hotly in the eyes. "Now," she demanded softly as she quivered for him.

Moving his hand up her shapely thighs to her flat stomach, he continued upward to massage her breasts with skillful fingers just as he plunged his shaft deeply inside her core with one powerful thrust.

They gasped hotly. Quick, hard, and fast they worked their hips with grunts and moans, giving in to their primal lust. Both sought to please and be pleased in a hurried but pleasurable fashion that was completely electrifying.

Caress met him stroke for stroke, using her tight walls to pull him deeper inside of her. She released all of her inhibitions and gave in to pure and raw sexual pleasure.

Julius grasped her shapely hips with trembling hands and thrust hard and deep inside of her like a piston, his pumps fast and furious as her moans pushed him to the edge.

Both of their movements became intense as the first wave of their climaxes warmed them from their toes to their loins. It was the first of many to come.

* * *

Caress's body definitely felt like it had been made love to all night. Her thighs ached, her breasts were tender, and her core was decidedly sore. She grimaced as she remembered all of the things they did and said last night.

But it had all been good. Damn good.

Rolling over in bed, Caress was surprised to feel the coolness of the sheets and a piece of paper instead of the warmth of Julius's body. Confused, she sat up in bed and picked up the note to read.

Caress,
   I had an early flight to catch so I didn't want to awaken you. I'll give you a call when I'm back in town in three months.

                                                   J.

At that moment the weight of her actions hit home. What happened between them, good as it had been, was not the start of a wonderful relationship like she hoped . . . but a one-night stand!

"Oh . . . no," she cried out dramatically, filled with embarrassment at what she did last night on the table . . . and in the shower . . . and on the floor.

"Oh, God . . . no," she moaned again, falling back in the bed to cover her mortified face with the sheet.

Julius handed the airline attendant his boarding pass. "Here you go."

"Have a good flight Mister, uhm . . . Jones," the beauty said with a flirtatious smile.

Julius ignored the obvious invite and accepted his I.D. back. "Thanks."

As he settled in his first class window seat, Julius felt absolutely drained of energy. Caress wore him out last night until he felt like he could be knocked over by a toddler. It took all the strength he could muster to get out of her bed so he could go home to shower and grab his suitcases and make it to the airport on time.

He didn't want to meet any new women.

He didn't want to talk with anyone.

He didn't want to do a damn thing but sleep off last night.

Julius cushioned his head with the pillow he requested from the flight attendant. Just before he drifted off to sleep, he thought of one of the moves Caress put on him in the shower as she straddled him with her feet braced against the wall. A shiver raced from his toes straight to his head.

"Damn it, girl," he muttered to himself.

Chapter Three

Three Months Later

Julius was excited about all of the great photos he took while in Africa. He was anxious to get home, unpack, and get right into the darkroom he set up in his basement for times he didn't feel like driving to his studio.

His agent was expecting the photos in two weeks and that wasn't a problem. He had hundreds of rolls of film that Dwayne and he were going to work overtime to get printed.

For the past three years, Julius had been throwing around the idea of a book. At first he hadn't known the particulars of when and what, but he knew he wanted to do it. Finally choosing Africa as his backdrop made perfect sense. It was a land rich with his culture, his history, and his ancestry. *Julius Jones: My Africa* would be in bookstores everywhere next year.

A fabulous career. A fabulous three months in Africa. Now a fabulous book. Life couldn't be any more . . . fabulous.

"Thanks, man," Julius told the driver who double-parked the green-and-white taxi in front of his house.

As the man hopped out to remove his passenger's luggage from the trunk, Julius dug enough money from his wallet to cover the fare and a hefty tip.

He was just about to climb out of the cab when his cell phone rang. It was an unusual sound to him since his phone hadn't worked while he was out of the country. Julius flung his leather carry-on onto his shoulder and reached into the inside pocket of his leather blazer for his tiny silver flip phone as he climbed out of the cab.

"Julius Jones here."

"Welcome back, Julius Jones. You truly have been missed."

He had to pause for a moment to catch the sultry, feminine voice on the line.

"This is Karina, silly boy."

Julius smiled as he envisioned the model. "Of course I recognized your voice," he lied, as he moved to allow the driver to place his two large suitcases on the sidewalk.

"I hope you haven't forgotten our date tonight."

Damn. He had.

"We never got to finish what we started at the photo shoot and you told me you'd be returning today and to give you a call."

He remembered it now.

"I'm naked in my big Jacuzzi tub and just thinking of you. I've been waiting three whole months for some of you, Julius. Don't let me regret waiting."

Julius waved the driver off. "I won't, I promise."

"Good," she sighed huskily. "Oh, and Julius? Your assistant sent me the photo. It's hanging over my bed. Don't worry you'll get to see it. I love it almost as much as you're going to love the real *thing*."

He smiled broadly. "Really?"

"Definitely."

"I'll pick you up, say around—" Julius began, glancing down at his Jaeger-Le-Coultre watch.

"No, *I'll* pick you up around six," she asserted.

"Oh . . . okay."

"See you then."

Julius smiled, shaking his head as he closed the phone and slid it back into his pocket. What the hell. His time in Africa had been more work then play. A date with Karina would be a good way to cap off his return home.

Then again so would a home-cooked meal at Kendrick and Tamara's.

Or another date with Caress, Julius thought, as he carried a suitcase in each hand up the stairs. He had to admit that she had drifted into his thoughts on more than one occasion during the past three months. He wasn't looking for a relationship, but he *damn* sure would love to touch base with her again.

Putting his key in the lock of the front door, he thought, *It'll be real good to see her.*

Julius set his bags on the hardwood floor of the foyer. Immediately he noticed that there wasn't one piece of mail on the floor beneath the mail slot on the front door. He hadn't bothered to discontinue his mail or his utilities because he didn't want the hassle of getting them reconnected. He merely prepaid his utilities three months in advance. When he traveled he liked to return to his life just the way he left it.

Even after three months, there should be mail. Plenty of mail.

Since he traveled so often, Tamara and Kendrick had a key to keep an eye on the place whenever he was out of town. *They probably piled up all the mail for me*, he reasoned, immediately put at ease.

Leaving his luggage by the door, Julius jogged up the

stairs, then stopped suddenly and backtracked two steps. He frowned at the odd angle of the picture hung on the wall. Correcting it quickly, he nodded in approval before continuing up the stairs.

As he walked into his bedroom Julius again frowned. He knew it sounded very cliché but . . . someone had been sleeping in his bed. Tamara and Kendrick. Their lackluster attempt at making it was definitely not up to his good-enough-to-be-in-Architectural-Digest par.

"Did those two . . . in my bed?" Julius asked himself aloud, already crossing the room to pick up his cordless phone. Quickly he dialed Kendrick's work number.

"Kendrick? Hey, what's up?"

"Julius? Welcome back. How was Africa?"

"Great, but look I got something to ask you? Have you and Tamara used my—"

"Actually, I got something to tell you," Kendrick began, sounding decidedly unlike his usual calm and collected self. "Uhm, it's about—"

The bathroom door opened and Julius whirled around to see who in the hell was in his house. His eyes widened in surprise. "Caress?"

"Yeah, as a matter of fact. It's about Caress," Kendrick said on the phone.

Julius disconnected the call as he faced Caress standing unsure in a white-fitted tank top and his pajama bottoms that were rolled up to her knees. Her hair was up in a ponytail and a toothbrush was in her hand. Her face was free of makeup. She was braless and the cotton of the tank top clung to the hardness of her nipples and the soft curves of her breasts. She bit her bottom lip and smiled nervously as she looked over at him.

He thought she looked absolutely gorgeous.

"Hi, Julius," she began, rubbing her free hand over her—no correct that—over *his* pants leg.

Julius frowned deeply.

"I guess I should explain," Caress began.

The phone in his hand rang suddenly and loudly. He held up a hand to her and then looked down at the phone to check his caller ID. Just as he thought, it was Kendrick. "Kendrick and Tamara in on this?" he asked, his voice stern.

Caress nodded, her face resembling a child about to be punished.

Hitting the TALK button, Julius raised the phone to his face. "I'll call you back," he said shortly, before disconnecting the call again.

"Julius—"

"Why are you in my house, Caress?" he asked, studying her and noticing that her plum-sized breasts were definitely larger than the last time he suckled them.

Shaking his head to free his mind of sudden erotic images of her naked astride him, he focused on her slow coming words.

"First, let me apologize for moving in without your—"

"Moving in?" Julius balked, his eyes darting around the room to take in the unkempt bed, the gossip magazines on his usually clutter-free nightstands, the red brassiere flung carelessly over his leather chaise lounge.

Noticing everything his eyes took in, Caress moved quickly to gather the magazines and bra into her hands. "Sorry. Look, Julius—"

Suddenly, her face paled and she dropped everything in her hands to dash into the bathroom. Curious, Julius walked over to pick up the items she dropped and then followed her.

Caress was kneeling over the toilet, retching horribly. Her back arched as she heaved up her stomach's contents. Frowning, Julius moved to grab a folded washcloth from the shelf to dampen with cold water. "Here you go," he told her, squatting down next to her.

She flushed the toilet before she shut the lid and moved to sit atop it. Accepting the cloth, she wiped her face, frowning at the awful taste in her mouth. "Thanks," she told him, careful to cover her mouth so that the smell of vomit on her breath didn't offend him.

"Are you sick?" Julius asked, rising to stand over her. Looking around, he immediately noticed the total disarray of his bathroom. He swallowed down a deep wave of irritation.

"No," she answered softly.

Too softly.

Julius's body immediately tensed. Their eyes met and locked. He swallowed despite a huge lump in his throat. "Are you pregnant, Caress?"

Her eyes dropped.

So did Julius's stomach.

Caress thought of the pained expression on Julius's face when she disclosed her condition. She couldn't really be angry with him about looking exactly like how she felt when she saw the little plus sign appear in the window of the pregnancy test. This wasn't the greatest news for her either. Especially having been evicted from her apartment three weeks ago.

"How are you feelin'?" Tamara asked, walking into Julius's bedroom where he left Caress while he went downstairs to talk to Kendrick.

Caress smiled half-heartedly, tossing her shirt into the open suitcase on the bed. "As fine as I can be pregnant, homeless, jobless, and husbandless."

Tamara winced visibly. "Besides all of that, how are you

doing? How's the baby, Caress?" she asked, moving over to pick the suitcase up off the bed. "Why are you packing?"

Caress's expression was odd as she watched her best friend set the suitcase on a luggage caddy by the door and then sit on the chaise lounge adjacent the bed. "I'm packing because he's going to put me out. Why'd you just do that?" she asked, pointing to her luggage.

Tamara made a face. "Girl, Julius is so anal about his things. He'd pass a stone big as both our heads if he saw your suitcase on his suede comforter."

Caress smiled. "I kinda noticed that he is very . . . organized."

Tamara sucked air between her teeth. "My daddy's a career military man and he's not as orderly. Trust me, Julius is a neat freak bordering on obsessive compulsive."

Caress felt sadness weigh her shoulders down. "I don't know anything about my baby's daddy," she wailed, dramatically dragging out her words as she flopped back on the bed.

"You know his name, right?"

"Yes."

"And you know his address?"

"Yeah."

"Then you got the most vital info girl, so hush."

The two women fell silent.

"I told you this was a bad idea, Tam-Tam."

Julius paced back and forth across his living room. Every time his friend tried to speak he silenced him with an agitated wave of his hand. He had a lot on his plate to swallow, and it was sticking in his throat like bile. Finding out he may have a baby on the way *and* an unexpected roommate was quite a bit to handle all in one morning.

Caress is pregnant with my child.
Is it my child?

He paused in his therapeutic pacing. Okay, it was very possible that it was. He couldn't deny that they had sex. Great sex. *Focus, man, focus.* Nor could he deny that although he carried two condoms in his wallet, he didn't use either of them that night. Everything had been so hot. So fast. He never had unprotected sex. But the one time he did—zip bam BOOM—he was going to be a daddy.

What was I thinking?

Julius continued his pacing. He was slipping. This type of thing didn't happen to him. He was too together for a baby mama. And with a woman he knew nothing about except that she was awesome in bed, homeless and jobless, and had taken residence in his home.

Julius felt like screaming as the control he cherished slipped through his grasp like sand.

"I know what we did was a little presumptuous—" Kendrick began from his seat on the sofa.

Julius swung around to gawk at him. "A little?" he scoffed. "Negro, please."

"Look man, I was just as shocked as you are when Tamara told me that you, Mr. Magnum, had gotten Caress pregnant—"

"Gotten?" he asked sarcastically, piercing his friend with angry eyes.

Kendrick held up both of his large hands. "I didn't mean it that way, Julius. All I'm saying is that you were in Africa and we couldn't reach you. Caress hadn't found a job yet and was getting evicted. Hell, Tamara was on my neck like a flea. What was a brother to do?"

"Certainly not give her keys to my home and tell her to move on in." Julius's voice was filled with exasperation and some resentment.

Kendrick went on the defensive. "What? You'd prefer that in your absence I let the woman who is pregnant with your child move into a shelter . . . or worse?"

"Why couldn't she stay with you?" Julius countered.

"Man, please, our one bedroom is tight enough quarters for me and Tamara."

The two men were at a stalemate.

"Look, Caress fell on hard times but she's not one of these chicks out to gank a brother for his cash. She's an independent, working woman. Hell, we had to bribe her into staying here."

"With?"

"Huh?" Kendrick asked, obviously confused.

"What'd you have to bribe her with?"

"Not telling you she was pregnant if you happened to call."

Julius frowned.

"What are you gonna do?" Kendrick asked, loosening his tie.

Julius walked over to the mahogany bar in the corner of the room and poured himself a shot of Courvoisier. Thinking of his predicament, he tripled it. "Now he asks me," he muttered into his drink murderously, before he gulped it down in one swig with a wince.

Julius released a heavy breath. "So this is what it feels like between a rock and a hard place?"

Kendrick rose to walk over to the bar. "It's just until she gets on her feet, Julius."

Julius felt the tension increase at the back of his smooth neck. "What exactly are you suggesting?"

Kendrick poured himself a glass of ginger ale and looked over at Julius in astonishment. "I'm suggesting that she stay here. What were you thinking?"

Julius reached down to pull a can of Pepsi from the

mini-fridge, taking a healthy swig to kill the aftertaste of the liquor. "I'm suggesting paying for an abortion."

"No abortion. Tamara already asked."

"No?"

"No."

"Damn," Julius swore, rubbing his beard. "If I agreed to the absurdity, where's she supposed to sleep? My only other bedroom is set up as my home office."

Kendrick wiggled his eyebrows suggestively and Julius immediately shook his head, adamant. "No. No. Hell no. I'm not looking to play house. Sex and living together adds up to one sticky ass situation."

Footsteps echoed on the stairs. Julius's eyes darted to the entrance of the living room just as Caress appeared.

This woman was going to be the mother of his child . . . *if* the child was his. *Were prenatal paternity tests safe?*

She walked straight up to him, her eyes swollen and red from tears. "I'm sorry."

Julius swallowed back a desire to pull her into his arms. "For?"

"All of this," she said, looking pointedly down at her stomach.

Julius nodded. "It took both of us, so don't apologize."

Caress nodded.

Instinctively, Julius could tell that she was embarrassed by her situation. He looked over her head to Kendrick. His friend's eyes said, "Do the right thing." He looked to Tamara, who now leaned against the doorframe, and her eyes said, "Don't make me whup your ass!"

"Come on, Kendrick," he said reluctantly.

"Where we going?"

Julius looked down at Caress. "To buy whatever I need to change my office back into a bedroom."

He strode out of the living room before anyone could say a word.

Kendrick hopped up, moving to kiss his wife before leaving the house behind Julius.

Tamara moved over to hug Caress's petite frame close in a motherly fashion.

Caress swallowed back hormonal tears.

"I'm going to have a baby." Caress whispered the words softly as she lay resting on Julius's bed.

Because the furniture for the other bedroom wouldn't be delivered until tomorrow, Julius had given her use of his bedroom for one last night. Caress would only admit to herself that she was a little disappointed that they wouldn't share the same bed and pick up where they left off.

Obviously Julius didn't feel the same way. That night clearly meant nothing to him, and a relationship was the last thing he wanted. In fact, since Julius returned late this afternoon he had kept his distance.

If that's how he wanted it then that was fine. Caress was not a woman to force herself on any man. Not even one she was pregnant by.

Truthfully, she was happy about the pregnancy. Okay, not at first. But once she realized that she couldn't bear to have an abortion and would have a beautiful baby after about nine months, well she got happy.

Tamara's assertion that Julius was not the kind of man to be a deadbeat dad had pleased her even more.

"As long as he's a good father to you," Caress spoke to her child, her hand on her still-flat womb. "Then I'll be fine about everything else."

She wasn't any less anxious about giving up her space and independence than Julius was. But the first rule of motherhood—as far as she was concerned—was you do whatever, whenever for your child. She would give her child something she hadn't had since she was two years old. A mother.

Caress was climbing out of the bed when someone rang the doorbell. Knowing Julius had secluded himself in his darkroom in the basement, Caress made her way out of the bedroom and down the stairs. She was just opening the front door when the door leading from the basement opened.

A tall and beautiful dark-skinned woman stood on the porch in a massive sable that was open and showing that she wore absolutely not a stitch of clothing underneath it. Obviously she thought Julius was going to open the door.

Well she thought wrong, Caress thought, frowning. "Excuse you?" she asked with attitude.

The woman didn't even bother to close her fur as she stepped past Caress into the foyer. "Julius?" she asked, her tone obviously confused.

Caress turned, realizing that he stood behind her.

Julius looked from Karina, his forgotten date, to Caress, the woman pregnant with his child, and then looked heavenward.

Chapter Four

Julius forced his eyes away from the sight of enough T&A to make *Playboy* look G-rated. He just didn't have the courage to face Caress if he acted on the temptation. Not that he owed her anything. Right? Okay, fine. He felt like he did.

Julius leaned forward and gently pulled the edges of Karina's coat together. "Karina, I—"

She gave him a look to kill as she whipped the fur back open with flare. "Julius," she said with plenty of question and annoyance and every other piece of drama that he didn't want to deal with right now.

"Don't let me interrupt," Caress said softly, before she pushed through Julius and Karina and dashed up the stairs.

"Are you married?" Karina snapped, looking past Julius's broad shoulder at Caress's retreating figure. "Shacking? Involved? Looking for a ménage? Hell . . . *busy?* What's going on?"

Julius shook his head. "Karina, plans have changed. I meant to call you earlier—"

Karina looked offended before she nudged her fur opened a bit wider. "Do you know how many men would die to be you right now?" she asked with a slight jiggle and wiggle of her breasts.

Julius took a very deep swallow over a suddenly huge lump in his throat. He lightly grasped her elbow and steered her back toward his front door. The brown tips of her hard nipples poked just past the edge of the fur, tempting him, but Julius ignored the stirring below his waist as a need to check on Caress topped anything else he might feel. "Trust me, I know, but it can't be avoided."

"Three whole months Julius." Karina finally closed her fur and tied the thick leather belt around it snugly. "No one has ever made me wait so long."

Julius felt relief and a little regret, but he pressed on. "Different time. Different place. Different . . . situation. I would be all over you like white on rice but it is what it is."

Karina's shoe caught on the edge of the bamboo rug as Julius eased her across the threshold onto the porch. His grip tightened on her elbow to make sure she didn't trip. "I'll call you," he said, just before he flashed her his winning smile and politely closed the door on her stunned, open-mouthed expression.

Julius made sure to lock the door before he turned and jogged up the stairs to his—correction Caress's—bedroom. He knocked twice.

Nothing.

He knocked twice again using his knuckle, the gold from his fraternity ring flashing. "Caress?" he called out softly, leaning his head forward a bit.

The door suddenly swung open and she walked out, sending a cool breeze over his body as she passed him dressed in her leather coat and snug woolen cap. "I guess we should work out something for moments like this. Maybe a tie on the door or leaving the porch light on," she told him over her shoulders as she walked like she was trying to win a marathon.

Julius's head swung to the right to watch her head and body slowly disappearing as she headed down the stairs. He followed her. "That's not necessary—"

Caress was at the front door pulling her keys from her pocket. "I'll head to Tamara's or the movies or something to give you privacy."

"Caress—"

SLAM.

Just like that, Julius was left with nothing but the wind breezing against his face as Caress left the house quicker than he could stop her. Moments later, lights flashed in the depths of his eyes as she backed her car out of the driveway.

He didn't bother opening the door and attempting to chase after her. Caress was gone and there was no stopping her. Besides, he didn't ask her to make assumptions.

Truth? He didn't ask her to move in here and interrupt his life either.

Yes, he had wanted to hook up with Caress again, but live with her? Have a baby with her? That all went *way* beyond another steamy X-rated sexfest that made his toes curl up and his dick straighten out.

Releasing a deep sigh, he tried to maneuver his neck to release the tension he felt across his broad shoulders as he made his way back down into his darkroom. As soon as he reached the basement floor he flipped the switch to bask the room in darkness. The red-colored safelight gave him just enough light to see what he was doing without exposing the paper to brighter light that would destroy it.

His darkroom was his savior. Every element of the process of developing film was a challenge to him. Digital photography helped to make the actual need for film developing archaic, but like a true artist and appreciator of his craft, Julius used any opportunity he could to develop his own photography. From taking the shot to seeing it on print, he was the master of his craft . . . and that was just the way he wanted it.

For now, the only thing he wanted to focus on was developing the reels and reels of the black-and-white film he brought back from his trip. His color films were all digital since the process of developing was far more complex than black-and-white film. His book would have an eclectic mix of pictures representing everything he discovered, loved, and cherished during his days in Africa. *His* Africa.

For the next two hours he became lost in his work. His photos were about more than just the tribal shots and the large stretches of wilderness. He had those and more. The culture. The food. The modern day amenities. The art. The architecture.

In moments the slowly developing images in the citric acid stop bath would make him smile at a memory—like the laughing faces of the students at Oprah's Leadership Academy in South Africa. Or make him feel inspired— like the school in the Njala Kendema village. Or make him sad—like the many faces of the women and children dying from AIDS.

He would never forget his time there, and he hoped those who purchased his book would feel inspired to experience it all for themselves. There was no denying that a trip back to the motherland was something any and all African-Americans should experience.

One day when I have kids I'll take them, he thought.

His gut clenched.

One day wasn't as far off as it had been yesterday.

Caress was supposedly pregnant with his child. In around six months he would be a father. Jesus.

Growing up in Stellar Home projects to a mother

addicted to dope and never really missing a father who was never around, Julius had made a better life for himself . . . by himself. His goals were accomplished. He was a college graduate. He was a celebrated and noted photographer. He owned his own homes—one here in his beloved hometown of Newark and an apartment in Miami. Not bad for a orphan kid from the projects whose mother only gave him two things he cherished before she died of an overdose. The first was bringing him into the world, and the second was a used Poloroid camera from a yard sale at some church.

But now everything was on the verge of changing because baby mama drama had never been a part of his plan. Still, he would never be the deadbeat his own father was. Ready or not, Julius Jones would soon add the label of father to his biography.

Feeling the tension in his shoulders and neck again, Julius gave up on trying to get any more work done. He crossed the floor to bask the room with light before he washed his hands in the small black sink in the corner of the basement. Before he climbed the stairs, he cast one last look over his shoulder at the dozens of photos drying on the lines stretched across the ceiling.

In the foyer, Julius checked out the window to see if Caress's battered little Jetta was parked out front. He frowned a little and glanced down at his watch before he turned and strode slowly to his study. It was a little after midnight and Caress was still making herself scarce for him.

At this exact moment, Caress was somewhere out there thinking he was with another woman. The whole damn thing was crazy to him.

The only thing about to get wet was his tongue.

Julius headed down the hall to his kitchen—his first time in it since his return from Africa. What he saw made him want to walk back to the Motherland. His newly renovated kitchen, complete with Viking appliances, granite countertops, and tiled floors looked like a tornado had gone through it.

A tornado named Caress.

Irritation caused his jaw to tighten as his hawk-like eyes took in every infraction on his peace.

The dishes on the counter. The wet dishcloth balled up on the edge of the sink. The few sandwich crumbs in the center of the island. The row of empty Snapple bottles lined up by the back door like prisoners. The haphazard way the slats of the wooden blinds hung at the window over the sink. The random items atop his normally clear and clutter-free countertop. The boxes of cereal atop his fridge. The sticky stains on the floor in front of his fridge.

Julius's frown deepened. *Is that Kool-Aid?*

He thought back to the night he spent at Caress's apartment. True, most of his focus had been on tasting and touching every inch of her body, but he hadn't missed that her little studio apartment could use some work.

At first he attributed the mess to a working woman rushing to get ready for a date; now, however, he realized he'd sniffed out a slob.

Julius turned on the WBGO's Jazz88 station and turned up the classic Miles Davis joint as loud as it would go before he got to work making his kitchen look like it was ready for a photo shoot in *Architectural Digest* again. He couldn't help but mutter to himself as he worked. He felt like a bear coming back to find Goldilocks had taken up residence in his house.

A piece of him was tempted as hell to leave the mess for Caress but maybe this *was* clean to her. The thought of that made him nervous as hell. He'd left the rats and roaches behind a long time ago. Living in a hellhole was not his idea of upward mobility. Far from it.

"Damn," he swore, as he continued to work.

Caress left the movie theater and couldn't for the life of her describe the flick she'd just sat through. Images of Julius making love to Karina with the same ferocity and passion he had with on her all those months ago had her head good and messed up. Especially since she left them to do the do.

What right did she have to throw Karina out on her ass?

What right did she have to demand that Julius send her and her too tall, too thin, too hungry-looking self from there.

No, instead she took the high road and left her baby's daddy to his booty call . . . and he let her go.

Caress rolled her eyes as she felt the need to pee. That and the constant morning sickness—that wasn't isolated to just the mornings—was her reminder of the baby she carried. She wasn't showing yet at just twelve weeks but her body was starting to feel it.

She turned around and went back inside the movie theater on Springfield Avenue and Bergen Street. She decided that trying to risk getting back to the house before she relieved herself was risky.

"What's up, mami?"

Caress saw the tall dark-skinned brother trying to get her attention as she practically ran to the ladies room, but she ignored him. She didn't mean to be rude, but when you gotta go . . . you gotta go.

She was walking back out of the bathroom when she almost walked into the same man. She stopped short and the bathroom door swung closed and bumped her solidly against her full behind.

"How you doing?" he said, his white teeth shining brightly against his smooth, dark complexion.

"Uhm, I'm good," she said with obvious hesitation before she took two steps over to get some space.

"I—"

Caress held up her hand and released a breath. Her nipples were starting to throb and she really wanted to climb into bed and forget about Karina, Julius, Karina and Julius, and everything else too. "Listen, I'm pregnant and I live with my baby's daddy," she told him with no nonsense. His whole face changed just like that as his eyes darted down to her flat belly and back up to her face.

Caress bit back a smile. *Poor baby*, she thought as he turned and walked away. *He was cute, too*.

She slid her hands deep into the pockets of her jacket as she made her way out of the movie theater again and into the cold winter air. As she made her way to her car, she thought about just what her situation meant in terms of dating. She snorted as she pulled her keys out of her purse.

"Let's see . . ." she said aloud to herself as she unlocked the driver's side door.

"I'm unemployed. Homeless. Pregnant." Caress slid inside her car and laughed, just a touch bitterly, as she said a quick prayer she'd have a drama-free start of the engine. "Yes, men of the world, bring . . . it . . . on."

The car started without major fuss and Caress was more than glad to drive her little Jetta out of the busy parking lot and onto Springfield Avenue headed toward . . .

Toward where? Home? Well, it wasn't her home and she was very aware of that fact. Just as aware as she was that Julius was not her man.

Was Karina gone? Was she spending the night?

Caress felt her cheeks warm noticeably as she pulled to a stop at a red light. She thought about heading to

Tamara and Kendrick's when she left Julius to his date, but her embarrassment pushed her to come up with something else. Who in her right mind would want to admit the truth about why she had to leave the house?

As she accelerated her little car forward, Caress thought of the other woman. Humph. So *that* was his type? Tall, thin, flashy . . . pretty as a model.

Caress couldn't deny the woman's beauty no matter how much she wanted to. Of course, Julius wanted her . . . had her . . . was having her right now.

"Oh shit," she muttered, tapping her hand against the steering wheel.

The radio had long ago stopped working, and needing a distraction, she pushed play on the CD player. Soon the sounds of Lauryn Hill's voice filled the interior.

Living with Julius was just not going to work. In fact, the whole idea of it was almost as stupid as them having unprotected sex and making this baby that neither was ready for. And now? Now they were in one hell of a fix.

She had to get another job and find her own place. No doubt about it.

Caress was relieved to see Karina's flashy silver Benz gone from the spot where it was parked in front of Julius's house. Perhaps the tryst was over.

Or maybe it was more than a tryst?

She paused as she sat in the driveway and looked up at the house through the windshield. She did know from Tamara that Julius didn't have a steady girlfriend, and during her brief time at the house she didn't answer his phone, but she'd overheard plenty of sultry-voiced women leaving messages before she finally turned the volume down on the machine.

It was hard to swallow being one of many.

Shaking her head at the shame of it all, Caress left her

car and made her way into the house through the side entrance leading directly into the kitchen. Her steps faltered at the sight of Julius standing at the kitchen sink.

He looked up and their eyes locked.

She immediately noticed that he looked annoyed.

"Welcome back," he said, his tone short.

She stiffened. Her eyes shifted quickly about the room. She was looking to see if he was alone.

"She's gone," he said with finality.

Caress's lips formed an *O* and she looked apologetic as she stepped in and softly closed the kitchen door. "Listen, Julius, I'm sorry about all of this. Please don't think I'm out to trap you or screw up your life—"

"Caress."

She shifted her eyes up to his and then shifted them away just as quickly. "This shit is . . . all of it is . . . is . . . embarrassing, frightening, foolishness . . ."

Julius nodded as he turned sideways and leaned his hip against the sink to cross his strong arms over his chest. "I won't have women over while you're living here, Caress," he told her as he cast those intense eyes on her.

"That's not necessary—"

"Yes, it is," he insisted in a strong voice.

She hated to ask. She really did . . . but she had to. "Karina?"

"Left right after you did."

He continued to watch her closely, and it made Caress feel nervous. "I appreciate you helping me out, Julius," she said, not sure what else to say. "I know you don't know me, but it's been awhile since I've asked somebody for help or even had anybody that I could ask."

His eyes squinted as he continued to watch her.

She ran her hands over her hair as she felt tears build.

Damn hormones, she thought, hating the feelings she had officially designated as "the weepies."

Julius pushed off the sink and Caress couldn't help but notice everything about him.

The way the soft hairs on his chest peeked above the open buttons of his linen shirt. The strength in his walk. The soft and subtle scent of his cologne. The fullness of his bottom lips. The intensity of his eyes. The man was impossibly sexy.

She saw his hands reach out to take her. Comfort her. Hold her.

It was way more than she could handle in that moment. Way more.

"I'm gonna turn in," she said softly, shifting past his embrace to walk fast as hell out of the kitchen. She never looked back as she raced up the stairs and into the bedroom. As soon as the door closed, she pressed her back to it and slid her hands down to lightly rub her belly as she waited for the longest time for her heartbeat to slow down.

Something as simple as a hug from Julius would have turned her knees to jelly and her senses would have flown out the window *again* and she would have easily snuggled her lips against his. Something about that man was dangerous to her common sense and until she found her own spot she had to find a way to avoid that same electric pull from that night they shared.

Caress's hands flew to her mouth as she felt the greasy hotdog she'd had at the movies work its way up. She dashed to the adjoining bathroom just in time to reach the toilet.

As she felt that steady thump-thump of her core ease she was actually glad for the morning sickness.

* * *

Julius leaned his head closer to the bedroom door as he listened to the awful sounds of Caress retching. He came upstairs to retrieve fresh linens from the hall closet and overheard her. He fought the urge to barge in and go to her. It was obvious she wanted distance from him.

Still, it wasn't until he heard the toilet flush and her moving about with normalcy inside the bedroom that he finally moved away from the door to retrieve his linens and make his way back downstairs to sleep on the couch.

Chapter Five

Caress was tired with a capital T.

She used her key to enter the house and dropped her purse and winter coat on the foyer table before she made her way to the guest bathroom to relieve herself. She had two interviews today—and that made four this week—and Caress was praying like crazy that one of them panned out. Looking in the papers for apartments was all well and good but without money it was all just a dream.

She was just finishing up when she heard her cell phone ringing from her purse in the hall. Hurrying to wash her hands, Caress made it back out to the hall in record time. "Hey, Tam. What's up?" she greeted her friend after seeing her number on the caller ID.

"Just checking on you. How'd it go?"

Caress kept the phone pressed to her ear as she jogged up the stairs to her room. "Girl, to hell with complaining pimps. It's hard out here for everybody."

Tamara laughed. "Tell me about it."

Caress bent over to dig a pair of sweats out of her hamper of clean clothes that she still had to fold. She saw a yellow tank and she grabbed that too. "I just can't believe I'm in this mess."

"Shit happens."

"Yes, I know and usually to me," Caress drawled as she put the phone on speaker and then set it on the nightstand next to an unfinished bottle of Snapple.

"How's everything at the house?"

Caress quickly removed the black sweater dress and high-heeled boots she wore. "If our baby is half the neat freak his father is then my womb is spotless."

"Julius can be very . . . *particular*."

Caress started to say anal was the better word, but who was she to complain? The man was doing her a huge favor and she hadn't forgotten that once in these last two weeks since his return from Africa. "Well, I hardly see him. We just do our own thing you know. We pass each other like ships in the night."

Tamara got silent.

Caress gladly slipped on the sweats and tee. She instantly felt better. "Tamara? You there?"

"Umm-hmmm."

Caress froze in pulling her hair up into a ponytail. "What?" she asked, waiting for whatever it was Tamara *wanted* to say.

"Nothing," her friend said simply. Too simply.

Caress arched a brow. "Oh, it's something."

"Well . . . I just wondered how you guys feel, you know, being around each other and . . . stuff and you know memories and . . . stuff comes drifting back and . . ."

"Yeah, I know. Stuff?" Caress bent down to the floor to find her left slipper somewhere under the pile of shoes under the bed. "We're not screwing, Tamara, if that's what you're getting at."

"Hmmm. Pity."

Unable to find the slipper, Caress settled on a fresh pair of thick white ankle socks instead. "Pity?"

"You told me that morning after y'all's big night that the sex was *amazing*. That was your word, right?"

Caress bit her bottom lip. "And your point is?"

"None of that old fire has blazed up between y'all . . . yet?"

Caress looked up and caught sight of her reflection. There were a gazillion wrinkles in her clothes from being balled up in the basket after she took them out of the dryer. Her ponytail was as crooked as a politician and she had a zit as big as Mount Everest on her chin—she added acne to her list of side effects from pregnancy. "I don't how Julius can resist all this," she said sarcastically.

When it came to their interactions in the house, it was as if that night at her apartment had never happened. There was nothing remotely sexual between them. Most of their conversation was limited to greetings or general pleasantries. Most of their time was spent either passing each other in the house or closed off in their own worlds—him in the darkroom or his bedroom and she in the living room or her bedroom.

Caress barely knew much more about the father of her baby than she did before.

He listened to jazz music.

He was a neat freak.

He liked sports.

He didn't have much company.

He liked to read mystery novels.

Oh and the one fact she knew from the first night. The man was devastating . . . absolutely devastating in bed.

Caress winced just a bit as she thought of this hot little move he did with the tip of his tongue. She shivered at the memory of it on her neck, her nipples, her clit. Caress fanned herself. Yes, his tongue should be licensed to thrill.

"Uh . . . earth to Caress."

Her eyes darted to the cell phone on the dresser as Tamara's voice filled the air. She picked it up and left the room in search of her favorite past time. Television. "I'm here, girl," she said, taking the phone off of speaker.

"So . . . no nookie?"

Caress rolled her eyes heavenward. "Maybe you and Kendrick need a little freakfest because you sure have sex on the brain."

"You might be right," Tamara agreed. "He's been working a lot of overtime lately."

Caress jogged down the stairs and walked into the kitchen to grab a fresh bottle of her beloved fruit punch Snapple. "Well, tell Kendrick to stop punching that time card and put in some work at home."

"Sounds to me like Julius has got some cleaning up to do around there," Tamara shot back playfully.

Caress opened the bottle and took a deep swig of it before she headed back out of the kitchen to the living room, the lone room in the entire house with a television. "Yes, but Julius is not my husband. Hell, he ain't even my man. Hell, he ain't even my friend with benefits."

"Aww, poor baby," Tamara teased.

Caress grabbed the remote from atop the leather ottoman in the center of the spacious masculine-styled room. "Listen, you're using up my minutes. Call me later," she said, turning on the flat screen over the fireplace.

"Let's go to Mahogany's Friday night. My treat," Tamara added softly.

"Okay," she agreed reluctantly. Caress had her pride and she hated charity, but during her working days she and

Tamara had treated each other often. Besides, she could use a night away from the house.

She closed the phone and set it on the arm of the chair as she used the other hand to flip through the channels.

She had just settled on a rerun of *Run's House* on MTV when she heard the front door open and close. Julius. He was home early. She looked over her shoulder expecting him to peek his head inside the living room, but all she heard was the sound of him jogging up the steps.

Caress tried to ignore the sting of disappointment she felt.

Maybe he had a date and just came home to change before he went back out. It had crossed her mind over the last two weeks just how much time he spent away from the house. She knew having an unwanted housemate (who was pregnant with his child) had to be cramping his style.

Suddenly feeling hungry, Caress threw off the mink throw she had put across her lap and made her way back to the kitchen. She wasn't sure if it was the baby or the emotional mess that made her crave a snack, but she wasn't going to deny it. She grabbed a big bowl and heaped it with Rum Raisin ice cream and then added tons of caramel and whipped cream. The very thought of digging into it made her do a little dance. As she slid a big scoop of the cold and creamy delight into her mouth, she did The Wop, an old school dance move.

A chuckle from behind her made her whirl around in surprise.

Julius was leaning in the doorway watching her with a huge grin on his face. He looked good in the fitted white sweater he wore with loose-fitting dark denims. The color perfectly emphasized his dark complexion.

Caress felt a flutter in her chest as she looked at him. "Hey, Julius," she said.

"If it's that good, than I need to try some," he teased as

he strode into the kitchen with that cocky, bowlegged swagger of his that only hinted that he was well endowed.

Caress picked up the bowl from the counter and grabbed a clean spoon from the drawer to offer to him. "It's good to me, but I'm pregnant and loving pickles wrapped in cheese right now."

Julius stood before her and the scent of his cologne surrounding her caused her pulse to race. He accepted the spoon and dug out a heap to slide in his mouth.

Caress's mouth opened just a bit at the short flick of his tongue against the base of the spoon as he ate the ice cream. Her heart was beating so fast and hard that she worried he would hear it. "Is it good?" she asked, immediately hating the breathlessness of her tone.

Julius nodded and looked down at her.

Caress's cheeks warmed and she felt a warm tingle start at her toes and explode deep within the walls of her core. She intensely remembered the last time she asked him that very same question. The memory made her shiver.

She had been sprawled out before him in the middle of the bed, her hands caressing the back of his head as he used his tongue to give her core that first intimate stroke.

"Is it good?" she had asked him then too.

Julius's eyes dropped down to her mouth and Caress licked them nervously. Anxiously. Expectantly.

It would be so easy to fling the bowl of ice cream to the floor and strip Julius of just enough clothing to taste his nipples while she rode him on the floor.

But she couldn't.

She wouldn't.

Caress shifted past him and used her spoon to put another scoop of ice cream in her mouth. It melted like snowflakes against fire. Considering how hot she felt for Julius, she didn't doubt it. "You're home earlier than usual," she said trying to diffuse the chemistry. Ease the ache. Cool the flames.

Jesus.

"I finished selecting all of the photos for my book today and decided to give myself and my assistant a much-needed break."

Caress smiled genuinely as she looked over at him as he made himself a bowl of ice cream. "Congratulations, Julius."

He glanced over at her. "Thanks. I'm really excited about it."

"I can't wait to see it," she said with honesty.

Julius leaned his hard buttocks against the counter as he ate his ice cream. "Traveling to Africa was really a dream come true for me. I can't wait to go back."

Caress slid onto one of the black leather stools beside the island. "I've never been farther than New York. I can't even imagine what being in Africa would be like."

Julius pushed off the counter and swaggered over to stand on the opposite side of the island. "I love to travel. I've been to Europe, Asia, all over America. It's good to see other worlds, other people. It helps to broaden your scope of possibilities for yourself. It lets you know what's possible. What's attainable."

Caress nodded. "For me right now I just want to attain a job and my own place."

Julius set his bowl down on the island. "I'm not rushing you, Caress," he told her in a serious tone.

"I know . . . I'm rushing myself," she insisted with truth.

The comfortable mood in the room switched.

Both of their thoughts were filled with the baby she was carrying. Their addition to the world. Both wished it could have been under different circumstances.

In the silence, Caress's stomach grumbled loudly.

Julius made a face before he flung his handsome head back and laughed. "I don't think that ice cream is going to do it."

Caress chuckled as she stirred the concoction that was beginning to melt. "Me either. I guess the baby is hollering for more."

"Why don't I cook us all something?" Julius offered, reaching across the island for her bowl to carry to the sink along with his.

"You can cook?" she asked.

"I'm not G. Garvin or anyone like that but I do all right."

Caress smiled, admitting only to herself that it felt good to chill out with Julius. She was enjoying just being in his company. But then that made her acutely aware that feeling comfortable like this around Julius was addictive and not a good idea.

The night between them was a one-night stand—her first, last, and only. It might have lead to other sensual hook-ups but definitely was not the starting point for a relationship.

And now they were having a baby together.

It definitely went against the whole equation of dating then marriage then a family. She was a child of foster care and she learned from Tamara that Julius's familial background wasn't much better than hers with a daddy who was MIA and a street-loving mother. If anything, they both should have been the poster children for the whole Huxtable scenario.

Emotions began to swarm her. Mostly the fear of the unknown.

Their date had been entertaining. Fun. Needed.

The sex with Julius had been intense. Gratifying. Satisfying.

But hindsight is 20/20 and she would gladly . . . *gladly*

give up that night if she had known she would wind up pregnant.

Gladly.

Julius heard Caress get up from the island and he looked briefly away from the grilled cheese sandwiches he was making to watch her leave the kitchen. His forehead furrowed at the downward slope of her shoulders.

His immediate instinct was to go to her, but did she want his comfort?

Tonight was the most conversation they shared with each other since their initial meeting upon his return from Africa. He knew it couldn't be easy for her. He knew she had to be scared. She had to be nervous. She had to be stressed.

None of it was good for the baby.

As he finished up the grilled cheese sandwiches and warmed up a large can of vegetable soup, he made a mental note to talk to Tamara.

Or I could just ask Caress myself.

Honestly, he was holding back from getting to know her even more because he didn't want to give her the wrong impression. He wasn't looking for a relationship. He wasn't ready to be a family man.

And he had the distinct feeling that she wanted to make sure he understood that she honestly wasn't trying to trap him into anything more. She avoided him around the house like the plague. At times he forgot she was here except . . .

The laughter that spilled from her as she watched those crazy ass celebreality shows. Really, who cared who Flavor Flav dated?

Or the sounds of her I'm-a-woman-singer-whose-been-done-wrong-by-men music that she always sang along with off-key.

Or when he was tripping over random piles of those damn Snapples she was always drinking, or other odd items she left about the house.

Other than that, the actual woman was pretty scarce whenever he got home.

Funny, it didn't stop her from staying constant in his dreams at night.

Oh, he still wanted Caress with an intensity that scared him. That night—their night—was just as fresh in his memory as if it happened last night. All the while in Africa and even upon his return he awakened at night with dreams of her riding him with her small, but beautiful breasts dangling just above his mouth as he held on for the ride.

How many nights had he awakened in a sweat with his dick as hard as a brick with the memory of her words still clinging to the air.

Is it good?

Tonight when she asked him about the ice cream, her words had sent him spiraling right back to their night. To that moment just before he tasted her. To the taste of her on his tongue. Again. And again. And again. Until he tasted her very liquid essence. Suckled on it. Feasted on it.

His dick stirred to life between his thighs and there was no denying the ache the memory caused. Shit.

Julius bit his lip and shook his head as he moved about the kitchen preparing a tray. Even as he carried it out of the kitchen and up the stairs his rod still hung heavy between his strong thighs just waiting for one touch, one look, or one other memory to shoot it straight to full hardness and heat.

Outside her door, Julius held the tray with one hand and knocked briefly with the other.

"Come in."

Julius didn't know if he was just a horny toad or what but her permission for him to enter sounded more like "coming" instead of "come in." He shook off the thought and turned the knob to step in the room.

Seconds later, he wished he had stayed downstairs and never crossed the threshold into what had to be the secret hideout for clothes. It looked like a dryer threw up in the place. That familiar tension that seemed to be with him lately settled on his shoulders and the back of his neck. He forced a smile and tried to rotate his neck and shoulders to shake it off.

Caress was lying in the middle of the unmade bed on her back with her knees bent and her arms crossed over her shoulders. She shifted her arm just enough to look over at him with one eye. "Is that for me?" she asked.

Julius was too busy wondering how on earth anyone could be comfortable in a room where there wasn't one neat spot to sit. He nodded as he fought the urge to treat her like a teenager who needed to be ordered to straighten her room.

A vision of his baby sitting and waving atop a pile of clothes in the crib flashed before him.

In order to reach the bed, he kicked a path in the clothes littering the floor. "Caress, listen, I can't hold my tongue any longer," he said, using a hand to make enough room on the bed to set down the tray.

"Yes, Julius?" she said, sitting up to position the tray in front of her.

He opened his mouth. Closed it. Opened it again. And then finally closed it for good. "Nothing. Nothing at all," he said, turning to leave the room with one last shove of a stack of magazines from his path before he closed the bedroom door.

Chapter Six

"Say you want me, Caress. Say it."

"I want you, Julius. I want you."

In the next moment his lips, those divinely soft, yet masculine lips, were pressed to the sweet hollow at the base of her neck as his skillful hands shifted up to caress the sides of her bared breasts. Caress moaned with a little cry that only hinted at the intense pleasure she felt. She shivered uncontrollably as she opened her legs wider before wrapping them around his strong, muscular waist.

Julius laughed softly against her neck as he shifted his body down on the rose-covered bed to press his face in the sweet perfumed valley of her breasts. He inhaled deeply of her sweet scent before shifting his head just a bit to suckle her nipple just as deeply.

"Julius!" Caress cried out achingly as she squirmed her hips against the bed beneath him.

He suckled the brown bud into his mouth again.

And again.

And again.

Caress arched her back, pressing his head closer as she bit her bottom lip and let her eyes drift closed in sweet *ecstasy as he shifted his mouth with ease to the other nipple. The first feel of his moist tongue and mouth made her take a sharp intake of breath.*

Julius shifted his hands, the muscles of his arms straining, as he took her bared ass in his hands to massage deeply as he circled his skillful tongue around her nipple and dark aureole swiftly. Erotic swirls. Devastating circles. Pleasure. Sweet, aching pleasure.

"Yes!" Caress cried out.

Julius rose to his knees on the bed. The electrified air between them coursed over the sudden gap in their bodies as he looked down at her heatedly.

Caress opened her eyes, looking up and devouring every inch of his muscled frame—including the eleven inches of pure muscle that curved away from his steeled body with dominance. The weighty tip was thick and just a touch lighter than the rest of the dark rod springing from a mass of soft curls and Caress was filled with a need to taste it. Suck it. Deeply.

She brought her hands up from tightly clutching the satin sheets to massage her own soft body as she watched Julius take his hardness into his own strong hands. "Come," she ordered softly, as her body tightened at the first feel of her slender fingers spreading the thick lips of her core to him.

Julius obeyed her without question bending down to bury his head against the soft trimmed curls covering the plumpest fruit he ever saw on a woman.

Caress raised a foot to his hard, hair-covered chest to stop him from tasting her.

He looked up in disappointment. Her scent—that warm, sultry, womanly scent that was uniquely hers—filled the air and he wanted to taste her essence. Drink upon it. Thirstily.

With a cocky smile and desire-filled soft eyes, Caress

raised one moist hand from her core to make a circle motion with her finger.

Julius's eyes darkened. His dick surged with renewed life. His heart pounded like a wild tribal drum just before the meanest war.

Caress removed her foot from his chest and raised an eyebrow almost as a dare.

The bed groaned under the weight of his movement as Julius shifted his taut frame so that he was on his knees above her backwards with face above her spread legs and his heavy erection now hanging down above her mouth. Anticipation made the muscles of his stomach tight.

Caress brought her hands up to massage his lower back and his hard buttocks as she looked close up at his beautiful dick. Feeling naughty she lifted her chin and released her moist tongue to run from the thick base of his dick along the weighty vein on the side to the thick tip. She circled it, loving the feel of the smoothness against her mouth and tongue as he shivered and tightly grasped her ankles. Her soft chuckle blew against the moist tip and he shivered again.

Raw electricity shivered over their bodies as she kissed the tip before she opened her mouth wide and suckled it deeply. Just the tip. That's all she wanted . . . for now.

"Damn!" Julius swore as his hips jerked above her.

Caress suckled his rod and then circled the tip with her cunning tongue. Her nipples ached and her clit swelled with renewed life because she knew she pleasured him. In that moment, it was all she wanted in the world. Nothing else mattered.

Julius fought for control as he felt himself harden to steel in her mouth. He throbbed and his sacs tightened as he felt the surge of his cum pulsating inside him. "Don't make me cum," he begged hoarsely as he pressed his face against her thigh and fought hard for control.

Caress shifted her head back letting his dick slide out of her mouth. She was nowhere near ready for the end of this sexual odyssey. Not at all.

With a playful slap to his backside, Caress spread her legs wider and made a little motion with her hips.

Julius was very obedient.

With his heart and dick still pounding, Julius brought his hands around her soft thighs to open her core to him. He quickly bent his head and with a dart of his tongue he stroked her clit. Caress sighed.

He stroked again.

Caress spread her legs wider until her plush buttocks lifted just a bit from the bed.

He stroked again.

She called out his name like he was her savior.

With a wolfish grin he suckled the whole of her into his mouth.

Caress arched her hips high until her feet were pressed deeply down into the softness of the bed and her buttocks were completely free of the bed. Rose petals lifted slightly in the air before dropping back down to the bed.

Julius wrapped his arms around her tighter and held on for the simulated rodeo ride as she bucked against him wildly with every lick, every kiss, and every suckle of her intimacy.

Caress gasped hotly as his tongue pressed deeply inside her to circle her walls. She felt like her heart stopped, but she knew she was alive. More alive and vibrant and electrified than ever. Beads of sweat coated her body. Her pulse raced through her body. She was on fire.

She was alive, and right now Julius was her lifeline.

His dick stroked her mouth as she thrashed about and she swiftly turned her head to the right to capture it in her mouth. Deeply. Wetly. Hotly.

With a deep moan she lifted her head from the pillow and sucked it in an iniquitous, piston-like motion that caused slurping noises to rise up into the heated and electrified air. Fast. Furious. Freaky.

Caress brought her legs up to surround his head as she held onto his waist tightly as they pleasured each other intensely, accepting the shift in their play.

Both trembled like fiends as they felt their climaxes steadily rising. Powerfully aware of the pleasure they gave and received, Julius and Caress were lost in one another. Captured by their desires. Blinded by their passions. Addicted to the heat.

Chemistry coursed over their bodies as they both cried out hoarsely and jerked their hips against each others' mouths as white hot spasms racked their loins, warmed their bodies, and exploded in their chests as they sent each other to orgasmic heights that was far beyond anything either one had ever felt . . .

Caress's eyes popped open wide where she lay in the middle of the bed. Sweat covered her body causing the sheets to coat her body like a second skin. Her pulse raced. She was warm. Okay, she was far beyond warm. She was hot. Everywhere.

She lifted her hands to her cheeks as she felt that undeniable moistness between her thighs and that steady thump-thump of her bud.

A wet dream.

It had felt so real. So erotic. So satisfying.

Not like the real thing, but good. Damn good. *Too* damn good.

Shit.

Caress flung the coverlet from her body as she sat up on

still-shaking legs. She leaned over to the beside table as she pulled her white nightie away from her body. The clock said it was just after six in the morning.

She was an early morning riser. She had been working since she was fifteen, so her body didn't know anything but rising and shining early.

Caress had an early appointment to get ready for. She reached in the nightstand for the white leather journal she kept there. A few weeks ago, she'd made the decision to keep a journal for her baby. It was one of those weepy, sentimental things Caress didn't usually to go for, but her pending motherhood must be softening her.

She pulled the pen from the middle of the book and turned to the last entry.

Possible Names

Girls	Boys
Marvel	*Cole*
Hope	*Marc*
Serene	*Julius, Jr.*

She laughed at herself. The names needed some serious work. Her eyes drifted down to Julius, Jr. How would Julius feel about that? Would he be surprised? Pleased? Annoyed?

It would be nice to know what the hell Julius thought about anything concerning the baby.

Closing the book, she pushed thoughts of baby names and indifferent baby fathers away. Right now her little escape into eroticism and the clear knowledge that she had to spread her legs wide in some stirrups to give birth had her in major need of a nice, hot bath.

Julius was lounging in the kitchen with a cup of coffee and *The Star Ledger* when Caress walked down the stairs.

Over the rim of his cup he took her in. With each passing day her face was filling out as well as her belly, and Julius honestly thought she looked more beautiful than ever. With the eye of a photographer, he absorbed the brightness of her eyes and the glow of her face.

Pregnancy suited her.

"Good morning, Caress," he called out, folding the paper and setting it on top of the island.

His brows drew in at the way she visibly jumped and whirled to look at him.

"Mornin'," she said, looking at him before her cheeks flushed and she looked away.

Julius watched as she grabbed her coat and keys before heading out the door. He was curious about where she was going. He knew from Kendrick that she was out looking for a job and doing interviews. Maybe she had one today.

He returned his attention back to his paper and coffee. He didn't have any photo shoots scheduled for today so he was leaving everything in Dwayne's hands for the morning. He deserved a lazy start just chilling, and he was going to have it.

The loud-and-angry strangle of a car not turning over filtered through the windows. He moved over to the door leading out to the driveway and pulled the wooden blinds apart just in time to see Caress banging her fist on the steering wheel in frustration. With an amused grin on his face he watched as she bit her bottom lip, released a deep breath like she was counting to ten, and then reached down to try and start the car again.

The same strangle erupted from beneath the hood.

Caress got out of the car, slammed the little door, and released a string of expletives that would make a west coast rapper blush. Julius didn't think he had ever heard a car addressed as "rusty, beat down, tore up, two-toned son-of-a-bitch." Biting a laugh as she kicked the tire like it was a purse snatcher, Julius opened the door and walked out into the brisk and biting winter air.

"Car trouble?" he asked, sounding amused as he shoved his hands into his armpits to help block the cold.

Caress looked up at him in annoyance at his amusement, and he dropped his grin.

"It won't start and I have a doctor's appointment," she said, moving back to bend inside the car and pop the hood.

Miss Independence, he thought.

Julius wasn't one of the let-me-take-a-look-under-the-hood kind of men. Nor was he interested in being in twenty-degree weather trying to figure out what was wrong with her ancient car. What he was was a gentleman. A gentleman who believed in paying those who enjoyed doing certain things in life . . . like fixing cars.

"What time is your appointment?" he asked, walking down the slanted drive to stand beside her in front of the car.

"In thirty minutes," she answered, pulling the stick to check the oil.

Julius shook his head. "No, no, no," he told her in a stern and deep voice that invited no argument—or so he hoped. He gently removed the stick, stuck it back where it belonged, and then closed the hood. "Give me five minutes to dress and call a mechanic. I'll take you to the doctor."

Caress instantly shook her head. "I can't afford a mechanic—"

Julius felt like rolling his eyes but he didn't because maybe he was hanging around Dwayne too much. "Caress, let me do this for you," he requested in a serious tone as he looked down into her bright eyes that were filled with water from the January cold winds beating around them.

Caress's gaze was one of refusal.

Julius nodded in persistence.

"I'll pay you back for the car," she told him with determination that made him want to smile.

Julius wanted to take her to the doctor anyway. Maybe hearing from the doctor's mouth what her due date was would help ease the questions that still remained with him as to his true role in Caress' unexpected pregnancy.

Caress settled deep onto the sand leather-heated seats of Julius's Range Rover. She couldn't lie—it was a far better ride than her chilly, in-need-of-shocks-real-bad hooptie. Still, she hated to think that Julius thought she was pushing herself or her baby onto him. Of course she'd be happy if he would get happy about the baby at least, but nothing else was foremost on her mind . . . during her working hours at least.

She shivered at the heated memory of her erotic dreams of him at night. Pregnancy obviously didn't cool her desires any because one thing she couldn't deny was that Julius Jones, debonair urban man of the new millennium, turned her the hell on without even trying. And Lord knows he wasn't trying worth a damn.

"Thanks again," she said, glancing over at him as he drove with ease and confidence. "I wish I didn't have to bother you."

Julius glanced over at her as well and their eyes met briefly before she looked away. "It's not a bother, Caress."

They fell silent and the soft strains of some instrumental jazz filled the interior of the luxury vehicle again.

"I guess if your car hadn't broken down this morning you wouldn't have told me about this appointment either?" he asked, adjusting his position in the driver's seat.

"Of course not," she answered. "I clearly see our situation for what it is and nothing more. So the whole happy picture of us going to doctors' appointments and shopping for the nursery . . . and . . . picking names together is not what I'm looking for. And I ain't trying to push it on you either."

She felt Julius's intense eyes on her and it made her feel electrified, but she ignored looking in his direction again.

"This is a hard situation for us both, Caress," he told her.

"I agree, Julius," she answered.

They fell silent again.

"You still not sure it's your baby?" she asked, finally voicing a question that had been haunting her since his return. She chanced a look at him out of the corner of her ebony eyes.

"Honestly?" he asked, as he turned the weighty vehicle right on Springfield Avenue.

A pang echoed in her chest. "Yes. We're both grown."

"I hardly know you so I can't lie and say I don't have doubts," he admitted in a low voice that let her know he wished he hadn't had to say that. "I'm sorry."

Caress nodded. "I understand your position. I watch Maury and all those talk shows. There are plenty of men being fooled . . . but please know that my last relationship ended months before our date that night. I hadn't been intimate with anyone for months before that night, and for the life of me I'm trying to figure out why the hell I lost my mind that night."

"*We* lost our minds, Caress," Julius insisted in soft and husky tones. "We lost our minds together."

Caress closed her eyes as a wave of awareness shimmied over her body. She nervously licked her lips as her heart fluttered. Everything in his tone let her know that he hadn't forgotten what they shared that night either . . . and that was dangerous. "There's my doctor's office on the right. You can just let me out and I'll catch the bus back," she told him, struggling to bring all of her senses and those physical cues of desire under control.

Instead of pulling in front of the brick building, Julius turned into the fenced parking lot on the side. "Actually, I wanted to come in, if that's all right," he said, turning the car off like the decision was already made.

Caress hid her surprise well. "Okay," she agreed, picking her purse up from the floor to leave the SUV.

"Howdy!"

Startled, Julius whirled around and eyed the short woman who walked into the examining room like a mini whirlwind. He hated to be rude, but a piece of him wanted to tell her to bring it down a notch.

"And who is this?" Dr. Dillinger asked as she washed her hands, her short dreadlocks framing a pretty, round face and wide, bright eyes behind frameless glasses.

From on the examining table, Caress glanced over at Julius standing by the window. He looked over at her too.

Neither knew what to say.

"He's a friend," Caress answered, turning to look away.

Julius tucked away the bit of annoyance he felt that Caress had just disclaimed him as the father. But what other choice did he give her when he wasn't prepared to claim it himself . . . yet?

"Well, welcome friend. I'm Doc Dillinger," she said enthusiastically with a big grin that was hard for anyone to resist.

"Nice to meet you," he told her in pleasant tones as he crossed his strong, chiseled arms over his chest in the suede blazer he wore well.

"You've had your labs drawn and so far everything appears within normal levels." The doctor slid on a pair of gloves and sat down on a stool positioned at the foot of the table.

Julius wondered if he should leave.

"I'm going to examine you and then it's . . . dah-da-dun-da-da-dun . . . ultrasound time, Mommy-to-be."

His eyes shifted up to Caress's face, and he didn't miss the twinkle of excitement in her eyes. He bit his lips, feeling like he was missing out on something big.

Since Caress didn't ask him to leave and he didn't necessarily want to, Julius remained by the window as the doctor examined her. Thankfully all of her private business was pointed in the opposite direction. Not that he hadn't seen it, touched it, tasted it . . . dreamt of it for the last three and a half months.

We both lost our minds, Caress.

That moment in the car came drifting back to him. He'd have to be deaf and mute to miss the electricity that surrounded them. In that heated moment he knew they could have easily lost their minds again.

He had hardly had enough Caress. *Nowhere near enough*, he thought.

Still it was a line he would not cross. Things were way too complicated now . . . but that didn't curb the desire he had for her. One sexy night was all he had to hold onto after all these months and he could remember every moment, which was more than he could say about women he'd bedded dozens of times.

Julius shook himself to push away thoughts of how much fun it would be to bury himself deep inside of Caress. He looked over as the Doc lifted Caress's printed hospital gown.

Her stomach was exposed and perfectly round though small. She was just starting to show. He wanted to know if it was his child. The last thing he wanted was to stick around like some naive fool buying up a bunch of baby stuff and proclaiming his fatherhood all during the pregnancy . . .

only to have the baby born and the blood tests done proving it wasn't his. Hell, men had feelings too, and there were plenty of brothers hurt because of some woman lying about paternity.

It was bad enough the woman—no matter how fine— was living with him rent-free. Hell, he already felt like he had a sucker sticker on his damn forehead.

"There's the baby!" Doc Dillinger said excitedly, like it was the first time she saw a baby on an ultrasound.

Julius's eyes shifted to the screen to the distorted image of the baby moving inside Caress.

"Everything seems normal for fourteen weeks gestation," the Doc said as she leaned forward to study the screen as she pressed the gel covered probe over Caress's stomach.

Fourteen weeks gestation. The time matched up to that night. That still wasn't a guarantee, but it damn sure seemed more likely than before. Likely but not definite. He moved forward slowly with his hands falling to his sides.

"Girl or boy, Doc?" Caress asked.

"Even with the 4D ultrasound, it's too early to be anything but a guess that it's a boy," Doc warned, pointing to a spot on the screen.

Caress smiled softly.

Julius's entire neck and face warmed at her words. It was a boy . . . clearly.

Was that his son? His seed? His legacy for this earth? He couldn't deny that it was possible and just that possibility caused emotion to clog his throat.

Chapter Seven

One Month Later

Julius was at his studio reviewing his schedule for the next couple of weeks when Dwayne knocked twice on the wall before pulling back the chocolate leather curtain. Julius looked up and had to blink twice to fully take in that Dwayne who was six feet tall, slender, and had broad shoulders, was now wearing his head permed and spiked. This was the first he had seen of his assistant this morning.

"Jordan Banks is on line one and I'm going to pick up breakfast. You want me to bring you something?" he asked.

"Yes, thanks."

Dwayne twirled dramatically through the curtain.

Shaking his head, Julius dropped his pen and picked up his phone. "Holla at your boy, big time *New York Times* best-selling author. How's Oprah?" Julius joked, leaning back in his leather swivel chair.

Jordan laughed with him. "Real funny. Besides I haven't seen O in months," he joked back.

Jordan Banks was a famous mystery writer who lived just blocks over from Julius in Newark. Like Julius and many other prominent Newark residents who remained loyal to the Renaissance city, Jordan also refused to believe the hype that Newark was some uninhabitable, savage city filled only with poverty and depression and nothing good.

In truth, Julius looked up to Jordan. As a single man, Jordan had adopted five children and raised them alone for many years until he met and fell in love with his wife, Mia. She was just as special to take on a ready-made family of five kids and then give birth to their biological son. After thirteen years of marriage, they were still going strong.

They were two of Julius's favorite people and among his closest friends.

"What's up?" Julius asked.

"Mia's getting on me to get some updated headshots so you know I had to call my boy."

"No problem," Julius said, pulling forward to the desk to flip through the large leather-bound calendar on his desk. "When's good for you?"

"If you can do it here in my office then I'm good for whenever your schedule permits."

"How about next Friday afternoon?" Julius offered, picking up his pen.

"Works for me and then you have to stay for dinner afterward."

Julius laughed lightly as he tapped the pen against the calendar.

"I'll cook," Jordan offered, his voice filled with amusement.

"That's a relief," Julius drawled.

"Hey, hey!" Jordan protested.

"No offense. Your wife is one fine ass woman who has made me a lot of money with all her investment advice, but she can't cook worth a damn."

Jordan laughed. "Oh, she burns where it's important, believe that," he bragged.

"*That's* TMI."

"One of those women of yours will get your nose wide open and you'll be around her bragging on your baby too," Jordan told him.

"Whatever, pimpin'. I'll see you Friday." Julius hung up the phone and wiped his hand over his mouth as he leaned back in his chair again.

Nose wide open. Please.

Julius jumped up from his desk and walked out of his office area. The large loft was clearly divided into separate areas. To the left was a showroom for the original photography he sold. To the right was the section where he did most of his portrait photography, and in the middle was the stylish reception area where Dwayne's glass and metal desk was the centerpiece—just the way his young assistant liked it.

Julius busied himself hanging some of the photos of Africa that he had blown up and framed. His selection from his trip was so varied that these prints were entirely different from the ones going in his book. He was standing back giving a critical eye to a photo of a topless woman covered nearly head to toe in colorful beads with a baby on her hip. He was proud that even with partial nudity—something Westerners were more prudish about—that his immediate focus went to the life in her bright and wide eyes.

The sounds of footsteps and clapping echoed in the large area.

Julius looked over his broad shoulder, and his eyes widened a bit in surprise to see Karina strutting across the polished wooden floors toward him.

She looked the part of a model in the black blazer she wore over a fitted white tee and ultra low-rise jeans with boots. Her hair was pulled back from her face in a loose ponytail. A black fur casually hung on her shoulders.

There was no doubt that Karina was a definite diva.

"You are so vain, Julius Jones," she said, coming to stand beside him in front of the photo.

"Then we have something in common," he mused, lightly placing his strong hand on her waist as he kissed her offered cheek. The scent and taste of her foundation made it a very quick and very light one.

She just laughed. "Haven't heard from you, Julius. I was coming from a meeting in the city and decided to swing by and check up on . . . unfinished business," she concluded with a leisurely and thorough look from the top of his head to the tips of his shoes—and at everything in between.

Karina and Julius had danced this dance before. Yet, they hadn't managed to close the deal so to speak. She was undoubtedly a beautiful woman but now Julius had no interest in discovering the pleasures in Karina's bed between her slender thighs.

Their time had come and passed and they'd missed it.

It was funny but the drama, the makeup, the loud perfume that arrived before she did, the over-the-top wardrobe and stunts, the whole I-want-to-be-Eartha-Kitt voice and mannerism. All of it was boring as hell.

Karina grew up in Newark's Pennington Court housing projects but she browsed around town like Paris was her birthplace.

Shoving his hands into the pockets of his Sean John slacks, Julius shifted past her to walk over to the reception area. "What can I help you with, Karina?" he said, busying himself straightening the contemporary leather waiting room chairs.

He heard her footsteps bring her over to him. "As much

as I would love to discuss rescheduling our date . . . I'm here on business."

Julius looked over at her, waiting for the rest.

Karina turned, offering him her shoulders in a silent request. Julius ground his teeth as he removed her fur and slung it over his arm. She turned back to him with a pleased smile.

"I've been offered my own calendar, and I want you to shoot it," she said, easing down into one of the chairs and crossing her long and slender legs.

Julius's interest was definitely piqued.

"In Jamaica," Karina added, turning sideways in the chair to strike a model pose as she flipped her long and undetectable weave over her shoulder.

He nodded, already calculating his fees for shooting an entire calendar and traveling. He wasn't in need of money, but this would be a sizeable hit and from the look in Karina's eyes she knew it too.

The metal elevators leading up from the street opened and Dwayne strutted in carrying two large brown paper bags. At the sight of Karina, he rolled his eyes before he reached them. "Hi, diva," he said, false as all get-out, showing every bright white tooth in his mouth.

Dwayne had no qualms admitting that Karina irked his nerves. In his own words, he swore the model "made his butt itch."

"Hey," she said off-handedly with a weak, almost dismissive, wave of her hand.

Julius had a distinct feeling she had planned to pull one of her I'm-gonna-make-you-sex-me stunts on him, but Dwayne ruined all of that.

"So I'm headed out now but someone from the agency will call with all the details."

Julius didn't bother to point out that he hadn't said yes.

Karina stood and turned again with a little wiggle of her shoulders.

Dwayne stepped forward with his hands outstretched like he would like to choke her from behind.

Julius stepped in his path and shook out the fur on his arm to place back on her shoulders. She gave him a wink and blew a kiss over her shoulder, then adjusted her fur and strutted to the doors as if her own personal runway music was playing in her head. Once she stepped on the elevator, she turned dramatically and struck a pose with her feet splayed wide and her hands on her hips.

The men shared a look long as the door closed.

"I wish you'd go on 'head and give her just what she's looking for so she'll stop coming here," Dwayne said, unwrapping a bacon, egg, and cheese sandwich at his desk. "She makes my butt—"

"Itch. Yes, you've told me that before," Julius drawled in amusement as he opened his own sandwich and took a healthy bite.

Things were definitely looking up.

Caress placed her hands on her widening middle as she did her official happy dance—a mix of the Wop and the Cabbage Patch. Tamara laughed at her friend at first, but soon she hopped up off the bed and joined her.

"I got a job . . . I got a job," Caress sang.

"She got a job . . . she got a job," Tamara mimicked.

Caress felt a tiny twinge in her back so she gave up on the dancing, but she couldn't stop the smile on her face to save her life. "Julius might even break-dance when he hears the news," she joked, moving to sit down on her bed.

Tamara laughed. "Girl, you stupid."

Caress raised her long sleeve thermal to rub her belly.

"We have settled into this nice friendly zone and that's good for the baby, but I know the man wants his house back. Hell, I want my own spot. God bless the child that has its own."

"I know that's right, but that's not going to happen tomorrow. Job or no job," Tamara reminded her as she started to fold the clean clothes in the hamper at the foot of Caress's surprisingly made bed.

"I'm creeping right now, but watch a sister crawl and then walk very soon." Caress leaned forward to grab a handful of the clothes to fold herself.

Tamara eyed the room. It wasn't up to Julius's standards but it was a marked improvement from the wrecked state Caress usually existed in. "Julius rubbing off on you?"

Caress shrugged. "When in Rome . . ."

Ever since the doctor's appointment things in the house had settled in nicely. They still lived separate lives but they talked more and joked more whenever they were in each other's company. She was well aware though that the only show of irritation or aggravation he showed was about her messiness—well and her love of reality TV and rap music. Loving the serenity and peace, she made an effort to tidy up more.

Plus, with the baby coming it was time for her to get in the habit anyway.

She didn't want the man thinking his baby would be crawling around on wrinkled piles of clean clothes and knocking into empty Snapple bottles. She'd never kept a nasty house—mice, roaches, trash, unwashed dishes filled with food—but she knew it was . . . untidy.

"We have to celebrate," Tamara insisted, stacking the folded shirts in the hamper.

Caress shook her head, causing her ponytail to swing from left to right. "My titties are heavy as hell, and the only clothes that fit these days look like this," she complained, waving a Vanna White-like hand up and down her current ensemble of baggy green sweatpants and a red tank top that was overfilled with her growing breasts.

"I see you're in the Christmas spirit, Mrs. Claus. Too bad it's not December." Tamara shook her head as she reached in the back pocket of her slacks for her cell phone. She ducked to avoid the throw pillow Caress chucked at her head.

"I can't wait till you're fat and pregnant."

"Not as long as I'm popping my pills, baby," Tamara assured her.

Caress playfully stuck out her tongue.

"So since Mrs. Claus isn't up for going out, we'll stay in. No biggie, boo," she said, dialing her husband.

Caress got off the bed and made her way to the bathroom. She felt an excited energy as she relieved herself. More than anything she couldn't wait to tell Julius about her job. It was important for her to assure him that her time here in his house was temporary and that she was working on lessening his burden.

Caress remained seated long after she finished. She needed a moment to herself. Tam-Tam was the best kind of friend but her girlfriend could talk and somewhere during her pregnancy Caress had developed a love of peace and quiet. She'd even found herself turning off the television to snuggle under the covers to read. Julius had an extensive book collection and right now she was devouring a book by Jordan Banks.

Pregnancy was changing her. Motherhood would change her even more.

Would fatherhood change Julius too?

Caress frowned as she leaned forward as much as she could and placed her elbows on her knees. *If* it did, how would she know? She hardly knew any more about Julius than she did that night . . . even after almost two months living with him.

In essence they really were still strangers.

Air whished against Caress's bared bottom as the bathroom door suddenly swung open. Her eyes got big as she squealed.

"Shit. Sorry," Julius swore, stepping back to swing the door closed.

He was home.

And he just caught a live action view of her on the john.

"Great," Caress drawled, finally pulling her sweats and panties up as she rose to her feet. She washed her hands and opened the door to step into the hall. Julius and Tamara were standing in the hall. *Oh great, an audience*.

"Tam-Tam said you have good news," Julius said, putting his hands on his narrow hips as he looked down at her petite frame.

Caress shot Tamara a look that made her friend focus her attention on the cell phone in her hand as she moved past them to jog down the stairs.

"I got the job at the insurance company," she told him, unable to hold back her smile.

Julius's smile matched her own as he picked her up with ease and twirled her. Caress squealed as she instinctively snaked her arms around his neck to hold on for dear life. She kicked her feet and pressed her face into his strong, warm neck.

Wrong move.

She inhaled his warm and spicy scent. Awareness filled her, and her body literally tingled from being so close to him.

Julius stopped spinning and looked down at Caress just as she drew her face away from the addictive and dizzying scent of his neck. They paused. Their eyes locked. Their mouths were just a few inches apart. Caress could smell the gum on his cool breath.

Caress still wanted Julius. She'd never stopped. She wondered if she ever would.

His eyes, those heated and intense eyes, dropped to her mouth and then to the tops of her breasts. She opened her mouth as she panted slightly like she needed air to breathe—and that was simply because he made her breathless.

Tamara's feet climbing the stairs brought them out of the spell.

Caress licked her lips as she shifted her arms down from around his neck. Her hands eased over his chest, and she didn't miss the thunderous pace and pounding of his heart. Even as he placed her back on her feet she couldn't draw her eyes from his. Instinctively she knew the beating of his heart—which matched her own—was not from physical exertion.

That excited the hell out of her.

"Oops. Sorry I didn't know I was interrupting," Tamara said, already turning to walk back down the stairs.

"No!" Julius and Caress hollered out together rather dramatically.

That caused them both to laugh nervously as they moved farther apart.

Tamara peeked her bobbed head over the railing with a knowing look. "Is it just me or is it hot up here?" she teased.

Julius gave Tamara a hard look before he turned and walked to his bedroom. "I'm taking a shower."

"Kendrick's bringing food and some movies . . . unless we're in the way," Tamara called behind him, as she winked at Caress.

His bedroom door closed solidly behind him.

Tamara continued up the stairs and moved over to bump

her thick hip against Caress. "Girl, it's so obvious you two want to get back in each other's pants."

Caress pinched Tamara. "Stop it. You're being childish," she scolded.

Tamara winced and then pinched Caress back. "You two stop it. You're being foolish. I can cut the sexual tension with a knife," she said dramatically as she sliced her hand through the air.

Caress released a heavy breath before she turned and walked into her bedroom. She wanted to put on a less-revealing top. Her breasts had surged from a B-cup to a C and her fitted tank top made her look more like Pamela Anderson than she wanted to.

Tamara walked into the room, predicting Julius and Caress would be going at it like rabbits really soon but Caress tuned her out. The only thing on her mind was the memory of that furious beating of Julius's heart.

Julius left the steam-filled bathroom loosely wrapping a towel around his waist. The length and breadth of his male-ness, even at rest, was impressive and it pressed against the towel with strength. He released a deep breath before he sat down on the leather bench at the foot of his bed.

This was a dangerous dance Caress and he were doing. His move to pick her up was innocent but in an instant it had changed. Switched. Flipped.

Pregnant or not, Caress was still sexy as hell.

He was fighting it . . . but he wanted her. He was curious to know if it would be just as good as that night. Or maybe even better?

That had to be impossible.

Caress living under the same roof with him was a wreck to his senses.

Of course the scent of her perfume wafting through the house messed with both of his heads.

Of course walking by the bathroom and hearing her in the shower evoked erotic images.

Of course the sight of her breasts near spilling out of one of those damn spaghetti strapped tanks she loved so damn much made him dumbstruck like a horny teenager.

He felt like a horny teenager anyway—he hadn't had sex since the sexy flight attendant he met while en route to Africa and four months was a record for him. Plus Caress had singed her memory into his brain and his body was calling for more—even if his brain told him "don't you do it."

Caress. Beautiful, exotic, complicated, sexy as hell, Caress. He felt his dick stir between his thighs and slightly tent the towel.

Knock knock.

Julius looked over to the door as he loosened the towel over his growing erection. "Come in," he ordered, opening his legs wider so that hopefully his arousal wasn't revealed.

His bedroom door opened slowly. He looked up from where he sat. His eyes smoldered as the sight of Caress stepping into the doorframe.

She wore nothing except for a sequined pair of sandals and a sultry smile.

His eyes took in everything. Missed nothing.

Her beautiful face free of makeup.

Her petite but shapely frame.

Her small but plump breasts with the darkest and fullest nipples and aureoles.

Her wide hips made for a man's hands.

The soft ebony curls covering her plump mound.

His dick surged even more with heat and strength, pressing against his towel.

Caress walked into the room slowly, crossing one shapely leg in front of the other as she brought that sexy little body to him like she had nothing else to do in the world.

"Say you don't want me . . . I dare you," she said softly as she straddled his hips with ease on the bench.

Julius breathed in and out deeply as he looked into her eyes. "I can't," he admitted, as his eyes dropped down to drink in the sight of her breasts.

He swallowed over a sudden lump in his throat at the sight of her nipples hard like pebbles as they pointed at him. Tempting him. Calling him.

Caress brought her hands up to trace a hot trail from the top of his strong thighs up to the back of his head. With her other hand she gently lifted one of her breasts before guiding his head toward her. She purred as she stroked her nipple against his mouth.

His tongue darted out to lick it . . .

"Julius . . . Julius . . . why the hell you looking at me like that?"

He shook his head and the hot image of Caress on his lap disappeared like a mist. Instead there was Kendrick standing over him. "Damn," Julius said softly, wiping his mouth with his hands as reality sunk in.

"Man. Throw some clothes on before Tamara thinks we on the damn down-low or some shit," Kendrick complained, before he turned and left the room.

Julius could only shake his head. Even in his daydreams Caress was hard as hell to resist.

Chapter Eight

Tamara licked the back of her card and then stuck it to her forehead with a "Bam!" before she then slapped it on the center of the card table. "Can y'all handle that?" she asked Caress and Julius, pointing to the ten of hearts. "Ain't nothing they can do with it, baby," she said, turning to Kendrick.

Caress and Julius eyed each other from across the table. There was nothing worse than a cocky whist player.

Caress shook her head shamefully when Julius tossed out his last card, a King of Diamonds—he was out of trump. Kendrick threw out a low piece of diamonds. Caress couldn't do a thing with the piece of club in her hand—face card or not.

Trumps were all played and everyone threw off the suit Tamara led with. Her piece of heart was nasty.

Kendrick and Tamara stood up and started their obnoxious high fives across the table. Caress was confident they would've bumped chests if the table wasn't blocking them.

Caress stood up and started to gather their wine and highball glasses. "Oh, man, please y'all act like you ran a Boston or something."

"Ain't it," Julius agreed, rising to stretch.

"Whateverrrrrr," Tamara said, glancing at her watch. "Come on, baby, let's go home and celebrate by spankin' dat ass."

"You two really need more victories to celebrate," Julius drawled as he started picking up their plates and empty Chinese food containers.

Kendrick retrieved their coats from the foyer closet. He helped his wife into hers before he shrugged his own on. "Congrats again, Caress," he said, as she walked into the foyer with her hands full. He bent down quickly to kiss her cheek and give her a one-armed hug.

"Thank you."

"Yes, congrats, girl," Tamara said, rubbing Caress's belly before she leaned in close to whisper in her ear. "I had a good time. It was a nice couples' night."

Caress started to protest but Tamara just laughed a little and walked out the door behind her husband.

Julius strolled out of the living room with his hands filled as well. "I wash. You dry," he offered with a charming smile.

Caress started to tell him that he was the one to insist on using regular plates instead of paper ones, but she just turned and headed for the kitchen. Julius followed behind her. While she filled the deep sink with water and detergent, Julius scraped the plates before placing them next to the glasses already on the counter. Caress shifted over, giving him the sink while she grabbed a dish towel.

They worked together in a comfortable silence, the soft strains of Julius's constantly playing jazz music floated in the air.

At times their arms or legs would brush from being in such close proximity. Each innocent touch was building a slow burn between them. The air surrounding them was charged with electricity.

Caress's entire body was alive from his nearness. His closeness.

Their hands accidentally touched, and they both jumped like they'd been shocked with high voltage.

Caress swallowed over a sudden lump as she grasped the edge of the sink tightly.

"Caress, we need to talk about this," Julius said.

She closed her eyes as she waited for her heart to resume its regular pacing. "About what?" she asked, proud of herself for sounding like the man wasn't turning her into jelly with nothing . . . *nothing* but his presence.

"We want each other. We *still* want each other."

Caress chanced a look up at him. He was leaning against the sink looking down at her with his arms folded across his defined chest. She licked her lips nervously and Julius threw his hands up in exasperation.

"Don't do that," he said.

Caress was confused and looked it. "What?"

"Lick your lips," he said in a deep voice. "You're not helping."

"Oh be serious, Julius. I am not trying to seduce you. I'm pregnant for God's sake," she said, whirling to poke her stomach out at him.

Julius shoved his hands into the pocket of the loose fitting—but still stylish—sweatpants he wore with a wifebeater. "Pregnancy hasn't made you any less sexy Caress."

Or less horny, she thought as she started to lick her lips again at the husky tones of his voice, but when his eyes darted down to her mouth she quickly tucked her lips inward. "Okay, Julius, Mr. Sexy Cologne, and shirts with just enough muscle exposed and that bowlegged walk—can you stop all that?" she asked.

"My walk?" he spouted.

Caress leaned her shapely hip against the sink as she looked up at him with more boldness than she felt on the inside. "You walk like you holding, and if memory serves me right . . . you are," she admitted.

Julius frowned deeply. "I can't help how I walk."

"And I can't help that our baby has given me . . . *these*," she waved her hand rather dramatically across her breasts. "But I catch you looking."

Julius bit back a grin. "They're pretty hard to miss."

Caress laughed too, putting her hands on her small, round belly as she did.

And there was that comfortable air around them again. The kind of comfort a man found with his woman and a woman found only with her man. It was a zone Caress was afraid to find comfort in and she felt Julius wanted no part of. "I'll be out of here soon," she reminded him. "Me and all this sexiness."

She was joking but when she looked up at Julius his eyes had darkened. That awareness between them returned like the snap of a finger.

"Fuck it," he muttered low in his throat, before he took one step forward, squatted down, and lightly grasped the sides of her face with a deep, guttural moan that was telling.

Caress sighed in the heated moments just before Julius pressed his mouth down upon hers. Their lips fit like puzzle pieces as they shared one long and passionate kiss. And then a dozen rushed and heated pecks. And then an erotic and sizzling twirl of their tongues in that minute space between their damp and open mouths. And then that frantic and deep kiss like they were trying to draw life from each other.

Julius broke the kiss long enough to pant deeply as he kept his face pressed to hers. "I wanted to do that all while I was in Africa," he admitted. "I dreamt about that little move you do with your—"

"Julius! We have to fight it," Caress reminded him, even as she brought her hands up to massage the back of his head.

Julius nodded. "Too many complications."

"Too many expectations," Caress added before she turned Julius's head toward her to briefly taste his delicious mouth again. *Just once more.*

"Caress, I don't know how much more I can fight—"

"No, no, no, no, no," Caress insisted, whirling away from Julius and quickly moving over by the island. "I will admit it, Julius Jones. I have not forgotten that night either. It was good. It was *real* good. Addictive. Delicious."

Julius ran his hand over his mouth before he whirled and walked over to the fridge to pull out one of her Snapples. He tossed his head back and drank the entire bottle nonstop. Her eyes shifted down to his throat and just the movement of his Adam's apple put Caress on edge.

"But . . . I am not a one-night freakum or booty call kinda chick, Julius," she said in a rushed voice like she was trying to convince herself why her pregnant behind shouldn't strip naked and hike her heels to the ceiling. "I'm a girlfriend, committed girl kinda chick. You're not looking for that . . . but I am. And sex would mess me up, so no matter how many wet dreams, no matter that you turn me the hell on, no matter that . . . that . . . night was the best . . . sex . . . I ever had . . . no more na-na for you, Julius Jones."

He nodded as he laughed low in his throat. "And no more for you, Caress Coleman."

They fell silent again for a little while and a haunting jazz song took prominence. They moved back to their positions at the sink and quietly finished up the dishes. As Caress put the dried dishes back inside the cabinets, Julius used the dishcloth to wipe down the countertops and the island.

"Caress."

She closed the cabinet door and looked across the kitchen at him.

"If that's my baby . . . I want you to know that I will be there for him. I will be the father that I never had. You won't have to raise him alone," he told her, his hands on the top of the island as he looked over at her with a serious expression.

She nodded as her right hand instinctively went to her belly. "I'm happy to hear that because he is yours. And I want you to know that I won't be one of those crazy, always-causing-drama baby mamas. I will put just as much energy, love, financial and emotional support into our child as you do. I'm not looking to use my baby as a meal ticket or as a way to stay in your pockets. We made him and we *both* will work together to take care of him."

Julius licked his lips and nodded in understanding. "That's good to know."

Caress removed the rubber band from her wrists and pulled her hair up into a sloppy ponytail. "And I promise I won't try to interrupt your home once you finally meet the one to make your whoring little butt settle down," Caress teased.

"I don't whore," Julius balked.

Caress snorted in derision.

"I am a single man enjoying the opposite sex."

"A *lot*," Caress stressed before she headed out of the kitchen. She smiled as Julius followed behind her.

"Women judge single men too harshly," he said from behind her.

Caress glanced over her shoulder as she moved toward the living room. She stopped and turned at the sight of his eyes dipped down to watch that up and down move-ment of her buttocks. "No more of *that*, Julius," she chided him, before she turned and continued.

His husky laughter reached her.

Caress busied herself folding the chairs around the card table they put up. She felt his heat as he stepped close to her and took a chair from her hands. Her skin burned where his hand lightly brushed hers.

"I got it. You go to bed."

Caress looked at the remnants of their night still scattered about his usually pristine living room. "But I can help—"

"Caress," Julius said sternly.

She looked at him.

He looked pointedly downward at his obvious erection straining against the zipper. "*Please* go to bed," he stressed.

Her mouth formed a circle as her cheeks flamed and the nestled, moist bud between her legs throbbed to life. "Oh . . . okay . . . good night then," she said, her voice shaky as she hurried from the room.

Long after she snuggled beneath the covers of her bed, Caress thought of Julius. Their attraction. Their baby.

She wished like hell that things could've been different.

Julius allowed Caress's image and her memory to seduce him as he massaged the length of his hardness beneath the hot spray of his shower. He gave in to his want of her as he worked his hand tightly around his shaft in a fast left and right motion around the thick tip. The water from the shower made the movement slick and easy.

As he felt the pressure rise from his loins, he bit his bottom lip and began to pant, inhaling deeply of the steam surrounded his hard, chiseled frame. He pressed his back against the wall and arched his hips as his heart beat furiously. "Caress," he moaned, allowing her image to caress his tense thighs as she suckled the tip of his dick with her mouth beneath the spray of water.

"Caress," he cried out, arching up on his toes as he

worked his hips in motion with the jerking movement of his hand. A tortured cry filled the glass interior of the shower and mingled with the steam as he spilled his seed in a series of long spasms that soon left him spent.

It was a sore replacement for the real thing.

Tamara turned on her side in the middle of the bed. She propped her head up on her hand as she looked down at her husband sleeping peacefully. His snores were evidence of that. *Awww, he looks like a big old baby*, she thought.

"Kendrick," she said loudly.

He jumped visibly as his eyes shot open. "Huh? What? Who? What?"

Tamara placed her hand on his chest to settle him down. "What does Julius say about Caress when y'all talk?" she asked.

Kendrick leaned back from her and gave her a look like she had three heads and a penis poking out of her forehead. "You woke me up in the middle of the night to talk about Julius and Caress?" he asked, with plenty of attitude. "Woman, are . . . you . . . *crazy?*"

Tamara shook her head innocently. "No," she answered him simply.

"Humph." Kendrick flopped over onto his side, giving her his back—and probably his ass.

Tamara spooned her body against his, pressing her soft and warm breasts against his massive back. "Well . . ." she asked.

He tensed. "Well what?"

Tamara smiled and slid her leg over the top of his. She eased up a bit to press her face against his neck. "Tonight I kept catching Julius and Caress checking each other out when the other wasn't looking. You know . . . a tittie peek here and a butt glance there."

Kendrick reached up for Tamara's hand and pulled it down to wrap around his hardness. "First, Julius and I don't talk about Caress so I can't help out with whatever schemes or fantasies you've cooked up this time. But don't worry, baby, it's not for waste."

"Huh?"

He turned to face her, his beefy hand easing down to raise the hem of her short nightgown. "You woke me up so no excuses, wifey, it's on like popcorn. You got it up so now you got to get it down."

Their husky and playful laughter soon was replaced by the sounds of their passions and one squeaky bed.

The next morning Julius was headed out for a location shoot when he overheard Caress releasing several expletives from behind her closed bedroom. The sounds of something crashing to the floor echoed next.

The baby, he thought frantically, dropping his briefcase and turning to burst into the room. "Caress, are you—"

She gasped loudly as she covered her upper body with her arms. "Julius," she snapped, giving him a look that made Aunt Ester from *Sandford and Sons* look friendly.

He held up his hands as he turned his back to her. "Sorry. I thought you fell or something," he told her. "Are you okay?"

"As good as I can be trying to fit all this baby in my old clothes. You can turn around."

Julius did so. He immediately bit his bottom lip to keep from laughing out loud.

Caress eyed him. "Are you laughing?" she asked in disbelief.

Julius shook his head but his eyes were filled with the

laughter he was fighting hard not to let spill through his lips. Caress wore dark denims that would be stylish if the zipper didn't stop midway, leaving the top of the jeans open and framing her stomach. And her top was a button-up black shirt that she *was* able to button, but was unable to get entirely over her stomach. It was a sight.

"My nipples hurt. My back is starting to ache. I pee all the damn time. I have a black line up the middle of my damn stomach. My nose is swelling and this is *only month five*." She stalked over to him with her eyes blazing. "On top of all those goodies of pregnancy, Mr. All I Did Was Bust A Nut, my clothes don't fit. So . . . I'm gonna ask you 'gain, Julius Jones. Are you laughing?"

That pushed Julius over the edge and he did laugh because Caress's whole reprimand was comical—whether she meant it to be or not. "I'm sorry I'm not laughing at you. I'm laughing with you."

Caress made an astonished face. "Funny, I don't remember me laughing nor do I plan to laugh."

Julius bit his mouth again as he crossed his arms over his chest. Caress eyed him before she caught sight of herself in the mirror on her dresser. She did a double take and then cut her eyes over at Julius before she felt her own laughter bubbling to the surface. "I look like Mr. Brown from those Tyler Perry plays."

They burst out in laughter together.

Caress bent over and two of her buttons popped, flying across the room to hit the opposite wall.

They really roared with laughter then.

"Caress, you need maternity clothes," Julius said simply, as they settled down.

"No shit, Sherlock," she drawled.

Julius turned and headed out the door. "I'm going out. See you later."

"Bye."

He closed the bedroom door behind. As he bent down to pick up his briefcase a thought came to him. He felt a bit callous in hindsight. Caress had a new job but no new clothes for her newly pregnant body.

And no money to buy any.

He stopped in his tracks and turned and looked at her door for a few thoughtful seconds before he turned and continued down the stairs and out of the house.

Caress walked in the house and started to drop her purse and coat on the foyer table but thought twice about it. She was beat from trudging through the clothes she had packed in her storage unit. Her steps were defeated. She had hoped the few items she had with an elastic waistband would fit. She'd been wrong. Nothing fit.

Of course Julius was right that she needed maternity clothes, but with only her last fifty bucks to her name it looked like all she could get were some big tops to wear over her regular-size bottoms buttoned and zipped only as far as they would go. Like some teenage mother or something.

She walked into her bedroom, but she stopped in the doorway at the sight of the five huge Motherhood Maternity shopping bags sitting in the middle of her bed. Curious, she walked to the bed dropping her coat, keys and purse at the foot. She reached for the note hanging from the bag in the front.

C.

I guessed on the size. Hope it all fits.
Good luck with your job.

J.

Caress's mouth fell open in surprise. She opened bag, after bag, after bag pulling out outfits she could wear to work. "Julius," she said softly to herself as she dropped down onto the bed.

She didn't know if it was her hormones or just how deeply touched she was, but Caress couldn't stop the tears that filled her eyes and then raced down her cheeks.

Julius noticed the folded piece of paper sitting on the center of the island as soon as he entered the house through the kitchen door later that night. Setting his camera case on the floor he picked up the note.

TO: Julius Jones
FROM: Caress Coleman
RE: Repayment of Loans
I Caress Coleman agree to pay Julius Jones $200.00 per month, beginning with my first paycheck, for the following items:

Car Repair	*379.92*
Clothing	*400.00 (est.)*

SUBTOTAL	*779.92*

Rent/Food/ Utilities	*200.00/month*
(Until I move)	

TOTAL	*??*

Caress Coleman

Julius just laughed and shook his head. He didn't take offense. He was fast learning that Caress was just as independent as Tamara and Kendrick had said. He balled the promissory note into his hand and tossed it into the trash before he grabbed his camera case and headed to his darkroom, still shaking his head.

Chapter Nine

"The renovations to the rest of the house look good, man," Julius told Jordan after they finished up the photo shoot in his office. "Can I assume this museum was off limits?"

Jordan chuckled as he removed the ebony suede blazer he wore over a matching silk shirt for the headshots. "I love my office just as it is. This is organized confusion, my brother."

"You sound like Caress."

Jordan used his index finger to push his wire-framed glasses up on his nose as he looked over at his friend. "And Caress is?" he asked, before he settled down in the leather chair behind his cluttered desk.

Julius didn't know what to say.

Caress is the woman living at my house, pregnant with a baby she claims is mine from a heated one night stand about five months ago.

Or . . .

Caress is this girl I can't seem to get off my mind . . . no matter how hard I try.

Or . . .

Caress is the woman I am fast beginning to hope is pregnant with my child.

"A friend of mine," was all that he said.

Jordan leaned back in his chair and placed his square chin in his hand. "You should have invited her to dinner."

Julius began packing up his equipment and ignored the look in his friend's eyes. "There is no mystery for you to snoop out, Slim Willie," he said, referring to the lead character in Jordan's best-selling mystery series.

"Umph."

Julius scooped up an open box of Jordan's latest book, *Death by Midnight*, from a chair and put it on the floor. He settled down into the chair and let his head hang back over the edge.

"I might have a son on the way," Julius finally said.

"Might?" Jordan asked.

Julius turned his head to look over at Jordan who was watching him intently. With one deep breath he began to tell the story of *that* night—his and Caress's night.

"That good, huh?" Jordan asked, bemused.

Julius made a face. "I left that morning and went to Africa."

"Weren't you there for like two or three months?" Jordan asked, as he reached to turn on the desk lamp. His arm accidentally hit his cup of coffee and he swore as he rushed to clean up the fast-moving spill.

Julius just shook his head. Jordan was and would always be a klutz. He sat up in the chair as he retold the rest of the story. "Anyway, I came back from Africa and . . ."

Jordan let out a long and drawn-out whistle. "So mama's baby, daddy's maybe?"

Julius shrugged. "To be honest, I really think it's my baby."

"And how do you feel about that?"

"To be honest, I don't know," he admitted. "You know my childhood was jacked up and even though my mind wasn't focused on having kids I just kinda always pictured me settled down when it happened."

Jordan leaned over to toss the coffee-soaked napkins into the trash. "So settle down."

"I don't want to be with somebody just because she is having my baby. That's relationship suicide."

"What if you two were destined to be but your hormones messed up the whole equation?" Jordan asked.

"Naw," Julius disagreed. "Caress and I are different as night and day. She is *nothing* like the women I usually date."

"And?"

"*And* . . . I hardly know her."

"And yet you're confident enough to know she's not like any other woman you've dated," Jordan drawled. "So you're going by the physical? Umph."

Julius gave him a hard stare as his friend hit a flyball out of the ballpark.

"Any other woman make you forget your jimmy?"

"Jimmy? What are you stuck in the eighties?"

Jordan said nothing else as he waited.

"No," Julius answered.

"Any other woman ever been pregnant with your child?"

"No."

"Any other rendered you celibate for months?"

Julius hopped to his feet. "Listen, Caress and me have this physical thing that blows my mind—I will admit that, but baby or no baby, we are not made for each other. Period."

Jordan leaned forward in his chair. "Let me put it this way. My son is his twenties and I would better imagine having this conversation with him than with a man ten years his senior."

Julius frowned, not sure if he should be insulted. "Your point is?"

"Don't be one of those whack ass, fifty-year-old players out there still chasing Miss New Booty." Jordan pushed his glasses up on his head and pinched the bridge of his nose.

The phone rang and Jordan hit the speakerphone button. "Yes, baby."

"Five of our six kids are here . . . and very hungry. There are ten eyes on that one roast. 'Nough said, gentleman?" Mia asked, her voice echoing into the room.

Jordan and Julius laughed as they both rose to their feet. "'Nough said, baby. We're coming."

"Good," she said sweetly before she disconnected the line.

Caress was in the kitchen eating a salad and flipping through a celebrity gossip magazine when the doorbell rang. Julius was out for the evening—and she was proud that she had trained herself not to wonder where and whom with. Her flip-flops dragged against the floor as she made her way to the front door.

"Who is it?" she asked, as she raised up on her toes to look out the window.

"Boo."

Caress frowned at the sight of the extremely tall and thin man she saw. "Uhm . . . Julius isn't home. You want to leave a message?" she called through the door.

"Uh . . . no. I'm his assistant and I wanted to drop off this package from his agent."

Caress crossed her fingers that she wasn't letting in an axe murderer as she unlocked the door. Her intention was to crack it open just enough for him to give her the FedEx envelope he held, but Boo bumped his hip against the wooden door and strutted into the house.

He twirled rather dramatically and pointed one finger at Caress, his mouth opening a little at the sight of her belly. "*Who* are you?" he asked.

"I'm Caress," she said, wondering if she was about to get in the midst of some down-low drama.

"You live here?" he asked, waving a finger.

"Yes."

"Are you related to Julius?" he asked.

"No."

"Ooh, Julius you slick little devil you," he said, holding the package to his chest as he grinned at her with lips that were just a tad bit shiny.

"You're Julius's assistant?" she asked, closing the front door since it appeared he wasn't ready to leave.

"Yup. Let him know I dropped this off for him, please."

She took the package. "I will."

Boo gave another look at her belly before he turned and left the house.

Caress closed the door, and her heart was beating fast with nervous anticipation. She wondered if Julius would be angry that his secret was out. It's not like he told her not to tell anyone she was living there temporarily.

Wanting to put the package in a safe place, Caress went up to Julius's room. The phone began to ring, but like always Caress didn't answer it. She always gave people her cell phone number to reach her so she felt she had no reason to answer Julius's phone.

"This is Julius. After the beep, leave a message."

Beep.

Caress set the package on his bed, trying hard not to let the lingering scent of his cologne entice her too much.

"Julius, this is Karina—"

Caress's steps faltered and she stopped to listen to the

message being left. She knew it was wrong and rude, but she couldn't help herself.

"I am so excited about Jamaica. We are going to have the best time. Believe that. Anyway call me when you get this message."

Beep.

So Julius was still seeing Karina.

Caress continued out of his room, closing the door behind her. She hated seeing the images that flashed in her head like a amateur porno of Julius making love to Karina. "Ew," she said, knowing she was being childish.

She walked into her bedroom and dropped down onto the chaise lounge in the corner. *Is that where he is tonight?* she wondered, as she tucked her feet beneath her. *No, she wouldn't be calling if he was, Caress.*

Maybe Karina offered him more than Caress could. Maybe she liked jazz music and sipping on fine wines. Maybe she was more his type. All refined and bougie. Maybe she was better in bed. Maybe she was the one he wanted to settle down with.

"Where was Miss Karina when he made love to me all night long?" she snapped, admitting to herself that she was jealous.

She let her head drift back to rest on the top of the chaise. Her eyes closed as she pressed her hand to her belly. "I'm just the mother of his child," Caress said aloud and then instantly regretted it. She couldn't have expectations about Julius concerning the baby. Not when neither of them planned it.

Caress let out a frustrated sigh. If Julius and Karina were making plans to live it up in Jamaica then it had nothing at all to do with her.

Needing a distraction, Caress headed back down the stairs to the living room to zone out on television. She had to get the images of Julius's sexy chocolate body wrapped intimately with Karina's tall and slender frame. It was driving her crazy.

She settled into the corner of the chair, snuggled the mink throw over her lap, and grabbed the remote. She found a celebrity gossip show to get lost in because there was nothing like somebody else's business to help you forget your own.

Julius entered the house and it was entirely dark save for the light flickering from the television in the living room. He dropped his keys and the autographed copy of Jordan's new book on the table in the foyer. He headed for the stairs, figuring Caress was vegging out on those crazy reality TV shows she loved so much. But after a few steps he turned and headed back to stroll into the living room.

"Hey . . ." the rest of his greeting drifted off when he saw that Caress was fast asleep on her side.

Julius looked down at her and something primal filled him. It wasn't desire—although Caress was still deep in his bones. It was a need to take care of her. She didn't want him to, and in the beginning he didn't want to, but that's how he felt now.

It felt good to take care of her. It felt right.

She shifted in her sleep and lightly smacked her lips. He smiled at the adorable sight she made. She was even prettier with her face relaxed in sleep. Something about her tugged at his heart.

He wondered for the first time if the baby would look like her or more like him. A mix of both? Her shortness or his tallness? Her love of rap or his love of jazz?

Removing the suede coat he wore, Julius picked up the mink throw that had obviously slid off of her to the floor.

He debated waking her or carrying her up to bed. Folding the throw over the arm of the chair, he decided on the latter.

Julius slid his hands under her and lifted her with ease into his muscled arms and against his chest. She snuggled against him with a little sigh. Careful not to trip, he used his hands to turn on the lights in the foyer and hall.

The scent of her perfume—something sweet and powerful, drifted up to him. It was the same sweet scent she wore that night. He would never forget it.

With his elbow he pushed the door to her room open. He settled her down on the bed and then used the blanket folded at the bottom to cover her. Nearly tip-toeing, he headed for the door, closing it softly behind him.

Julius stripped off his clothing as soon as he closed the door to his bedroom. He didn't bother turning on the lights. He was beat and all he wanted to do was shower and crawl into bed. Naked, he pressed play on his digital answering machine before walking into the bathroom.

"You have four new messages. First message . . ."

Julius turned the shower on full blast. Soon steam began to fill the glass enclosure as he listened with half an ear to those annoying customer service reps trying to sell him something.

Beep.

"Julius, this is Karina. I am so excited about Jamaica. We are going to have the best time. Believe that. Anyway call me when you get this message."

Having no plans to call Karina since he'd already worked out all the details with her agency, Julius pushed any thought of her out of his mind as he stepped into the shower and let the spray rain down on him. The heat and pressure of the water felt good against his chiseled body. Turning, he bent his head and reveled in the feel of it pulsating down on his shoulders, back, and buttocks.

Tonight watching Mia and Jordan together after nearly thirteen years of marriage had caused a little envy in him. He saw that same connection between Tamara and Kendrick. Would he ever have that? Would he ever put in the work to have it?

"Don't be one of those whack ass fifty-year-old players still out there chasing Miss New Booty."

Was he setting himself up to be one of those old players?

"I'm a girlfriend, committed girl kinda chick. You're not looking for that . . . but I am . . ."

Julius turned again, closed his eyes and let the spray hit his upturned face as he inhaled deeply. He placed his hands on the wall in front of him, the muscles of his arms straining.

Caress was getting to him.

He had to deal with the facts because he felt himself slipping. He wanted her. She aroused him without even trying, but did great chemistry and the promise of mindblowing sex make for a good relationship—especially when he wasn't ready for a commitment and she made it clear that to get in her bed meant getting into her life?

Julius grabbed his washcloth and soap. He washed himself thoroughly, and rinsed off. He was just drying off with a thick and plush towel when his phone began ringing. Folding the towel to hang on the rack, he strode into his bedroom naked, his maleness swinging as he moved.

He checked the caller ID making sure it wasn't Karina.

Dwayne. He hit the talk button.

"Whaddup?" he said into the phone, pressing it between his shoulder and ear as he pulled back the covers and sat down on the bed.

"Your agent sent a package to the studio and since you left early I dropped it off at your house."

Julius frowned. Dwayne had been to his house? "I'm sure it's here."

"Yes, I see you have a lot of new things at your house," Dwayne said.

"Good night, Dwayne," Julius said.

"I will work for free if you let me tell Karina about the baby," he pleaded.

"Good night, Dwayne."

"Please, Julius. I am beg—"

Julius ended the call, setting the phone back on its base before reaching to turn on the lights. It was then he noticed the package in the middle of the bed. He already knew it was the contracts his agent wanted him to sign. He reached over and set it on his bedside table and then lay down naked enjoying the crisp feel of the expensive sheets against his body.

Although he was tired, sleep eluded him as he tossed and turned in the bed. His thoughts were full. Needing a diversion he thought of Jordan's new book. Flinging back the covers, Julius didn't bother covering up his nudity since Caress was fast asleep. Besides in the days before his roommate, Julius would roam around his house naked all the time—one of the perks of living alone.

He dashed down the stairs in the darkness and grabbed the book. Jordan was an excellent writer. Very descriptive without being long-winded. Realistic dialogue and situations. Lots of character development. Great mystery plotlines that always surprised you with the whodunit. Julius couldn't wait to dig into it.

"Uh hum."

Julius looked up just as he reached the top landing. Caress was walking out of the bathroom and her bemused expression took in his nudity with a twinkle in her eyes. "I thought you were asleep," he said, slowly lowering the book to try and cover most of his jewels.

She pointed over her shoulder toward the open bathroom. "Potty called."

"Oh, okay," he said, pausing on the stairs and waiting for her to go into her room.

Caress covered her mouth with her hands and he knew she was hiding a smile. She was enjoying this. She thought he was afraid to walk to his room. *Shee-it. Well, let's see if this keeps the smile on her face*, he thought as he moved the book and looked her boldly in the eye as he walked across the floor with his rod swinging like a billy club.

As he passed her, it was his turn to smile at the way the laughter left her eyes, replaced by what he knew was lust. With one last look over his shoulder before he entered his room, he discovered her eyes squarely on his buttocks. Just for fun, he stopped, posed, and flexed the muscles of his firm rear and then walked in his room, softly closing the door behind him with a husky laugh.

The image of Julius's sculptured body was branded into Caress's memory. His body—those broad shoulders, hard chest, defined abs, square buttocks and all—was just as sculptured as it had been that night. Caress fanned herself as she lay in the middle of the bed. "Doggone shame to be that fine," she said aloud to herself as she pictured his cocky bowlegged strut as he paraded past her as naked as the day he was born. She never guessed he would do it.

But why wouldn't he? The man had nothing at all to be ashamed of. Even at rest he hung with thickness and length. Once hard it only got better, thicker, longer, curvier. She knew that firsthand.

How much longer could they play this little game of pretending not to want each other? How much more time before she carried her little pregnant self into his bedroom and laid out all her goodies for his delight?

But her feelings for Julius were beyond the physical.

Her heart was betraying her.

Against reason.

Against common sense.

Against her better judgment.

Deep down she held hope that Julius would want more, but it was time for her to put away the fantasy and move on with her life. She had to free her heart of him before he took more of it.

Chapter Ten

Two Months Later

"So what do you think?" Caress asked Tamara as they ended their tour of the one-bedroom apartment.

"I like. I like," Tamara said excitedly, grabbing Caress's hand on her way into the kitchen which was separated from the living room by a counter.

Caress folded her arms across herself, propping them on her belly as she looked around the apartment with excited eyes. It took two months to save up the first month's rent and deposit, but it was hers. It was even bigger than the studio apartment she used to have and in a slightly better neighborhood, just ten minutes away from Julius's house. The six-unit apartment building was clean and free of loiterers. With it being early May she even drove through the neighborhood a couple of nights ago and if a block was empty at night in the summer, then that was a telling sign. Caress was pleased with her choice.

"Eventually I have to get a two-bedroom place, but God bless this child that has her own again," she said.

"Has Julius seen it?" Tamara asked as she opened and closed the black refrigerator.

Caress shook her head. "He's not my man, Tam-Tam."

"You want him to be."

Caress's head whipped to the right as she pierced her friend with an angry look. "No, *you* want him to be my man."

Tamara nodded as she walked back over to Caress, her footsteps echoing against the wood floors. "Humph, we have something in common," she said, reaching to rub Caress's belly. "Godmother privileges."

Caress laughed as the baby kicked. Tamara jumped back in surprise.

"My son is telling you to stop working my nerves about his father," Caress joked as she placed her hands on her own expanded belly.

Tamara rolled her eyes and waved her hand at Caress dismissively. "Caress, you may fool yourself into believing you don't have feelings for Julius, but I can see it in your face whenever he is around and you think no one is looking. You've fallen for him, haven't you?"

"No," Caress said emphatically. "You know Kendrick is right. You do have a hard head."

"Damn, Caress, I thought you and I were better than that," Tamara said in a rare show of seriousness as she leveled her eyes on her friend.

Caress shifted her eyes away hoping to hide the truth. In the last few months, her feelings for Julius had grown. Against her wishes. Against her better judgment. Bit by bit.

The chemistry between them was just as strong. Their flirting had never stopped. They learned to laugh together. They had learned to talk and share with each other. They even learned to understand one another.

And with all of that Caress had learned to love him. Yes,

it stung a bit that he didn't want to be in a relationship, but she appreciated his honesty. A lot of men would have gone right ahead and slept with her, lied to her, taken advantage of her. And so far each time she tried to leave her loan payments for him, he would make sure he returned the checks uncashed. He was a good man and that was evident in his good friends and his charity work. He was a fabulous photographer. He was a great lover. Handsome. Stylish. Funny. Loyal. Compassionate. Passionate.

He was completely lovable.

Damn.

"Tell him I need him. Tell him I love him and it'll be all right," Tamara sang softly in her best Lauryn Hill impression.

How astute her friend was because there were many nights she lay with her thoughts wrapped around Julius as she listened to the raw emotions of Lauryn's voice and the deep convictions of her lyrics.

"Love on a one-way street ain't fun," Caress said softly.

"Ah-ha," Tamara said in sweet satisfaction. "So you do love him."

Caress pointed her finger at Tamara and her face brooked no argument. "I swear to God if you tell him I will never speak to you again," she warned her fiercely.

Tamara reached out and softly placed her hand over Caress's. She entwined her fingers with her friend's and held them tightly. "I wouldn't do that, Caress," she said with the utmost seriousness.

Caress let the tension in her body drift away. "Girl, if I knew your blind date would lead to an unplanned pregnancy and unrequited love I would have undone myself from that damn date."

Tamara laughed as they headed for the front door. "Hey, I planned the date, not the sex. I am a friend, not a pimp."

Caress just laughed and shook her head. "Girl, hush with your crazy self."

"So when is move-in day?"

"Just as soon as PSE&G gets the lights on."

"Well, I'm proud of you and I'm happy for you."

"Thanks, Tamara." Caress gave the place one final look before she began to pull the door closed behind them. "Let's go. I'm ready to sit my big ass down."

"How far along are you?" Tamara asked.

"Twenty-seven weeks."

Tamara quickly did the math in her head. "Wow, you are big for close to seven months."

Caress nodded, feeling the additional pounds on her lower back. "I know."

"Once he's born please stop the counting in weeks and months. Seriously, once he's a year just like leave it alone. It is crazy to say he's like eighteen months. No, he's a year and a half. Or he's fifty months. Oh God that works my nerve. I swear it does."

"Girl, shut up."

Julius followed Kendrick into his and Tamara's apartment. "Man, your game is falling off," Julius chided as they moved across the hardwood floors to settle in the kitchen.

"Man, I can't ball like I did ten years and thirty pounds ago," Kendrick said, as he reached into the fridge for two ice cold beers.

Julius cut his eyes up at his friend as Kendrick tossed him a can. "Tell me about it. To get those fleas off our necks, I had to pull out some tricks I haven't used since I was growing up in the projects."

Kendrick laughed. "I'm glad as hell my woman wasn't there to see me."

Julius took a deep sip of the beer, although he preferred brandy or cognac when he was in the mood to drink. Beer made him too tired unless it was lite. Just one can and he was somewhere sleeping with his mouth wide open—hardly an asset to his cool and suave persona. "Where is Ms. Busybody anyway?" he asked, pulling his basketball shorts away from his thigh where they clung because of the sweat.

"She and Caress went to look at Caress's new apartment," Kendrick said. "I know you're happy as hell to get your house back."

Julius didn't try to hide his surprise.

Kendrick paused, his beer can frozen at his mouth as he cut his eyes to Julius. "Caress didn't tell you she found a place," he stated more than asked.

Julius shrugged. "Not yet," he said, his eyes looking off into the distance at nothing as he let the news settle on him.

Caress was finally moving.

They'd both waited months for this to come to fruition. Now here it was.

"I love Caress like a sister but you should be celebrating . . . so why you looking all shell-shocked?"

Julius turned his head and leveled his eyes on the big and tall man across from him. "I'm just hoping she isn't moving into some roach-infested rat trap because she's rushing to get her own place."

Kendrick spew beer out of his mouth as he looked at his friend. "Rushing? A roach-infested rat trap?" he said with comical emphasis as he used a paper towel to wipe the beer from his chin and the table where it landed. "Why the hell do you care?"

"I don't want my son growing up in the kind of crap I used to live in."

The beer went flying again as Kendrick's eyes widened. "Your son? A first, ladies and gentleman. Julius Jones faces reality."

"Shut up," Julius growled. "I meant *if* he is my son and you know it."

"Playa down! Playa down," Kendrick hollered to the roof. "Call 911. A playa is down."

Julius eyed Kendrick like he was a fool. "You and Tamara are made for each other."

"Maybe you and Caress were made for each other," Kendrick retorted.

Just then the front door opened and the ladies walked in laughing at something. Julius's eyes immediately shifted to Caress. His heart tugged at the sight of her. She frequently joked that her nose was now the size of a 747 and her neck was getting dark, but Julius thought she was beautiful. She never did the pregnant woman waddle even though her belly was fast expanding. She was wearing one of the outfits he bought: a deep fuchsia button-up shirt and fashionable dark denims. The color brought out her complexion and made her eyes come alive.

He took a deep sip of the beer as he forced his eyes away from her.

"Hi fellas," Tamara said, setting her purse and keys on the kitchen table.

"Caress, my bad, I spilled the beans to Julius about your apartment," Kendrick admitted as he turned and reached for another can of beer from the fridge. He offered one to Julius, who declined with a shake of his head.

Caress looked over at Julius as she took a seat at the small round table. Their eyes met. They both looked away quickly.

"Congratulations, Caress," he said.

"I was going to tell you tonight," she said.

Their knees brushed under the table and Julius felt that same awareness between them. It had become familiar to him. "So where is it?"

"It's just ten minutes from your house, Julius. It's nice," Tamara said, easing the can from her husband's massive hand to take a sip.

Julius didn't move his knees from Caress's and he noticed she didn't move hers either. "So you like it?" he asked.

"Well, I would love a two bedroom better but I like it." Caress smiled at him. "I'm just excited to be back on my feet, and I know you'll be glad to get your house back."

Julius was acutely aware of Kendrick's and Tamara's eyes on him. He ignored them. "I'm more excited for you than anything."

Their eyes met and held for a few seconds before they both looked away.

"Thank you, Julius," Caress said softly, her hand rising to touch her neck.

The room fell silent. Both Caress and Julius slowly turned their heads to eye Tamara and Kendrick, who were both looking at them like they were putting on a play or something.

"Y'all are so cute together," Tamara said with a big goofy grin on her face. "I don't know why you two don't admit—"

"Tamara," Caress warned in a hard voice.

"What?" Kendrick said. "Julius was just in here—"

"Kendrick," Julius warned in a voice just as hard and ominous.

Caress stood. "Julius, can I catch a ride home?"

"Sounds like a plan to me," he said, rising to his feet as well.

"You don't have to go," Kendrick said, as they walked out of the kitchen.

"I want to start packing," Caress said opening the front door.

"I have to go over the proofs for my book," Julius said, reaching in the pocket of his shorts for his keys.

"Bye!" they said in unison before Julius pulled the door closed in Tamara's and Kendrick's faces.

Later that night, Caress left her room in search of Julius. She had walked every square foot of the upstairs and downstairs before it crossed her mind to try his darkroom in the basement. She knocked, not knowing if opening the door would ruin his film or not.

"Come in," he hollered up.

She opened the door and slowly made her way down the stairs. The red lights for developing were on, and Julius was removing dried photos from the line hanging across the rear of the darkroom. "I've never been down here before," she told him as she looked around.

Julius smiled at her over his shoulder. "Welcome to my world," he said as he continued to take down photos.

Caress walked around looking at the framed photographs on the wall. "You really have a way of pulling people into your photos, Julius," she said, captivated by the picture of a homeless man asleep on the top of a subway grate.

"Photography has been my passion since I was a kid with a second-hand—or maybe even third-hand—Polaroid camera."

Caress smiled and softened her eyes as she looked over at him. "I can't imagine you as a kid."

Julius glanced at her over his shoulder again. "Oh yeah. Why not?"

"I don't know. Today was the first time I've seen you in shorts and sneakers," Caress mused as she walked over to stand beside him at the waist-high table. "Guess, I imagine you twelve and decked out in a suit listening to Miles Davis."

Julius laughed. "Far from it. When I was growing up I was always in patched-up clothes, and I promised myself a different life when I was grown."

"Guess we both had it rough coming up," she said sadly.

Julius looked down at her, nearly towering over her with the difference in their height. "My Dad was MIA and my mom was caught up in her own life and the streets. I thank God for my grandmother."

"I grew up in foster care after my mom died when I was two. So I don't know who my daddy is, you know. All I have is this old photograph of her and this Spanish man— which is the only reason I even know I'm part Hispanic."

"Foster care can be rough. Were you okay all those years? You know, were you safe?" he asked, his eyes searching her face.

Caress's heart swelled at the genuine concern he was showing. "I guess I was one of the lucky ones, nothing too traumatic that I couldn't handle."

"Good," he said in that deep voice.

She waved her hand around the darkroom. "You did well for yourself though. Not bad at all for a kid from The Bricks."

"Thanks. That why I sometimes volunteer with Jordan as a mentor. I want kids to know they can have more, hope for more, and work hard for more."

"Jordan?" she asked, pushing her hair behind her ears.

"Jordan Banks—"

"The writer?" she asked in disbelief.

Julius laughed and nodded as he reached to the end of the table for his camera case. "The one and only. Real nice guy. He's good people."

"I read a couple of his books that you had," she said, turning to lean back against the table as Julius moved across the room with that bowlegged swagger. She allowed her eyes to dip down to the movement of his firm buttocks in the jeans he wore. "He still lives here in the city, right?"

"Jordan will never leave Newark. He's another Amiri Baraka." Julius squatted down to open the case and pull out his beloved camera. "Would you like to meet him?"

"Jordan Banks? Hell yeah," she said, excitedly.

"Done."

"For real? Wow. Thanks."

They fell silent as Jordan extracted the film from his camera.

"Julius, I really came down here because I have something to ask you," Caress admitted as she walked across the room to stand beside him as he filled trays with some liquid.

"Fire away."

"Why won't you cash all those checks I've been giving you?" she asked accusingly.

Julius looked down at her and under the red glow the intensity around him was only heightened. "Caress, I don't need the money," he said simply.

"And I do?" she asked with a bit of annoyance.

"Yes," he said with emphasis.

Caress bit back a smile. "Okay, yes I do, but I like to pay my debts. You were under no obligation to do all those things for me, and I want to pay you back, Julius Jones."

"I wanted to offer you all of the furniture I bought for your bedroom since I'm changing it back to my office," he told her, sounding exasperated. "Are you going to write me an IOU for that too? Why can't you accept a gift?"

"Julius, I can't—"

He locked his eyes on her like a dare. "Independence is

great and all that, but cutting your nose off to spite your face is childish and foolish."

Caress did one of those sista girl head motions as she poked him in the arm. "Are you calling me childish and foolish?" she asked.

"If the shoe fits."

Caress's mouth dropped. "You think you have the right to call me names, Julius Jones, but I can finish whatever it is you're starting in this basement."

"It's a free county."

"Maybe . . . maybe," she struggled for an insult to top the one he threw at her. "Maybe the reason you don't want to be in a relationship is because . . . because you're switch-hitting. Now there."

Julius frowned. "Are you calling me gay?" he balked.

"All I'm saying is there might be more to you and Boo than you're letting on," she said.

Julius's eyes glinted as he watched her for a long time.

Caress forced herself not to break his hard stare.

Suddenly the light in his eyes changed and she saw it. She took a step back. He took two forward. She took another back and he took several forward, until the table was pressing into her back.

He picked her up with ease, sat her on the table, and stepped between her open legs. It put their mismatched frames on a more-equal level, eye to eye and mouth to mouth. She said nothing as he quickly swooped his head in to lock his mouth on hers. She gasped hotly at the first electrifying feel of him, and he used that opportunity to delve his heated tongue inside.

With a moan from deep in her soul, Caress tilted her head to the side and brought her hands up to the sides of his handsome square face as Julius deepened the kiss. When his hands shifted down to her buttocks and he pressed himself close, it felt just fine for her pregnant belly to be pressed against his hard abdomen.

Under the light that was as red hot as their chemistry, Julius and Caress kissed with a slow and sexy intensity that allowed them to relish the goodness of it all. Their hearts pounded in unison. Electricity seemed to cause the very air around them to crackle. Their body heat made the room several degrees hotter. Their moans and the light smacking of their lips and tangling tongues echoed in the air.

Caress wrapped her arms around his strong neck and held him close as Julius used his tongue to trace her lips before he placed a dozen tiny but erotic kisses on and around her open mouth. "Julius," she moaned into the air with a whisper as she let her head fall back as he kissed a trail down to her neck. She shivered and moaned aloud as he twirled his adept tongue around her beating pulse.

Her nipples ached. Her clit throbbed. Her heart beat wildly. She was moist with anticipation.

Julius placed kisses up and down her neck, even nudging her blouse open with his nose to press his lips to her cleavage. He inhaled deeply of her scent and his erection seemed hard enough to press a dent into the table. "Caress, if we don't stop I'm going to make love to you," he admitted against her throat before kissing a trail back to her open and panting mouth.

She took the lead, grabbing the back of his head with her quivering hands as she used the tip of her tongue to lightly flicker against his mouth. She relished the feel of the tremble that shook his hard, chiseled frame. With a cat-like purr she eased her tongue between his lips and stroked his tongue with her own. "Just once more. Just for tonight. No strings," she whispered into his mouth as she opened her eyes to lock with his.

She saw the desire he had for her in the dark depths of his eyes. She saw him considering her indecent proposal.

"Caress, you got my dick so hard," Julius admitted, burying his head against her chest.

"Don't let it go to waste," she teased sensually as she slid her hand from around his neck to reach for the hem of his silk T-shirt. She pulled his shirt up exposing his chiseled chest to her. She moaned in satisfaction before lowering her head to twirl her tongue around his hard nipple. "Mmmm."

Julius honestly didn't know he could get so hard as he flung his head back and enjoyed the way Caress suckled his nipple between her pursed lips. "Damn," he swore, swallowing hard.

She laughed huskily as she brought her hand up to tease his other nipple. "You know if I ride you backward the baby won't be in the way."

Julius nearly came.

He stepped back from her. Not too far. Just far enough to break the delectable hold of her mouth on his chest. He looked down at her as he breathed like he just finished running a marathon. Her hair was mussed. Her eyes were bright. Her shirt exposed the fuller swell of the top of her breasts. Her lips were swollen and pouty.

Who knew a pregnant woman could look so damn sexy?

She was a woman in heat, and he knew that only he could cool her off. Just like she was the only woman who could ease the ache in his loins.

"Caress, we can't. I want to. I really want to. But I don't want you to regret this in the morning," he told her, putting his hands on his hips as his erection caused his pants to teepee.

She eyed him. Hard chest exposed with his shirt up under his armpits. Eyes glazed over. Rock hard abdomen. Dick hard and ready. "I'll regret it if we do. I'll still regret it if we don't. Might as well err on the side of pleasure," she told him, tilting her head to the side as she reached out and trailed her finger through the hard grooves of his eight pack.

"If you weren't pregnant, I would climb on that table and make love to you all night, Caress," he told her with conviction.

Her eyes dipped down to his hardness. "You're big but do you really think you can reach the womb?"

He gave her a half smile. "We wouldn't have even gotten this far if you didn't try to call me a down-low brother."

"I know you're not gay or bisexual or trisexual."

"Trisexual?" he asked, pulling his shirt back down.

"Willing to try anything," she said, both relieved and disappointed that their little rendezvous was over.

Julius moved to lean back on the table beside her. "If nothing else, I guess it's good you're moving out or we wouldn't be able to fight this thing much longer."

"Is that the only reason it would be good for me to move?" Caress asked as she pushed her hair behind her ears.

"I'm used to you being here now," he said with a smile.

"Yeah, right," she drawled.

They fell silent again.

"Thank you for being the voice of reason," she told him as she let her eyes shift over to him.

"If you can say thank you for that, why can't you say thank you for the things I've done for you and not worry about repaying me?"

Caress wondered if he would ever understand her. "Because that's different, Julius."

"You know I could have very easily made love to you down here . . . especially with you begging me," he said, crossing his arms over his chest.

She slapped his muscled arm. "I did not beg," she stressed. "I made an impassioned request."

Julius snorted. "Fine line, Caress. Very fine line."

Caress laughed huskily as she dropped her chin to her chest and let her hair cover her warm, blushing face.

"So I guess I kinda did you a favor by not taking advantage of you. So how about you do me a favor?"

Caress flipped her hair back and eyed him suspiciously. "What?" she asked.

"Very simple. Just say, 'Thank you for the bedroom furniture, Julius' and accept it as my gift."

Her shoulders dipped as she released a long breath. "No, Julius."

"Favor for a favor. Plus, I've already said I have to get rid of the furniture because I'm moving my office back upstairs. So that's two favors for a nice guy who has been a wonderful host and a gentleman for not sexing the hell out of you even though I have never been so turned on and so hard in all my damned life."

"Julius—"

"Thank you for the bedroom furniture."

"Julius—"

"Come on. You can say it. I promise it's not that hard."

She chuckled as she bit her bottom lip. She reached over and lightly grasped his chin, turning his head to face her. "Thank you for the bedroom furniture," she said softly as she leveled her eyes with his. "I really appreciate it."

Julius grinned as he reached over and quickly pressed his lips to hers. "You're very welcome, Caress Coleman. You are very welcome."

Caress just dropped her head and enjoyed the lingering taste of his kiss on her mouth.

Chapter Eleven

Two Weeks Later

Julius was feeling déjà vu.

Karina breezed right past him and stepped inside his villa, twirling to open the white cotton wrap she wore, and exposing her naked svelte body to his eyes. "Last time I tried this, we were interrupted," she said in a husky voice as she ran her hand from the valley of her breasts and down to stroke her shaved kitty.

"Well, looks like your luck has run out again, sweetie."

Karina whirled and her jaw dropped to find Dwayne sitting in front of the computer at the desk in the corner of the living room. She gasped and jerked the wrap closed as Dwayne pretended to cover his eyes with his hands but then obviously peeked through the break in his slender fingers.

Julius closed the door and then shot his assistant a warning glare—an unspoken warning to be respectful to his clients. Dwayne dutifully focused his eyes back on the digital proofs they had been reviewing on the computer. Julius's eyes dipped to take in the sight of the tightly held wrap formed to the slender but shapely outline of Karina's body.

She turned to him and he leisurely shifted his eyes upward. "Julius, can I speak to you . . . *alone*?"

Julius shoved his hands inside the pockets of his linen pants. "Can it wait, Karina? I was just about to e-mail some preliminary shots to your agency. They want them ASAP."

If there was one thing Karina understood or respected above all it was her business. With her back safely to Dwayne, who was far from interested anyway, she let the wrap hang loosely, leaving a glimpse of a hard brown nipple here and a flash of a thigh there. She stepped close to him and placed her hands on his strong shoulders as she whispered in his ear. "Dinner. Tonight. No excuses, Julius."

As she lightly licked his earlobe, his body—that primal male instinct—responded to her. Her seduction plot. Her obvious desire for him. The soft scent of her perfume. The heated feel of her body so close to his.

His desires stirred.

It had been months since he'd had sex. He couldn't deny that his level of sexual frustration was at an all-time high. With Karina steadily pouring it on him, it was hard to deny that if nothing else it would feel good to just make love to a woman. To release his pent-up frustration. To stop feeling like a virgin ready to explode all over himself.

Karina understood him. She knew this would be nothing more than a man and woman finding pleasure in each other's bed. No promises. No pressures. No strings.

It was just the arrangement he needed right now.

Julius brought his hand up to touch her lower back as he pressed his lips to the warm spot just below her ear. "In your room," he ordered, enjoying the feel of her body shivering from his words, his touch, and his promise of pure sexual gratification.

He ignored the sounds of Dwayne pretending to gag.

With a soft smile, she gave him a kiss on the lips. Her eyes full of promise, she tied her wrap closed and left the villa.

Julius made sure the door was secured behind her before he made his way back over to the desk. He could tell from the way Dwayne's lips were going in two different directions that his assistant was going to say something sideways. He reclaimed his seat next to Dwayne and began scrolling through the many photographs they took on the beautiful island locale of Karina in fashions from some of the top swimwear designers.

Suddenly Dwayne stretched his long limbs. "I heard Karina might be the face of a new perfume."

Julius knew Dwayne too well.

"Her essence might even influence the name," Dwayne said.

The build up.

"I'm thinking Desperation or Hopeless."

And the put down.

Dwayne chuckled. He had amused himself.

Julius gave him the kind of hard stare a parent gave a mischievous child.

"I'm sorry, but that woman is a stone cold mess and no Caress, sweetie." For that little zinger he did his signature four snaps in a semi arc.

Somewhere along the line, Dwayne had joined Tamara, Kendrick, and Jordan on the Caress-is-the-one-for-you bandwagon.

"You don't even know her," Jordan said, using the mouse to select a photo of Karina sitting on the edge of the water in nothing but a sequined bikini bottom as she covered her bare breasts with her hands.

Dwayne waved his hand dismissively. "Yes, but I know you and this whole 'I slipped one night and had unprotected sex' is a bunch of bull. Okay, there I said it," he proclaimed. "Somebody needed to."

Julius sat back in his chair and turned a bit to face his assistant. "Are you saying I got Caress pregnant on purpose?" he asked, astonished.

Dwayne turned his chair as well and then crossed his legs. "I'm saying that you are Mr. Responsibility to a tee. You are Mr. Condom kept anywhere I might need it— office, car, wallet. You are the epitome of thinking three steps ahead. You are the safe sex poster child. So why did all that fly out the window *that* night with *that* woman?"

"I got caught up."

"Yes, you did. In the connection. In the chemistry. In the destiny of it all. When you are part of a bigger picture and a bigger plan, things are out of your control."

Julius shirked away the familiarity of Dwayne's lecture. His words echoed Jordan's. When did everyone get bit by the damn love bug and this whole divine prophecy crap? "You're here to assist with this photo shoot . . . not my love life," Julius said, turning back to the flat screen monitor of the computer.

"What love life?" Dwayne asked, "There is no love anywhere in the equation of your life. Love surely is not what Ms. Karina is hunting up. Unless that's what you call your magic stick lately."

Julius focused on his work and pretended to ignore his assistant who might just be wiser than Julius was willing to admit.

Several hours later, Julius walked up the secluded walk to Karina's villa and knocked on the door before he could change his mind. Just moments later the door opened slowly and the flickers of a dozen lit candles illuminated in the depths of his eyes. He looked all around the elegantly styled living room as he stepped inside. He paused for just a second to find Karina in nothing but a pair of leopard heels walking toward him with two glasses of champagne in her hand.

"I decided, why waste time with dinner when it's dessert we're hungry for," she said huskily, coming up to stand before him and offer him one of the crystal flutes while she kicked her foot out to nudge the door closed.

Julius accepted the drink and took a sip of the liquid, immediately recognizing it. "Krug Clos Ambonnay?" he asked as Karina sipped her drink with her left hand and used her right to unbutton the black silk shirt he wore.

"Nothing but the best for tonight," she whispered against his mouth before she kissed him long and deep.

Julius used his free hand to grasp the back of her thigh, running it up to the soft swell of her buttocks to press into her lower back. He brought her body closer to his as their kiss deepened with a moan.

For him, tonight was all that mattered.

Caress was stirred from her position on the sofa as the microwave began to beep annoyingly. Her TV dinner was ready. She eased up off of the sofa as the lights from her nineteen-inch television flickered in her eyes in the dark living room. She was in the midst of a *Martin* marathon on TVOne and one of her favorite episodes from the nineties hit sitcom was on.

Still laughing as a commercial came on, she moved through the small living room back into the kitchen to grab her dinner and pour herself a glass of milk. She really wasn't hungry but knew she had to eat for the baby's sake. Thankfully the "all day" sickness had subsided and she was less tired than at the start of her pregnancy. Besides some lower back pain and learning to sleep on her side, everything with the pregnancy was going fine.

In fact, she loved her little apartment and had even worked hard to decorate it once she paid off her hefty storage bill and saved her furnishings from being auctioned off. Her life had settled back into a pattern. Everything was back to normal. She was officially back on her feet.

God was good.

Caress grimaced as her son kicked. "Hey you, settle down and stop using my uterus as your football," she said, giving in as always to her urge to talk to her baby.

"I love you so much," she said, her head down as she directed her voice toward her round belly. "You are everything I never knew I wanted."

The baby kicked again and Caress's eyes filled with tears as she thought of her own mother for the first time in years. Did she feel this same protective urge, this urgency to love, this fierceness to fight for her child?

It hurt that her baby would never have grandparents, but Caress was determined to give her son all the love she had in her plus some more. She just prayed that Julius lived up to the father she thought he could be because she never would want her child to feel the same disconnection as she did from her family and her past.

Instinctively, she felt Julius was the same way. They shared something through their troubled pasts, and only common sense and common decency would make them ensure their child had far more than they ever had. Not just the material, but the important things: the emotional support, the stability, the comfort of knowing his parents loved him and would never leave him.

As always, when her mind drifted to Julius, Caress felt that familiar ache. She missed him. She missed that comfortable vibe that in time had developed between them.

She even missed their flirtation. That little walk they often took across the line between admitting their desires and giving in to them.

Caress smiled and then laughed a little at the kiss and the heated moments they had shared in his darkroom. In the days following they would tease each other about their "red-light special."

Raising her T-shirt above her stomach, Caress massaged the mound and tried to pretend she didn't wish they were Julius's hands on her belly instead. She couldn't lie and say she didn't want him more involved in the pregnancy. He called to check on her at least once or twice a week. He had yet to cash the cheeks she faithfully sent him. The very day she moved in he hired a moving company to bring the bedroom furniture.

He was a man of his word.

He was a man of style and grace.

He was a talented photographer.

He was a good friend.

Well-liked.

Caring.

Loyal.

Intelligent.

Articulate.

Handsome.

Funny.

Sexy.

Caress closed her eyes and let herself get lost in the memory of the many moments they shared over the last several months.

The laid-back fun of their first date.

The heat and passion of their first night.

The shock of her moving into his home.

The stiffness of those first few weeks living together.

The undeniable buzz of awareness between them.

The revealing kiss in the kitchen.

The urgency of that "red-light special" in the darkroom.

Moment after moment after moment played in her head.

Brrrnnnggg.

Caress jumped out of her reverie and turned from the counter to pick up the cordless phone on her small kitchen table. "Hey, Tam-Tam," she said, having checked the caller ID.

"Whatcha doing?"

"About to eat a TV dinner," Caress said, turning to slide the dinner back in the microwave for a quick rewarming.

"I'm bored," Tam-Tam sighed dramatically. "Kendrick has a men's meeting at church."

Caress removed the Salisbury and mashed potato dinner from the microwave and made her way back to the living room to reclaim her seat. "You should have come over here. We could have been bored together."

"High as gas is? This local call is free, baby."

Caress laughed as she turned down the volume of the television.

"Heard from Mr. Lover-Lover?" Tamara asked while chewing noisily on something.

"We spoke last week," Caress said, wishing she didn't care that they didn't speak more often.

"He should be back from Jamaica tomorrow."

Caress froze, a spoonful of potatoes paused at her open mouth as her heart slammed like a door against her chest. Karina's words came back to her in a rush:

"Julius, this is Karina. I am so excited about Jamaica. We are going to have the best time. Believe that. Anyway call me when you get this message."

"Jamaica huh?" Caress said, shaking her head to free it

of explicit images of Julius and Karina. "Karina must be in heaven."

"Huh?"

Caress sat on the edge of the chair and leaned forward to alleviate the strain she felt in her lower back. "Julius's first night home from Africa, this woman shows up at his door with nothing on but a massive sable—"

"Girl . . . shut up!"

"Humph."

"Why didn't you tell me?"

Caress could imagine Tamara sitting on the edge of her own seat. The woman loved juice, "One word: EM-BA-RAS-SING."

"Girl, you should've slammed the door in her face."

Caress shrugged. "Not my house. Not my man."

"Still."

"Still that's who he's in Jamaica with." Caress grabbed a pillow and shoved it behind her back.

"No!"

"Yes."

"Dang, I really thought y'all woulda worked it out and got together." Tamara sighed. "I didn't know he was dating one of those models. He said he went to Jamaica for a calendar photo shoot."

Caress sucked air between her teeth. "He's working all right . . . from the waist down," she said sarcastically.

"Sound mighty jealous."

Beep.

"Hold on I got another call." Caress gladly clicked over. "Hello."

"Hi, Caress."

Her heart raced. She would know that voice anywhere. Julius.

"Caress?"

"Hi. Hey . . . hey Julius. How's Jamaica?" she asked and then instantly regretted it. *Don't let him know you care.*

"Beautiful. Relaxing."

His voice was deep and husky through the phone line. She hated that she felt the urge to press the phone closer to her ear. "It's nice of Karina to let you call your future baby mama on y'all vacation," she said, completely sounding just as jealous as she felt.

Julius only laughed. "You are one of a kind, Caress," he said huskily.

"Don't laugh at me, Julius Jones."

"And don't you try to play me, Caress Coleman," he countered in a warm voice still filled with his teasing. "I am in Jamaica. Karina is here. We are not on vacation."

Beep.

Dammit. She hated the intrusion. "I got another call. Hold on, Julius."

She clicked over. "Hello."

"Girl, how long you gonna leave me on hold?"

"Tamara, I'm talking to Julius—"

"Ooh-wee. Bye."

Click. Then nothing but a dial tone.

Julius poured himself a shot of cognac before he settled back down on the sofa in his villa. He was surprised how much he felt like a teenager calling a cute crush as he waited for Caress to click back on the line.

"Julius. I'm back."

His heart raced at the sound of her soft voice. He pictured her face and smiled a bit. "You were saying," she prompted.

Julius's smile broadened. "I just called to check on you," he told her, before lifting the glass to take a sip of the brown liquid. It burned a warm trail as it raced down his throat.

"From Jamaica?"

"I thought about you in Jamaica." He licked the remnants of the liquor from his lips.

"Anyway, that's not what we're talking about."

Julius set the glass on the bleached wooden table. "I figured you wouldn't want to talk about Karina," he said as he turned and lifted his feet up on the couch.

"And why is that?"

"You think we're together."

"And you think I care who you are with."

"Definitely."

Caress's laughter came through the phone line. "You sure think highly of yourself."

Julius tilted his head back and laughed, his straight white teeth flashing against his bronzed complexion. "If I don't love me first who else will?" he asked, feeling relaxed by his tropical surroundings, the liquor, and the laid-back flow between them.

"No vacation in Jamaica, huh? Does all work and no play make Julius a sad boy?" she teased.

He crossed his feet at the ankles. "More like all work and no play makes Karina a mad girl," Julius admitted, instantly wondering if he said too much.

"Awww," Caress sighed, sounding fake as hell.

Julius laughed again. "Try to sound like you mean it," he drawled.

"Whatever."

They both fell silent.

Julius could only wonder what was on Caress's mind as his own thoughts filled with the flight he made from Karina's villa earlier. He could only shake his head. Every single time Karina laid out the deal for him, Caress had stopped the show.

Months ago, in his office, when Tamara called to set up the blind date with Caress.

When he first got back from Africa and Caress opened the door to Karina and her near-nakedness.

And tonight, thoughts of Caress and how much he missed her and still wanted her made sleeping with Karina feel wrong.

They both were single. He had extra Magnums. He was eager. More than in need. So was she. But as soon as she loosened his belt and zipper enough to close her hand around his hardness, the whole thing felt . . . wrong. Odd. Out of place. A mistake.

It's not that his body wasn't willing because every bit of his manhood was rock hard and ready to roll. But images of Caress played in his head even as he tried to make his normal moves on Karina.

Caress's smile.

Caress playing with her earlobe while she read those silly celebrity gossip magazines.

Caress trudging around the house in those sweatpants and T-shirts she loved so much.

Caress's eyes all dilated-looking after he kissed her in the kitchen . . . or as he stroked deep inside of her that night at her house.

Whew!

Somehow, Mr. Living Life to the Fullest as a Bachelor had become comfortable coming home every night to a woman. The same woman. Caress. And Karina was not Caress. No way. No how.

"Karina, let's not do this," he had told her, even as her hands nearly clawed at him in her eagerness.

Once she caught on he was serious, he had barely made it out the front door of the villa before his pants and shoes came flying out behind him.

Still, the feel of the air breezing across his bare legs and ass as she slammed the door felt good. Damn good. Almost as good as that unmistakable buzz of awareness between Caress and him even when they were just passing one another in the house.

The first thing he did when he walked through the door of his own villa was pour a drink and then pick up the phone to call Caress.

"Julius? You asleep?" she asked, her voice filling the silence.

"No." He shook his head as if she could see him.

"Julius?" she called out softly.

He pressed the phone closer to his ear, expectant of her next words because the way she said his name sounded like she had something serious to say. "Yes, Caress?"

"Nothing," she mumbled. "Never mind."

Julius frowned a bit as curiosity nipped at him. "Go ahead," he urged. "Say it. Ask it. Demand it. Go."

"I don't have the right to ask it."

"Yes."

"Huh?"

He smiled. "I was answering the question you were going to ask."

"Okay, Mr. Know-it-All, what was I going to ask?"

"If I still thought you were sexy," Julius said, shifting his long and lean body for comfort on the sofa.

Caress laughed, and it made him smile even more. "Uh . . . no."

"So what were you going to ask?" Julius sat up long enough to take another sip of his drink.

"Nothing, Julius."

"Something, Caress," he urged in deep tones as he set his glass back down on the table. "Come on. Be a woman."

"Oh, I'm *all* woman."

A vision of her naked and sprawled before him on her coffee table flashed. "That I know."

"Okay, listen. What exactly is going on with you and Karina? Okay I asked. Now you go."

How honest should he be? Vagueness or half-truths would make sense if he and Caress were in a relationship or working on one. "I've photographed her a lot and we've flirted a lot. But it just never happened and I'm learning it's just not meant to be."

"In Jamaica?" Caress squawked in disbelief.

"In Jamaica," he countered in a serious tone. "I've never made love to her, Caress, and trust me, I've had *plenty* of opportunity."

"Check you out bragging, Mr. Billy Big Stick."

Julius chuckled. "I see you remember me well."

"Negro, puh-leeze."

"So it's not?"

"Not what?"

"Big." Julius loved messing with Caress.

"I don't remember."

Julius's eyes widened huskily.

"You know what? You do have a big head—it's sitting on your neck."

Julius suddenly pressed his mouth closed tightly as the words "Damn, I miss you, Caress" almost slipped through his lips with ease. "Everything good with the baby?" he asked, purposely changing the subject as he wiped his hand over his face.

"Yes, everything is fine."

"And the job?"

"It's real good."

They fell silent again.

"I guess I better let you go," Julius said, amazed by how reluctant he was to end the call.

"'Kay."

"Caress?" he called out huskily as he sat up on the sofa.

"Yes, Julius?"

He shook his head, before dropping it into his hand. "Nothing. Never mind."

"Oh, no. I'll tell you like you told me. Man up."

Julius turned his head and gazed out the open balcony doors at the beautiful island locale. "I was just going to say good night," he lied as his eyes reflected the emotions he was trying ever so hard to ignore. Deny. Push away.

"Good night then, Julius."

Long after they disconnected the line, Julius sat in that same spot with his thoughts and his heart filled with many what-ifs.

Chapter Twelve

Two Months Later

Caress tried hard to ignore the tiny twinges of discomfort occasionally radiating across her back as she shifted for comfort in her chair. Her doctor had already warned her that she was very large for thirty six weeks, plus her petite size was causing hell on her back. On top of that, the stifling city heat of July was making her pregnancy really aggravating.

"Everything okay, Caress?"

She tried to cover a grimace as she looked up at her supervisor Harriett Longe, standing beside her desk. Caress adored the woman because if for nothing else, this tall, red-headed white woman had hired an obviously pregnant woman who was in need of a job. "I'm fine, Harriett," she assured her as she reached for a stack of files on the edge of her desk. "Here's the information you requested for your meeting today."

Harriett accepted the files but her green eyes were filled with concern. "Why don't you go on home for the day?"

Caress started to deny the offer, but she felt a headache coming on top of the backache, and she did just want to lie down. "I'm sorry about this, Harriett," she said, as she reached into the bottom drawer of her desk and pulled out her purse.

"No worries. You haven't missed a day since you started working here, and half the day is gone anyway." Harriett stepped back to let Caress rise and slowly walk from behind her desk. "I'll call you later and check on you, sweetie."

"Thanks, Harriett," Caress said over her shoulder with a weak smile.

She reached out for the desk as the room spun suddenly and pain pierced her lower belly and the back of her head. She hollered out as her hand missed the desk and her body fell to the carpeted floor with a thud.

"Caress!" Harriett cried out, dropping the files as she rushed down to the floor to check on her. "Oh God, you're bleeding."

Harriett left her side just long enough to call an ambulance and Caress, filled with fear even as she felt unconsciousness claim her, told Harriett, "Call . . . Julius . . . on my . . . cell."

Julius's heart hadn't stopped pounding since he'd gotten the call that Caress was on the way to the hospital. He drove like a madman through the streets of Jersey City and then Newark to reach UMDNJ. He had never before blown his horn excessively, driven in the wrong lane, or maneuvered in and out past cars, but this was urgent.

Nothing had ever felt so important to him as getting to Caress's side.

Thoughts raced through his brain as he raced through the streets.

What if she lost the baby?

What if she passed on from complications?

He felt nauseous and weak at the thought of both.

Julius burst through the doors of the emergency room.

"Julius?"

He turned as a white woman came running up to him. He immediately assumed it was Caress's boss, Harriett. "Where is she?" he asked, not caring that he was completely drenched in sweat and nearly out of breath from running from the parking deck.

Harriett grabbed his hand and pulled him toward the nurses' station. "He's here for Caress Coleman," she said, her cheeks flushed and her eyes teary.

"Are you the father of the baby?' the nurse asked.

"Yes," Julius answered without hesitation. Now was not the time for what-ifs.

"Right this way."

Julius gave Harriett a thankful squeeze of the hand she had lightly resting on his arm, before he followed the nurse down the brightly lit hall to a small room on the right. As soon as he turned into the room his eyes locked on Caress lying in the bed looking pale, an IV in her arm, and hooked up to monitors that were beeping. Alone. In need of him.

He brushed past the nurse to stand beside the bed and take Caress's hand into his own. "Caress, I'm here. I'm here, Caress," he whispered down to her as emotions made his throat tight, and he felt his eyes fill with tears of happiness that she was alive and fear that she was still in harm's way.

Her eyes flickered open and he could tell from the dampness of her lashes that she had been crying. "The baby?" he asked, turning to face the nurse as panic clawed at his chest.

"Is fine," she assured him with a comforting smile. "That's his heartbeat you hear. It is slowing down and we've let the doctor know."

Julius went still. Listening. Needing to hear it.

"I'll let Dr. Dillinger know you're here," the nurse told him, quickly checking Caress's intravenous site and line before she left the room. Caress tightened her grasp on his hand just enough for him to glance back down at her. "My blood pressure . . . shot up. They might . . . have to induce labor . . . if they can't get it down," she said to him, obviously still weakened from the ordeal. "I'm so glad you're here, Julius."

Julius bent down, his elbows resting on the side rails of the bed as he locked his eyes with hers. "You scared the shit out of me, beautiful," he admitted, his thumb making light circles on the back of her hand.

"I'm scared, Julius," she admitted to him in a whisper.

In that very instant. That unforgettable moment. He knew. He welcomed it. He embraced it.

He loved Caress. He was in love with her. Completely.

Julius leaned in and pressed his lips to her forehead. He kissed the tears silently falling from her eyes. And finally her mouth. "I'll be right here and we'll get through this together, Caress. I swear," he promised, his words breezing lightly down the short distance to her trembling mouth.

The monitors began to sound an alarm and moments later Caress's room filled with medical staff.

Someone pulled him from the side of the bed but he held onto Caress's grasp until the distance between them was too wide for even their fingertips to touch.

"Mr. Jones, we're taking Caress in for an emergency cesarean section to alleviate the preeclampsia and take her and the baby out of harm's way."

As they wheeled her bed out of the room he drew his eyes away from Caress just long enough to notice Dr. Dillinger standing by his side. "I want to be in there," Julius told her, in a voice brooking no argument.

Dr. Dillinger smiled at him reassuringly. "Of course," she told him, leading him out of the room.

Tamara had never wrung her hands or paced so much in her life. Everything about the bland waiting room was a reminder that her best friend was in a hospital in surgery. She wrapped her arms around herself and released a heavy breath. Moments later, Kendrick's strong arms covered her arms and she was grateful for the wall of support and love he gave her. She turned into his embrace as he pressed a kiss to the top of her head.

"I just wish I knew what was going on," she admitted softly as she eased her arms around his waist and hugged him back fiercely. "I'm so scared that when someone does remember us they'll be nothing but bad news."

Kendrick bent his head, placing his mouth near her ear. "Our father, which art in heaven. Hallowed be thy name . . ."

Tamara closed her own eyes and joined her loving husband in prayer.

Caress vaguely noticed Julius in his operating room garb as he stood by her head in the operating room. She kept her eyes closed. Blocking the bright lights. Pretending the room wasn't cold. Trying not to visualize what was going on beyond the small curtain blocking everything from her view. Placing her mind on anything but the facts. Wishing for the best. Dreaming of the end result and not the road traveled to get there. . . .

Julius kept his eyes focused on Caress as the emotions of everything—the birth of the child, the risks to both the baby and Caress during surgery, his love for her—

overwhelmed him. He reached over and lightly caressed the side of her face. His heart swelled when she smiled softly at his touch.

What does this mean now? he wondered. *Where do we all go from here?*

"Okay, ladies and gentlemen. Here comes the star of this event . . . and it *is* a boy."

Caress opened her eyes and turned her head to look up at Julius. He stroked her forehead just as the sound of a healthy and strong wail of a baby filled the air. "Thank you. Thank you. Thank you, God," she whispered.

Julius watched as the baby was quickly wiped off and his mouth suctioned. Squirming, screaming, fat, and healthy. His hair a mass of tight curls. His complexion already a deep brown. *Like mine*, he thought. His eyes stayed locked on him as the nurse brought him around for Caress and him to see. "Here's Mommy and Daddy sweetie," the short and plump woman said.

"Hey, man," Caress sighed up at him, a smile on her face and in her eyes.

Julius couldn't deny that he could already see the baby had his wide bridged nose and cowlick hairline. No, he still didn't know for sure, but his heart surged with all the emotions a parent should have: fierce love, complete devotion, and total protectiveness.

"We're going to get him examined," the nurse told them softly, allowing them one final look before she turned and walked away.

Caress smiled as she closed her eyes again. "He looks like you, Julius. I just hope he's not as conceited," she teased.

Julius smiled, amazed that she could find a moment to joke even as the doctors sewed her back up. She was a remarkable woman and he loved her.

* * *

Tamara jumped up from the chair as soon as Julius walked into the visiting room. She felt relief at the huge grin on his handsome face. "They're okay?" she asked.

"Caress is in the recovery room. She did great and the baby is healthy and beautiful," Julius said with pride.

Tamara clenched her fists and jumped up and down excitedly before she turned and shook a sleeping Kendrick. "Wake up. Caress had the baby!"

Kendrick cocked one eye open. "Tamara, baby, bring it down a notch. This is a hospital, you know."

She slapped the side of his head playfully. "Shut up," she told him, walking across the room to hold Julius close. "Congratulations, Daddy."

Julius nodded several times as he smiled. "He has my nose," he said, a bit goofily and out of character for the suave man.

"Aww." Tamara sighed as she leaned back to look up at her college friend.

Kendrick walked up to them and soundly clapped Julius on the back. "Now do you forgive us for moving her into your crib?" he joked.

Julius eyed them both stoically as they began to giggle and then full out laugh.

In the recovery room, Caress lay on her side with the baby beside her as she finally got him to successfully latch on to her breast. He was busy sucking away and she just lay there, watching him and loving him. In the moment, she didn't let the nausea or the tenderness of her abdominal stitches disturb finally having her child in her arms.

She looked up as Dr. Dillinger walked into the recovery room. "Hey, Doc," she said, still a little weak.

"Hi, Mommy," she greeted Caress cheerfully as she cleansed her hands. "The nurses tell me you're requesting a paternity test."

Caress closed her eyes waiting for a wave of nausea to pass before she spoke, "Yes, his father wants to be sure . . . he . . . I . . . our situation—"

The Doc held up her hand. "No need to explain. We'll get it done."

Julius stepped into the room and Caress's eyes immediately shifted to him, but his eyes were on the baby. Their son. He smiled at the doctor before stepping up beside the bed to scoop the bundled baby up into his arms.

Caress didn't know why she felt any apprehension at all because Julius handled the baby with ease. As the doctor examined her, Caress felt her eyes getting heavy. Through the break of her full lashes, just before she allowed sleep to claim her, she saw Julius press a kiss to the baby's cheek.

When Caress stirred hours later she immediately noticed she was in a private room and out of recovery. The room was dark save for the light over her bed. The baby was pushed close to the side of her bed in one of those clear, plastic bassinets with wheels. With his striped cap and his body bundled snugly in his blanket, only his face was visible. One chubby brown fist was pushed against his mouth.

Caress reached over and lightly stroked his cheek with the side of her index finger. "You need a name," she said softly.

"Yes, he does."

Caress looked to the right and noticed for the first time that Julius was kicked back in the recliner chair. She was surprised to see him and her face showed it. "Hi, Julius. Everybody went home?" she asked, wishing the darkness didn't cloak so much of his expression.

"Your boss left when I got here. Tamara and Kendrick will be back in the morning," he said.

"Did they see the baby?" she asked, her heart still racing from the surprise of seeing him.

"Yeah, at the nursery."

Caress looked over at him, and she knew his eyes were on her. "You've been here the whole time?" she asked, shifting her head to instead focus her eyes on her baby.

"Of course."

Warmth spread over her entire body at the sound of his voice. Something about his tone in those two simple words electrified her.

"You like your flowers?" he asked, finally rising from the chair and out of the darkness. His usually trimmed beard was fuller and rougher. It made him look wild and sexy.

She followed his line of vision and gasped in surprise at the half a dozen vases of white roses and helium balloons in front of the window. How had she missed them? "They're beautiful," she gasped in pleasure.

"Not half as beautiful as you are, Caress."

She turned her head again to look up at him. "My hair is all over my head and my mouth tastes—and probably smells—like rotten eggs," she quipped, trying to cover the warmth and excitement his words evoked.

Julius laughed. "Dwayne actually went by your apartment for me and grabbed your bag. Tamara told us where to find it."

"Thank . . . God. I need a tight bra to help with these milk jugs that used to be breasts—and a toothbrush. In that order." Caress shifted her body up into a sitting position.

She tried not to notice how good his backside looked in his stiff denims when he turned to grab her bag from the small closet by the sink. She had to shift her eyes up quickly when he turned back to set the bag on the side of the bed by her legs.

"The baby and I had the mouth swabs done for the paternity test," he told her, as he unzipped the bag.

Caress began to undo the shoulder snaps on the generic print hospital gown. She avoided his eyes as she used one arm to drape the gown over her full and heavy breasts.

"I paid for the results to come back tomorrow," he continued.

Caress dug in the bag with her free hand and pulled out one of the bras she had packed.

"Caress."

She looked up at him. "Yes, Julius?"

He locked those magnetic eyes with her own.

The semi-darkness of the room, with that crazy and undeniable buzz of electricity and awareness surrounding them, was powerful.

"I know this isn't something we originally wanted, but I'm happy about my son and I want you to know that." Julius reached down to cover her hand with his own. "Thank you. Thank you for bringing my son—*our* son—into this world."

She smiled a little as emotions made her chest tight. "I'm happy too and I know we will give him a better life than our parents gave us."

Julius nodded as he returned her smile. "Definitely."

That vibe flourished between them and they both shifted their eyes away nervously.

Caress cleared her throat and Julius looked over at her again. She used her finger to motion for him to turn before she dropped the gown to her waist and took her time putting on the bra. The nurses claimed it would help ease the aching of her swollen breasts. "I'm done," she told him.

"You mentioned naming him. I like Justin for the first name," he offered as he turned back to face her, his eyes dropping down momentarily to her newly lifted breasts.

"Kinda want to keep the *J* thing going, huh?" she teased as she settled back against the pillows.

Julius, ever the neat freak, grabbed the bag and set in back in the closet.

Caress looked over at the baby. "Justin Jones," she tried out as she watched him suckle his fist. "Mr. Justin Jones. Justin Coleman Jones."

Julius walked up to the bassinet and looked down at their son. "Coleman, huh?" he asked, shifting his eyes over her.

Caress licked her lips as sadness softened her eyes. "Every baby should have a legacy . . . a history. I don't even know my own to pass on to him. The only thing I have in this world to hint at who I am and who made me is my name. I'd like to pass it on to him somehow."

Julius understood. "Justin Coleman Jones it is."

Caress instantly forgot the list of names in her pregnancy journal.

The door opened and a head full of braids peeked inside before a petite woman entered the room. "You're awake. Good. I'm Nyla and I'm your nurse tonight," she said, smiling up at Julius from across the bed.

Julius walked over to the window while the nurse examined Caress. He didn't move back to her bedside until Nyla left, pushing the baby out of the room to take back to the nursery.

Caress missed him already. "Everything is different now. All my life I just had me to worry about and now there's this little person who will rely on me."

"On both of us," Julius stressed.

Caress cocked her head to the side as she eyed him. "That's right. Both of us."

"I just want to thank you for not tripping or holding it against me that I wanted a blood test," he admitted, placing his hands on the side rail of the bed.

Caress picked up the wired remote control beside her on the bed as she diverted her eyes from him. The man was divine looking and distracting. She shook herself. "Uh . . . I, uh . . . I won't say I'm not a little insulted that you would think I would pass another man's child off on you . . . but I'm also a realist. I've seen enough *Maury Povich* and heard enough stories to understand any and every man wanting to be 100 percent sure. We really don't know each other and I'm partly to blame for this situation of ours."

"I feel like we know each other now," Julius said.

"Yeah, me too."

"I believe he's my son, Caress." Julius's voice was clear with his belief.

Caress pressed her head back against the pillows as she looked up at him. "Yeah, me too," she teased, her eyes twinkling.

Julius just shook his head and laughed. "I love you, Caress."

Time went completely still.

Julius looked as shocked by the words that seemed to slip from his mouth as Caress was to hear them.

She opened her eyes a bit as her heart raced. "What?" she asked in a small voice.

Julius's face slowly changed to seriousness as he slid his hands into the front pockets of his jeans. "I love you," he said simply as his eyes pierced her.

Caress closed her eyes. Breathed deeply. Counted to ten. Then she opened her eyes to look up at him again. "Julius, listen. I understand with the baby and everything, that emotions are running on high. And . . . and we don't have to live up to some stereotype to be his parents. You don't have to tell me you love me—"

Julius bent and swooped his head in quickly, covering her mouth with his and swallowing the rest of her words.

As he covered her mouth with a thousand tiny kisses, Caress melted. She brought her hand up to lightly hold the side of his face as she welcomed his affection.

Moans that were filled with all of the pent-up emotions, regrets, and unfulfilled desires that they shared, filled the air around them.

"I love you, Caress," Julius moaned against her mouth a dozen times in between electrifying kisses.

Caress felt dizzy as she opened her eyes and looked up at him. "Julius—"

"Do you love me, Caress?" he whispered against her lips.

Of course, she thought, but the words would not leave her mouth even as her heart pounded with so much love for him that she felt like she would explode.

A twinkle filled his eyes as he smiled at her with all of his Julius Jones charm. "I know you love me," he told her with the utmost confidence.

"Oh, you do?" she asked, as her eyes darted down to take in his mouth.

Julius tasted her lips again as he nodded. "Uhm hum. Don't you?"

Caress's hand rose to lightly grasp the back of his head. "Huh?"

Julius suckled her bottom lip into his mouth. "Don't you?" he demanded again in a soft, teasing tone.

Caress leaned her head back from him and met his stare boldly. "Yes, I do, Julius Jones. And?"

A grin as smooth as butter spread across his handsome face but Caress couldn't deny that even as he continued to bless her with his tender affection one nagging question remained: *Now what?*

Chapter Thirteen

Week One

Caress removed the last piece of chicken from the pan of grease. She looked over her shoulder as Julius walked out of the bedroom with the baby monitor in his hand, quietly closing the door behind him. "He's sleeping?" she asked, as she turned the burner under the mashed potatoes down to low.

"What else? Does he do anything else?" Julius asked as he walked up behind her and placed a kiss on her neck.

Caress shivered and laughed at the same time. "Soon I'm going to wish he'd sleep more."

"Like those nights we want to run around naked chasing one another," he whispered near her ear before biting her lobe hotly.

"You are a perv," Caress teased, turning to wrap her arms around his waist as she leaned back a little to look up at him.

Julius eyed her mouth as he placed his hands on the counter behind her. "I am horny as hell too," he admitted, with desire in his eyes.

Caress made a mocking sad face. "Nothing I can do for you for at least six weeks," she told him, planting a kiss near the corner of his subtle mouth.

Julius made a pained expression. "Pray for a brother," he said, dropping his head to lightly rest on top of hers.

Caress laughed. "Hell, pray for a sistah. Remember the last time we both did it was that night."

"Let's eat and talk about something else," he said, moving away from her to grab dishes from the cabinet over the fridge.

Caress eyed him, still unable to believe that they were trying the relationship thing. She was ready, but she couldn't help wondering if he was. Did she love him? Definitely. Did he love her? That's what he said.

Since she was released from the hospital they had spent each evening together at her apartment. A couple of times he had even stayed the night, seemingly content just lightly holding her in his arms as they slept.

Everything about their love affair was so jumbled and out of place. She was still getting adjusted to this new step. Her heart was his, she just wished she could believe his emotions weren't just based on their son. Still she loved him. She had missed him terribly after she moved out of his house. She wanted them to be together.

Julius lightly touched her back as he moved past her in the small kitchen and she looked over at him. He looked up suddenly and smiled at her. Her heart swelled.

She wanted this to work.

Week Two

Julius leaned back in his leather chair as the sounds of sultry jazz filled his office. He cast his eyes out the window before picking up his shot of brandy to sip. He bopped his head to the bass line as he thought about Caress and Justin. Love like nothing he had ever known filled him and he smiled.

"What has you looking so goofy?"

Julius looked over his shoulder as Kendrick walked in. "What's up, man?" he greeted his friend, reaching out with his fist to offer him a pound.

"Nothing, man." Kendrick settled his large frame in one of the chairs in front of Julius's desk. "You ready?"

Julius leaned back in his chair and fingered the rim of his glass. Tamara was throwing Caress a baby shower and had enlisted Kendrick to keep him out of their hair. "Where we headed?" he asked, looking out the window at the setting sun.

"Wanna catch a movie?" Kendrick asked, reaching for *The Star Ledger* on the edge of Julius's pristine desk.

Julius cut his eyes over to his friend. "Uh . . . no. I'm not going to the movies with a dude."

At that moment Dwayne strolled in with his hair in a spiky Mohawk and his slender frame damn near choked in his black skinny jeans. He set a huge shopping bag on the desk. "This is for Justin. Be sure to tell Caress to call me after she opens it," he said.

Julius eyed the bag and then shifted his eyes to Kendrick. With Dwayne, anything could be in that bag. "I'll tell her," he said.

Dwayne dramatically turned to leave, but paused at the entrance to turn back and point a long and slender finger at both of them. "I don't see anything wrong with two grown men going to the movies together."

Kendrick's and Julius's eyes locked over the rim of the paper partially covering Kendrick's face.

"Matter of fact, I can take you to a theatre where there ain't nothing but men—"

"I don't think so, Dwayne," Julius said, as Kendrick frowned deeply.

Dwayne laughed as he pushed past the leather curtain and left the room.

Kendrick shook his head as he folded the paper. "No movies."

Julius laughed.

Week Three

Caress watched Tamara as she changed baby Justin's diaper. "You better hurry, girl, he has good aim."

Tamara smiled down at the chubby-cheeked angel. "You wouldn't dare pee on your godmother," she said to him in baby talk.

"Humph," said Caress who was sitting on the sofa, folding baby blankets.

Tamara took the hint and finished up quickly. She scooped him up to her shoulder as she settled back against the chair. "I might have to have one soon," she cooed before nuzzling her face in his neck.

"He's a good baby." Caress pressed the folded blankets down into the hamper near her foot.

"And how's the daddy?" Tamara winked at Caress playfully.

"Counting down the days—if you know what I mean."

Tamara laughed. "Awww, poor little horny baby."

"I'll tell you what. Every day I feel better and better." Caress raised an eyebrow as she looked at her friend.

Tamara leaned the baby forward to burp him. "So Julius ain't the only one doing some counting."

"Three weeks, two days to go," Caress said without hesitation.

"Awww," Tamara sighed with a laugh.

"It's been a *looong* time, Tam-Tam."

Tamara made a comical face. "Okay, *that's* TMI but I understand."

Caress eyed her son, seeing more and more of both her and Julius in him everyday. "I just wish I didn't feel like I'm waiting for the other shoe to drop."

"Listen, Caress, if you live life looking for something bad to happen then it will. If you and Julius love each other everything will work out if you just let it."

Caress watched as Tamara gave baby Justin the rest of his milk. "Think you're ready to baby-sit all night?" she asked.

Now it was Tamara's turn to lift her brow. "Let me guess, in about three weeks right?"

Caress smiled big as day. "You got it."

"And you gon get *it*, huh?"

The ladies laughed together.

Week Four

Julius eyed Caress as she moved about his living room picking up the baby's things. It was hard to tell that she'd just had a baby a month ago. Her belly was back to its pre-pregnancy state and the black leggings she wore with a fitted tee hugged snugly to her petite and curvaceous frame.

His eyes dipped down to her buttocks as she bent over to pick up the container of baby wipes. He couldn't deny the hardening of the muscle between his thighs. Her body wasn't a picture of perfect proportions, but he liked every bit of it. He liked it and he was ready to feel it.

Julius smiled when Caress turned and caught him checking her out. She dropped the items she held into the baby bag before she walked over to lie down beside him on the couch. "I can see what's on your mind," she said, looking pointedly down at his erection.

Julius wrapped his arms around her and pulled her body close to his. "Those pants are giving me hell, baby," he moaned into her ear.

"I thought you hated all my sweats?"

"I thought so too."

Caress laughed huskily as she massaged her hand up and down the hard length of Julius's strong arm. "I'm so glad we found a good day care for the baby. I go back to work in two weeks."

"Uhm hum." Julius brought his hand up from her waist to palm and then massage one of her breasts.

Caress mouth shaped into a *O* as his touch made her entire body tingle. Nearly one year since that night and the chemistry between them was still stirring. Magnetic. Undeniable. She was finding it hard to ignore the warmth filling her core as Julius shifted his body to place kisses on her neck.

"Yeah, me too, baby."

She gasped hotly as his fingers teased and tantalized her hard nipple. "Julius," she said, starting to protest.

He lifted her shirt, exposing her lace-covered breasts. "This is nice," he said, even as he skillfully undid the front snap. "But this is nicer."

Caress arched her back from the couch as Julius licked a trail from one hard nipple to the other. "Julius," she said, in pure pleasure.

He circled the nipple with the tip of his tongue before suckling it into his mouth. "Caress," he moaned against her moist flesh as he felt her hands release his hardness from his pants. He arched his hips at the first feel of her soft and hot hands surrounding him and stroking him. Teasing him and squeezing him. Pushing him near the edge of free falling into a speedy climax.

He suckled one breast deeper as he teased the nipple of the other. He reveled in the shivers of her body and the sweet sighs of pleasure she released into the heated air as she massaged the sensitive tip of his length. "You're gonna make me cum, Caress," he groaned, feeling the pressure rising.

She looked down at him as he continued to ravage her breasts. "That's fine," she whispered huskily.

Julius's eyes shot up to her with his tongue resting on her nipple.

She licked her lips as she increased the speed of her stroke. "You'll just owe me one," she told him with glazed eyes.

Julius shifted his body back up and kissed Caress deeply as she stroked him to a mind-blowing climax that was just a hint of the pleasure he knew she had to give.

Week Five

"You look beautiful," Julius whispered into her ear.

Caress tilted her head back onto the sofa as the light-hearted chatter of their guest surrounded them. "Is it the make-up?" she teased, batting her mascara-covered lashes at him.

Julius covered her mouth with his own.

"Oh, good God. Get a room!" Tamara exclaimed.

Caress broke the kiss slowly. Raising her hand to wipe her sheer gloss from Julius's lips she eyed Tamara, Kendrick, Jordan, and Mia. "Sorry," she said sounding anything but.

"Jordan, remember when we used to be all over each

other like that?" Mia asked, running her manicured hand through her newly cropped mass of curly hair as she sat on the arm of the club chair where he sat.

Jordan wrapped his arm around her waist and then playfully swatted her full bottom. "You mean last night?" he asked, with boast.

Mia laughed as she presented her wine glass to him in a mini-toast. "You got that right," she said in her husky voice before bending down to taste his lips.

In the weeks since she and Julius had the baby, Caress had fallen for the clumsy but sexy writer, his take-no-bull wife, and their children. In fact, their teenaged twins, Amina and Aliya, were babysitting Justin upstairs.

Jordan crossed his legs as he continued to hold on to his wife. "Love is a wonderful thing. It's a powerful thing. And I don't know about all of you but I'm glad to have it in my life."

Mia smiled warmly at her husband with her eyes. "To love y'all," she said. "Black love."

Tamara and Kendrick touched their glasses before they shared a kiss.

Caress felt good sitting next to Julius and surrounded by their friends. She leaned back against the sofa to look up at him. "I—"

Julius shook his head. "This has nothing to do with our vibe, or our son, or anything except I think you are a strong, smart, independent woman who makes me laugh and makes me forget all of my rules."

Caress blinked away the tears his words evoked. "What am I going to do with you, Julius Jones?" she whispered against his mouth.

"Love me," was his simple reply.

* * *

Week Six

Julius walked into his studio, with his briefcase and monogrammed camera case hanging from his broad shoulder. "Morning, Dwayne," he greeted his assistant.

"Morning, boss." Dwayne handed him a stack of phone messages. "And there's some packages on your desk."

"Thanks." Julius headed for his office with his eye on the clock. He wanted to wrap up whatever work he had so that he could head out to Caress's apartment as soon as he could.

"One of the packages is from Karina," Dwayne called behind him.

Julius stopped short. Karina. He knew without a doubt that it was drama. He hadn't spoken to her since the photo shoot in Jamaica.

Resolved to not let anything ruin his day—especially this day—Julius continued on to his office. He knew the bright pink-and-white-striped box atop the generic brown boxes had Karina stamped all over it.

Julius put down his briefcase and camera before he picked up what Karina had sent. He opened it to find a mock-up of her calendar. Scribbled across the cover shot of her in nothing but a rhinestone-encrusted bikini with her bare breasts covered by her hands was a note:

Thank God you're better with the camera than you are with other "things."

Karina

Just what he thought. Drama. Dropping the calendar back into the box he tossed it into the trash where it belonged. The only thing he had his mind on today was Caress and the doctor's appointment. To hell with anything else.

* * *

Caress securely held baby Justin's car seat in her hand before she used her hip to securely close the passenger door of her car. The door squealed loudly.

Julius was nagging her to get a more reliable car but she was hesitant to take on a car payment, and without a lump sum of cash to buy something reliable, she would have to finance a better ride.

"Hi."

Caress looked up and smiled at the pre-teen girl of about twelve who lived in the large apartment building on the corner. She didn't know her name but Caress knew her from seeing her around the neighborhood. As always her hair was pulled back into a messy tail that was more pig than pony. Her clothes fit like they belonged to someone twice her size. And her eyes were wide and bright and haunted in her ashen, caramel-colored face. The girl was the portrait of urban sadness.

Caress smiled at her encouragingly as the girl showed the first sign of happiness in her face as she stooped down to look at Justin. "His name is Justin," she told the girl, feeling empathy for her—or at least the sad story she assumed the girl had. "What's your name?"

"Luretha," the girl told her in a soft voice as she stood up.

"I'm Caress."

"Hi," Luretha said again, before she turned and started walking away with one last glance at Justin over her shoulder.

Even after the girl continued up the cracked pavement to the corner store, Caress's eyes stayed locked on the back of the far-too-slender girl with the well-worn clothes and the look of a well-worn life.

She reminded Caress of herself.

With one last look, Caress continued up the brick steps and into her building. When she walked into her apartment, she took Justin out of the carrier and placed him in his bassinet. She was putting his beloved pacifier in his mouth when she heard heavy footsteps on the stairs.

She looked around the apartment, glad that she had straightened up before she left that morning. It wasn't spotless but it was clutter-free.

Caress turned her head as the key turned in the lock. Her eyes widened in surprise at the huge teddy bear and the dozen red roses Julius held in his hand. Her eyes took him in. The suave demeanor. The neat shadow of his beard. That bowlegged walk that was all too telling.

Her heart raced.

"For my baby," he joked with a delicious kiss to her mouth before he turned to set the bear in Justin's bassinet. "And for my baby boy."

Caress inhaled deeply of the roses as she watched him tease Justin with the bear.

"How was your day?" Julius asked, rising to his full height of over six feet.

Caress kicked off her flip-flops before carrying the baby bag into the kitchen. "I went by to visit the day care and I think he'll be fine there," she told him.

"Oh, that's good. And?" he asked, before following her into the kitchen.

Caress looked blasé as she started placing the milk and water bottles inside the fridge and out of the summer heat. "And what, baby?" she asked, enjoying teasing him.

Julius stepped over to take the baby bottles from Caress's hand before he gently turned her to face him. "Can I or can't I make love to my woman tonight?" he asked, before he lowered his head and kissed her.

Caress laughed huskily as she wrapped her arms around

his waist. "Yes, yes you can. And hopefully with all the passion and power I remember from our last night together," she whispered against his strong chin before she bit it lightly.

Julius used strong arms around her waist to lift her petite frame up so that their eyes and mouth were matched. With a wolfish grin, he kissed her deeply and soon their bodies were pressed together as their hands explored each other's backs and buttocks with a building energy that was frenetic.

He stepped back from their heat first. "If we don't stop we won't make our dinner reservation," he warned.

Caress shrugged as she removed the bind from her hair, freeing her ponytail. Next she began to unbutton the sleeveless white shirt she wore.

Julius's eyes watched the slow reveal of her cleavage in the black sheer brassiere that cupped her small but plump breasts. "Caress," he said suddenly, reaching out quickly to remove her hands from the rest of the buttons. "I'm going to take the baby to Tamara and Kendrick's, then go home and get dressed. I'll be back in a couple of hours."

With one last look at temptation, he turned and sauntered out of the kitchen as fast as he could without actually running. Her laughter followed him.

Julius couldn't believe that he actually felt nervous as he checked his appearance in the full-length mirror. It felt like that first night when he prepared for his blind date with Caress.

But this night was so very different.

Tonight she was the woman he loved. The mother of his only child. His new confidante and friend.

With an ever-critical eye, he made sure the hand-tailored charcoal suit and big knot, bold print tie fit him just so.

Cuff links and shoes polished. His face was clean-shaven. His head taped up perfectly. The scent of his Gucci cologne was noticeable without being overwhelming.

He was the epitome of a well-groomed urban sophisti-cate man.

A man ready to wine, dine, and woo his woman.

Caress was definitely a no muss and no fuss kind of woman. Sweats over silk. Jeans over jewels. Television over movie. Drive-thru over dine-in.

But tonight she went all out and she looked and felt damn good.

She twisted her shoulder-length hair up into a sleek top-knot that emphasized her high cheekbones and exotic eyes. And those she made smoky with eye shadow and heavy layers of lengthening mascara. Lip gloss highlighted her full mouth.

The pale pink wrap dress she wore with oversized gold hoops, necklace, and strappy heels worked to lengthen her shorter stature and emphasize her thick, curvy frame.

She didn't know what Julius had planned for the night but she was more than ready for whatever he had to offer.

Chapter Fourteen

Caress smiled in pleasure as Julius turned his Range Rover into the gated parking lot of Mahogany's. "Back to the beginning, huh?" she asked, enjoying the feel of Julius's warm hand on her thigh as he drove with his other hand.

"That's right."

Caress reached into her gold clutch bag for her cell phone. "I want to check on the baby."

Julius reached over, slipped the phone out of Caress's grasp, and slid it into the inner pocket of his jacket. "Justin is fine. Tamara is more than capable and completely in love with him. Kendrick is her sanity. Everything's fine, baby. Let's just enjoy each other tonight. It's been a long . . . damn . . . time. For real."

Caress nodded as he parked. "Just you and me."

"Just you and me," he agreed, hopping out of the car.

Caress climbed out before Julius could make it around. He eyed her as she looked at him curiously. "What?"

"Listen, Miss Coleman, it's okay to be independent and strong and still let me be a gentleman. Okay?"

Caress smiled at him. "Okay."

Julius placed his hand at the small curve of her back as they walked into the restaurant.

In only a short time they were seated across from each other at one of the more secluded balcony tables overlooking the already crowded dance floor. They ordered their drinks as they accepted leather-bound menus.

"I love it here," Caress said, looking around at the muted jewel tones of the brick-walled interior.

"Me too." Julius unbuttoned his suit jacket.

They fell silent but the music and atmosphere created a warm zone where the silence was far from awkward.

With a soft smile, Caress watched the people on the dance floor. She loved dancing and couldn't wait to get on the floor. She looked over at Julius and found his intense eyes resting on her.

"You look good as hell, Caress," he told her, the flickering light of the candle centerpiece illuminating his handsome face as he continued to watch her.

"Thank ya. Thank ya." Caress reached across the square wooden table and lightly stroked the back of his hands. "You're looking fine yourself, Mr. GQ . . . of course."

They fell silent again.

"I actually wanted to talk to you about something," Julius began, flipping his hands over to grasp hers.

Boom. To Caress that was the sound of that other shoe dropping. She felt that nervous anxiety and dread as she closed her eyes like that would block the blow of his words.

"I want you and the baby to move back in with me."

She opened her eyes. "Julius, I . . . uh . . . uhm. No. No."

His handsome face shaped into a frown. "Why not?" he asked, obviously confused by her answer.

"Being pregnant, jobless, and without a place of my own to live will forever be one of the worst time periods in my life, Julius," she began, her eyes filled with conviction. "I thank you for letting me stay in your house, but I'm finally back on my feet and if this thing between us ends I don't want to be back behind the starting line getting myself together. God always blesses the child that his—or her—own."

The waiter stepped up to their table and they gave their orders of oxtail stew and rice for Julius and fried catfish for Caress. Julius waited to say anything else until the waiter was out of earshot.

"So you're just waiting for this 'thing' between us to end?" he asked Caress with an edge in his voice.

Caress lifted his hands to place her face against his palm. "I'm waiting to see what this 'thing' is, Julius," she told him with complete honesty.

Julius stroked her cheek. "This 'thing' is the first time I've met a woman I can say I've fallen in love with."

"Because of the baby?" Caress asked, letting her doubts surface.

Julius's face hardened. "Give me more credit than that."

"And don't blame me for being afraid," she countered with attitude.

Julius locked his eyes on her. "Afraid?"

Caress nodded, meeting his stare.

"Of me?"

"Of love."

"Of me," Julius asserted, his anger and annoyance clear.

"Okay fine, yes, Julius. Of you," Caress admitted. "You have women coming to your door buck naked with a smile and calling you leaving messages just trying to throw their stuff on you like you have the last penis on the planet earth."

"It's up to me to catch it."

"Eventually."

Julius frowned. "Did some brotha dog you out and now I'm catching his hell?" he snapped in irritation as he sat back in his chair and fingered the rim of his drink.

Caress's mouth dropped open. "Oh no you didn't."

"Yeah I did." Julius picked up his drink and swallowed nearly half of it down.

Caress sat back in her chair and glared at Julius like she wished she could choke him.

The mood was shattered. The air was stilted and the distance between them was far wider than the table separating them. Each looked any and every way around the dimly lit interior. Anywhere but at each other. When their food arrived, they focused on their meals.

The sounds of the live band's sultry jazz rendition of Mary J. Blige's "I'm Going Down" suddenly filled the air.

Julius looked up at Caress.

Caress looked over at Julius.

They both looked away.

The music seemed to get louder like it wanted to be noticed.

Julius used his napkin to wipe his mouth while he chewed his food, with another quick glance at Caress.

She took another bite of her crispy fried fish while she fought not to sway to the music and get lost in the memories of their first night together.

But it was hard to forget for either of them. That night and all it encompassed was far beyond the physical.

Caress felt her anger and annoyance at Julius ease away. The man planned a romantic evening when she would've gladly let him take her right there on her kitchen floor. Not to mention his patience the last six weeks—or the last ten months for that matter.

Clearing away a piece of fish from her teeth with her tongue, Caress removed her napkin from her lap and dropped it on the table next to her plate. Clearing her throat a bit, she rose from her chair, smoothed her dress over her shapely hips and then held out her hand to Julius. Her friend. Her lover. Her man.

He bit back a begrudging smile before he too dropped his napkin on the table and then rose to take her hand.

Sparks immediately flew at their touch.

Caress dropped her head as she led Julius down the stairs to the crowded dance floor. They found a spot near the front, their bodies already swaying to the music as she turned and wrapped her arms around his waist.

Doubts about love and their relationship ceased.

Silly worries about possible infidelities in the future went away.

The moment—this moment—was all about Caress and Julius. Nothing else mattered as they got lost in the moment, the mood, and the music.

Julius watched Caress as she slowly walked around his studio. He was fascinated that she stopped and studied each and every photograph. Her face would show whatever emotions she was feeling so clearly . . . just like when he made love to her that night. Raw. Exposed. Unbridled.

After eating dinner and enjoying countless moments dancing in their own little piece of the world, Julius asked Caress what she wanted to do next. He offered her anything at all. Truly it was a rhetorical question because he assumed she would be ready to head to one of their homes and bed.

Her reply, "Take me to your studio," was a definite surprise.

So here they were.

As he walked up behind her, Julius tried not to notice how thick and shapely her petite frame looked in the dress she wore. "You've been looking at this one for a while," he said, taking in the black-and-white photo of children outside a village.

Caress reached for his hands from behind and wrapped them around her waist. "I was just remembering some of the stories you told me about your trip to Africa. I can't wait to have your book in my hands."

Julius pulled her body back close to his. "And I can't wait to have all of you in my hands," he moaned against her soft neck.

She lifted up on her toes to place her full bottom against his groin. She wiggled her hips as she arched her back. "In time," she teased, before breaking his hold around her waist and walking away from him with sass.

Julius shoved his hands into his pockets before he followed her.

"What's behind here?" she asked, pointing to the leather curtain.

"My office."

"May I?"

Julius smiled, thinking of the childhood game "Mother May I." He nodded his head and Caress disappeared behind the curtain. He followed at a slower pace, eventually leaning in the doorway as he held the curtain open.

Caress was standing in front of his desk with her hand at her mouth as she looked up at the poster-sized photo of baby Justin hanging on the center of the wall behind his desk. "Awwww," she sighed, moving around the desk to step closer to the image.

Julius smiled at the image as well.

"I really wanted to see your studio since it's such a big part of you," she said, touching the picture of Justin's face softly before she turned to Julius. "I like . . ."

Her words trailed off as her eyes fell on the five-by-seven photo on the corner of his organized desk. It was a beautiful snapshot of Caress breastfeeding Justin as sunlight streamed in through the sheer curtains at the window. The look on her face as she gazed down at her son and he gazed back was total love. "Okay, why don't I have a copy of this?" she asked.

Julius smiled when Caress finally looked up and focused her soft eyes on the gold heart-shaped locket hanging from his index finger. He walked over to stand behind her and placed the twenty-inch chain around her neck with a kiss to the soft hairs at her nape.

Caress shivered as she pressed the small latch on the side of the plump heart locket to spring it open. Inside was a small copy of the picture from his desk.

"I was going to give it to you at my house but the moment seems right."

She turned and kissed him passionately as she splayed her hands on his strong back. "Let's go," she whispered up to his panting and open mouth.

Julius grabbed her hand and pulled her out of the office without another word.

Caress laughed as Julius carried her up the stairs and into his dimly lit bedroom. As soon as she slid to her feet from his capable grasp, she kicked off her heels and crossed the room, pausing at the bathroom door to beckon him with a bend of her finger while she untied her wrap dress with her free hand.

Caress undid her bra, flinging it at him before she wiggled out of the matching sheep thongs. Julius strode across the room to reach for her but she dodged his embrace.

Ever aware of his eyes, Caress made sure to strike a few sexy poses as she bent over to start the shower. She turned and watched Julius step out of his pants and boxers like a stripper. A well-toned and sculptured stripper.

"You are one fine ass man, Julius Jones," she told him as the steam of the shower began to fill the room.

Naked and proud with his long hooked erection leading over to her, Julius placed one sinewy muscled arm around Caress's waist and picked her up to step into the shower. As the water pelted down on their bodies, Caress tilted her chin up and pressed her lips against Julius's with a soft grunt of pleasure.

With her body held close down the length of his, her feet floated above the floor of the tub. That plus Julius's kisses made her feel like she was floating on air. "Yes," she sighed as his hands shimmied across her wet, silken skin. The back of her shapely thighs. Her fleshy brown buttocks. The small curve of her lower back. The soft sides of her breasts.

Julius turned and pressed Caress back to the slick, tiled walls. He moved down to squat before her, leveling his lips to her twin peaks. Looking up at her as she looked down at him expectantly, Julius released his tongue and took an exquisitely slow time tasting her taut chocolate nipples. One to the other. Each stroke sent her senses reeling from something so seemingly simple.

Caress arched her back, pressing her hands to the back of his head as she brought her legs up to wrap around his back. The bud between her legs throbbed with a beating pulse all its own. "It's been so long, Julius," she admitted in a passion-filled sigh.

"Too damn long," he agreed against her cleavage before suckling the plump flesh of first her left and then her right breast.

Caress gasped hotly as he suckled the tingling spots until he left twin passion marks in his wake. Shivers wrecked her body as he licked a trail from one nipple to the other before pursing his lips and pulling one nipple deeply into his mouth.

He grabbed her knee and raised her leg to his shoulder shifting down with the heated water and steam to ease his movements. Julius then placed kisses from her knee to the sweet vee of her essence. Her core. Her ultimate pleasure zone.

Caress spread her legs wider as Julius blew a stream of air against her throbbing and moist lips. "Lawdy," she gasped, bringing her hands down to spread her lips and expose the pulsing pink bud to him to do with as he pleased.

And he chose to please.

Each stroke of his tongue.

Each suckle of the bud into his mouth.

Every tender nip of it with his teeth.

All of it sent Caress free falling into one delicious wave after another until she forgot everything but how good he was making her feel. Without shame she cried out in passion and release until she was hoarse.

Julius relished in the pleasure he gave her. Even as his hard inches throbbed and ached for release he denied himself so that she could be completely fulfilled. In that moment it was his job. His duty. His privilege to be all that he could be.

"Damn, Julius, damn," Caress said in between pants for air, as she placed her hand to her rapidly beating heart. Julius kissed her deeply, drawing her tongue into his mouth before offering her his own. And when she circled her tongue around it, tasting her own juices, he felt his dick harden to stone. A piece carved out just for Caress.

She climbed down on wobbly legs and came around to stand directly under the spray of the water with a beguiling smile. Julius took it all in as he watched her over his shoulder and then turned to face her.

Steam swirled around her body as water cascaded down it like an erotic waterfall. Drops raced down the slopes of her breasts to hang precariously like diamonds from the taut tips before plunging down to the floor of the tub. Her body simply glistened as the water soaked her hair and softened her makeup.

Caress is sexy as hell.

She grabbed the soap and gave him a coy look as she began to lather her body. The addition of the foamy suds was damn near his undoing as he stroked the length of his hardness as he watched her like a hawk over its prey.

Julius shook his head for clarity as Caress stepped closer to him, dropped down to her knees, and then brought her body up the length of his body. Her hands and breasts made a sudsy trail from his ankles and his thighs—pausing to cup and caress his hard length.

Julius's body went tense as she looked up at him as she held his shaft at the base to guide it toward her slowly opening mouth. Inch by inch she took him in with delicious swirls of her tongue. He hissed in pleasure as his hips arched from the wall at the jolt of pure electricity that shot through him. "Caress . . . Caress," he moaned as he reached out blindly, entwining his fingers tightly in the wet strands of her hair.

She grabbed his thighs as she continued her passionate onslaught with deep sucks to the thick smooth tip that was warm and throbbing in her mouth.

Julius felt his knees weaken as Caress circled the tip with her tongue like she was on a mission. His face twisted in pleasure.

Feeling, that nervous energy of his climax nearing,

Julius placed his palm to her forehead and pushed while he pulled his hips back, freeing him from her eager mouth.

"What?" she asked innocently.

Julius nodded even as he waited for his equilibrium to return. "Round one goes to you . . . but now it's my turn," he told her with cocky confidence, stepping out of the shower to turn and lift Caress into his arms.

She clutched him tightly as he almost slipped on the tiled floor. They laughed, but the laughter and the teasing quickly diffused as Julius sat down on the bench at the end of his bed with Caress straddling his hips. His healthy and hard inches stood up between them like the hands on a clock showing high noon.

Caress brought her hands up to Julius's shoulders before easing them up to touch his face lovingly as he placed his hands on her hips possessively. "I love you, Julius Jones," she promised him huskily as she lowered her face close to his.

"That's all I want."

Their kisses were filled with the love and desire they shared—running the range from tender bite, playful pats, and delicious deep thrusts to tantalizing tangos of the tongue. They enjoyed the electrified but easy energy they created in each other's arms. It was a chemistry between a certain man and a certain woman. Unique. Blazing. Addictive.

As Julius used strong hands to grasp her bottom, he raised her body until she was positioned just above his pulsating, shiny tip. He lowered her down and filled her in one swoop with his heat planted deeply within her rigid walls.

"Ah!" Julius hollered out hoarsely, lowering his head to rest on Caress's cleavage. He felt her racing heart beat against his forehead as he fought not to spill his seed deep within her tight heat.

Caress closed her eyes and bit her bottom lip as she

shuddered and clutched him close to her. "Julius!" she cried. "Julius."

He slid his hands from her buttocks to her legs to wrap them around his waist. Caress followed his lead and locked her ankles behind him.

"Hold on baby," Julius whispered into the heat surrounding them as he lifted her just enough to cross his legs Indian-style beneath her.

Caress's mouth shaped into an *O* as the move pressed the thick and rigid base of his shaft against her swollen bud. "Oh . . . my . . ."

He kissed her with a smile on his lips but clear desire in his eyes. "Now watch this," he taunted sexily, wrapping his arms around her hips.

On that bench, Caress and Julius defied gravity as they perched precariously on the edge and he guided her to rock her hips back and forth. Nice. Slow. Easy.

"Whoo!" Caress arched her back as she let her head drop back until her damp hair tickled her back as she rode him. Nice. Slow. Easy. Just the way he wanted.

Back and forth. Round and round.

Julius's mind was completely blown. Caress was a very quick study. He clenched his jaw as he pressed her upper body to his, enjoying the sway of her soft breasts against his chest and the soft purrs of pleasures echoing from the back of her throat. He was dizzied by the tight, wet feel of her walls gliding up and down his shaft as she rode him. Nice. Slow. Easy.

Caress sat upright, still working her hips, as she tipped Julius's head up with a shaking hand to his strong chin. Their eyes locked. She hotly licked his mouth like a thirsty cat to milk as she continued her ride back and forth. Nice. Slow. Easy.

Julius deepened the kiss as he arched his hips up from the bench, sending his length deeper inside of her.

"Yes!" Caress cried out.

Sweat coated their bodies.

Their hearts raced.

Moans blended like a chorus.

Heat radiated from them.

All the while Caress continued her relentless ride back and forth. Nice. Slow. Easy.

Together the heat of the sensual union began to build from their cores. The delicious end was nearing—they hated and loved that all at once. Trembling and clutching at one another, their movements intensified until they both felt the explosion from deep within them. Blinded and consumed by the waves pouring over their bodies, their sighs, moans, grunts, and shattered cries of pleasure shifted easily into harsh, guttural cries that mingled in the electrified air with the sounds of their release.

Spent and pleased beyond measure, Julius uncrossed his legs and held Caress tightly as he fell back on his neatly made bed with his tool still planted within.

And they lay there entwined, still lightly caressing each other, and lost in their own little piece of the world.

Chapter Fifteen

One Month Later

Caress settled baby Justin down into his portable bassinet by her bed. Feeling a slight bit of the October chill in the apartment, she snuggled another of his knitted blankets over his plump three-month-old frame. Once she was satisfied her sleeping baby was secure, she turned her attention to some fall cleaning of her wardrobe.

With Julius at his studio preparing for his book release party, Caress planned to spend the day doing something productive. She didn't have much space for clothes in her small closet and dressers, so it was beyond time to flush out all of the clothes that didn't fit. The baby had spread her in all the right places—according to Julius—and she had to buy clothes to fit her new size-twelve frame.

Caress glanced up at the portrait of her nude body strategically covered with a silk sheet from Julius's bed. She still couldn't believe she let Julius convince her to take the sultry photos just moments after they made love. He said the good sex had inspired him and Caress had to admit she looked sexy as hell with her hair tousled, her mouth swollen from his kisses, and her eyes filled with love.

The man had a way with a camera . . . and other things.

Whisking her hair up into a loose ponytail, Caress pulled a velour sweatsuit over the black unitard she wore. She wished she could turn on some heat to knock off the chill but the landlord legally didn't have to supply heat until the fifteenth of the this month—and since it was cheaper for him she knew he didn't plan to.

Wishing she had a TV in her bedroom, she compromised by turning on the radio on her alarm clock. She considered listening to the jazz station Julius favored but passed on the idea. Just because they were together didn't mean they had to like all of the same things.

As the sounds of Alicia Keys filled the air, Caress took her time sorting the clothes into either a trash pile or a charity pile. She wasn't getting rid of that much, but at least now her dresser drawers could easily open and close.

Stepping over the piles, Caress headed into the kitchen for one of her beloved Snapples. She walked over to the window, pulling back the sheer sage curtain to look down at the street below. Her eyes focused in on the apartment building on the corner.

Luretha was sitting on the stoop alone, still dressed in the clothes Caress saw her in yesterday. As always her heart went out to her.

Caress looked over her shoulder at the framed picture sitting atop the living room table. It was a connection to her history while being a reminder of her painful and lonesome past. She turned away from it, shifting her eyes back to Luretha only to discover she was gone.

Her cell phone rang and she moved across the room to snatch it up from the kitchen counter. She checked her caller ID.

"Hey, Julius." Caress walked back into her bedroom intent on seeing if any of her clothes could fit Luretha.

"Hey baby, let's bring Justin to the book release. I want my son there."

Caress nodded, immediately understanding this was a big night for him and baby Justin was all the blood family he had. "Good idea. He can wear that dang suit you brought him."

"And you said it would never come in handy."

They laughed together.

"I miss y'all."

She pressed the phone closer to her ear. "We miss you too."

"I see Dwayne coming in with a box of pink streamers so I gotta go."

Caress laughed. "Yes, you better."

Julius couldn't keep his eyes off of Caress, who stood out among the hundred or so guests filling his studio for the book release party. Her usually straight hair was a mass of curls. The pink-and-gold-print strapless dress was knee-length and showed off her shapely legs in the gold strappy heels she wore. With the elaborate makeup and her subtlety sexy strut, she was messing with both of his heads.

Caress stood with Tamara and Mia, two attractive women in their own right, but to him neither held a candle to Caress. "Damn, I love her," he thought, letting his eyes drift over her for the hundredth time that night. He couldn't wait to get her alone and kiss every drop of gloss from her mouth.

The elevator doors opened and he took a sip from his flute of champagne. He nearly choked on the liquid when Karina breezed in on the arm of a tall white man who looked like he could be a model.

"Shit," he swore into his drink, as his eyes cut over to Caress only to find her eyes already locked on Karina.

Drama.

Julius looked around the studio for Dwayne, ignoring his agent trying to catch his attention. Seeing blond-tipped spikes over the many heads in the crowd, Julius headed that way. He thought it appropriate that his assistant's head resembled a chicken's butt because if he found out that Dwayne had invited Karina he was going to wring his neck.

"What . . . the . . . hell?" Caress's hand nearly snapped the delicate stem of the crystal flute in half as her eyes burned into the back of the model strutting across the room like she owned the world.

"What's up?" Tamara asked, instantly at Caress's side.

"That's Karina," Caress said tightly, taking a deep sip of champagne.

Mia made a face before stepping in front of the women. "Ladies, I'm older than both of you and so I'm going to give out some advice."

Caress and Tamara shifted angry eyes to her.

Mia held up her hand. "Hey, I'm on your side," she exclaimed jokingly.

Caress's face softened a bit. "I'm sorry but this is the same woman who came to Julius's door damn near naked."

Mia cringed. "Yes . . . I heard."

"I have my Vaseline and Uptowns in the trunk, girl," Tamara said with spunk, already reaching to her ears to remove her dangling beaded earrings.

Mia rolled her eyes. "Ladies, this is a business event for Julius who is more than your man, Caress. He is a prominent photographer. There is press here. There are some local politicians in the house. This is not the place. Not the time, ladies. No. No. No."

Caress looked into Mia's eyes and somehow found the calm within herself not to go half-cocked in a jealous rage and ruin Julius's night. Well, unless she found out he was double-dipping—then it was on like popcorn! The rules had changed since the last time she laid eyes on Karina. *There's a new sheriff in town, chick,* Caress thought, as her eyes scanned the room and landed on Julius talking to Dwayne. In that same instant, she saw a flash of bright crimson red from the corner of her eye. Caress turned her head to see Karina striding across the room headed in Julius's direction.

"Oh, Lord," Tamara sighed, taking a deep sip—and then another—of her champagne.

"Keep it cool, Caress," Mia advised.

Caress plastered a smile to her face and smoothed her dress over her frame. "How do I look, ladies?" she asked opening her beaded gold clutch bag to remove a pack of breath mints.

"Like you're ready to wear somebody's ass out!" Tamara said emphatically.

"You look lovely and dignified and confident enough not to act like a fool," Mia said with emphasis.

Caress loudly chewed a couple of mints. "Yeah, uh-huh," she muttered distractedly, already strolling away from them with her eyes locked on Karina lightly touching Julius's arm.

"You better work, girl," Tamara hissed behind her. "Just throw up a sign and I'm right there."

"Honey, you need to breathe," she heard Mia tease Tamara.

Caress felt like she deserved an Oscar for the calm and easy demeanor she presented as she reached Julius, Karina, and Dwayne. She was so proud of herself for not jumping on Karina like the tree she resembled and snatching her bald.

Dwayne spotted her first and his eyes got as big as saucers as he stepped in her path. "Hey, Caress, girl—"

"Move," Caress demanded under her breath from behind her fake smile.

Dwayne nodded. "Moving," he said, stepping his tall and slender frame aside without hesitation.

"Hello," Caress said sweetly as she stepped next to Julius and wrapped her arm around his waist.

Julius did the same to her as he pressed a kiss to her forehead. "Caress, this is Karina—"

Karina's beautiful face became an imposable mask of coldness before she recovered quickly and put on a smile as fake as Caress's. "We've met," she said, eyeing Caress. "Remember?"

Caress felt her spine stiffen and her tolerance drop low. Real low. *Breathe, Caress.* "Not really."

Although she smiled, the truth of her emotions was clear in her eyes. "So you two are . . ."

"Very happy," Caress told her, locking eyes with the woman.

Dwayne made a sort of laughing noise in the back of his throat. He stood off to the side just enough to appear he wasn't listening, but clearly he was.

Karina waved her hand dismissively as she turned her eyes to Julius. "Can we talk . . . alone?" she said, looking like a she was ready to stomp her foot petulantly.

"Oh no she didn't!" Dwayne exclaimed under his breath.

She whirled toward Dwayne. "Will you shut up?" she hissed angrily, before turning back to Caress and Julius with her mask back in place.

The instant change made Caress lean back a bit.

"Karina, there's plenty to drink. Enjoy yourself," Julius said patiently.

"Poof. Bam. Be gone!" Dwayne hissed fiercely in a low voice.

Karina's eyes filled with tears and she stomped her foot. "Julius," she whined.

Caress eyed the other woman oddly.

"Oops!" Dwayne taunted from nearby.

"Dwayne!" Julius said sharply.

Moments later Dwayne moved away from them.

Julius reached down to entwine his fingers with Caress's. "Enjoy the party, Karina," he said with finality.

Her eyes dropped down and caught the move just as her companion walked up to her carrying two flutes of champagne. She corrected her pained expression in an instant and smiled up at her handsome date. "Vincent, baby, this is Julius Jones. Julius, this is Vincent Pavlov," she said in satisfaction.

It was obvious she wanted to make Julius jealous.

The two men shook hands.

Caress had long since resolved that Julius and Karina weren't dealing and thus was bored with the woman's company.

"Look who's awake everyone!"

Caress turned at Dwayne's loud enthusiasm to find him walking out of Julius's office with baby Justin in his arms. Her face immediately lit up with a smile. As Dwayne made a big show of handing the baby to Julius, she wondered *Did Dwayne wake my baby up?*

Karina's mouth fell open as she eyed Julius nuzzling his bearded face in the warm nook of the baby's neck. "Is that your baby, Julius?" she asked, trying her best to form her face into surprised pleasure . . . and failing. Her nostrils flared like she had dog poo on her upper lip.

The young woman's face was hilarious with her wide

eyes and Joker-like smile. Caress actually felt a little sorry for her.

She really had no reason to dislike her, and she was fast realizing that this was a spoiled and vain child wrapped in a pretty package. She was used to getting what she wanted and didn't know how to handle things otherwise.

Caress focused her eyes on her son who had become the center of attention. He was adorable in his little khaki suit as he held his curly head up and gave his onlookers a gummy smile. It was probably gas but everyone sighed anyway—including Caress and Julius.

Everyone except Karina.

Her jaw was tight enough to crack marbles between her teeth . . . especially when Victor leaned in and starting making comical noises as he gently poked Justin's rotund belly.

"Victor!" Karina snapped, forcing another tight smile when she drew curious looks.

Victor eyed her oddly as well.

"I'm ready to go, Victor." Karina turned dramatically on her designer heels, tilting her head up as she strode through the crowd like she was headed to war.

"Deuces!" Dwayne called out behind her.

Victor shrugged and shook Julius's hand again. "Congrats on your book," he said politely following Karina to the elevator at a more leisurely pace.

Caress could only laugh and shake her head at the woman's dramatics. "Is she for real?" she asked Julius as Tamara and Mia walked up to them.

Julius laughed. "Yes."

"I thought I was gonna have to check you or wreck you behind that woman," Caress said, watching as Tamara eased Justin out of Julius's arms.

Julius shook his head. "You're all the woman I need."

"Don't you forget it," Caress told him before turning to smile at the photographer from *The Star Ledger* taking candid shots of the event.

"Meet me in my office and help me remember it," he whispered near her ear.

Caress shivered instantly as she cleared her throat and smoothed her hand over her curls. "In ten minutes?" she asked.

"Make it five."

Jordan walked up to Dwayne, Tamara, Kendrick, and Mia sitting in Julius's reception area. "Has anyone seen the man of the night? His agent and publicist are looking for him."

"I'm not sure where he is but Caress must be with him," Tamara said, stroking the back of baby Justin as he lay across her lap sleeping.

"They wouldn't," Jordan said, voicing everyone's thoughts of a rendezvous.

"Why not? We have," Mia asserted as she looked up at her husband like she would love to slip off with him right then and there.

Jordan dropped his head with a smile as he massaged the bridge of his nose under his glasses.

Tamara handed the baby to Mia. "Bet I know where they are," she said, rising to her feet and heading to Julius's office.

The steam on the bathroom's mirror was caused by pure body heat.

Caress sat back on Julius's lap as she straddled him. She smiled down at him with her eyes glazed and dazed from their steamy encounter. "Will it always be this good?" she gasped, still out of breath.

Julius nodded and swallowed over a huge lump in his throat as he massaged Caress's buttocks beneath the dress pushed up around her waist.

"What's the matter, Julius?" she teased as she eyed him still fighting for control.

Knock knock.

They both froze as the doorknob rattled.

"Julius? Caress?" Tamara hollered through the door.

Caress held her finger to Julius's mouth as she climbed off his lap, being sure to keep her dress high until she cleansed herself.

"I know you two are in there."

Caress rolled her eyes.

Tamara rattled the door knob again.

"What, Tamara?" Caress finally snapped in irritation as she stepped over Julius's lap to step next to the door.

"What are you doing in there?"

Julius wiggled his brows suggestively.

"Something's griping my stomach," Caress lied.

"Well tell him to pull that something out, you couple of freak nasties."

Still holding her dress up, Caress stepped over Julius's lap again to reach the sink. She frowned. "Mr. Perfection doesn't have any washcloths in his bathroom?"

"I have no reason to wash at my office."

Caress dropped her eyes down to his now limp member lying against his strong and muscled thigh. "That's good to know," she drawled.

"Shut up, girl."

Grabbing a ton of paper towels and soap, Caress got to work while Julius looked on in amusement. "This is so not funny."

He just bit back a smile.

* * *

"I want to thank you all again for sharing this night with me," Julius said, looking out among his friends, loved ones, and business associates gathered in his honor. "I've spoken to just about all of you concerning how important my trip to Africa and this book are for me. Hopefully many others will understand, appreciate, and enjoy my vision of *Julius Jones: My Africa*. Thanks."

Everyone applauded him before raising their flutes in a toast.

Julius's eyes sought Caress and it was her face filled with pride that meant the most to him. Life was good. He had the career of his dreams, a woman who completed him, a son that fulfilled him, and friends that supported him.

He truly felt blessed.

Chapter Sixteen

Two Weeks Later

Caress parked her car at the corner and quickly hopped out to gather Justin from his car seat. She just wanted to grab some diapers for the baby and head home to start dinner. To celebrate the one-year anniversary of their first date—and the night they conceived Justin—Caress was cooking dinner for them.

Her motives for staying in and not going out were twofold. Besides it being more intimate and casual, she wanted to help Julius deal with her insistence on not moving in with him. She was happy in her little apartment and he needed to deal with it. He had come up with every excuse he could think of including acting like the area wasn't safe enough.

Caress held Justin's carrier with one arm and entered the corner store that was convenient because of the location and the fairly reasonable prices.

"Hey, Mami," Danny, the short Puerto Rican store-keeper, called from behind the counter.

Caress waved to him, avoiding the long, flirtatious stares he threw at her. She kept it moving, trying her best to maneuver through the cramped store with Justin's carrier. "Damn," she swore as she looked up at the diapers on the top shelf. She set the carrier on the floor at her feet and tried to lift up on the tips of her pumps to reach one of the packages.

"Mami, you need help?"

Caress looked over her shoulder at Danny. "Yes, please," she said, dropping back on her heels and stepping aside. "I want one of the green ones."

Danny used a long pole with a handle to knock the package from the edge. It landed in his open hands. Caress smiled her thanks when he handed it to her.

She ignored the silly wiggling of his thick brows and turned to pick up Justin's carrier from the floor. She gasped in horror because the spot where he peacefully sat was now empty.

Caress looked left and then right, shoving Danny aside and dropping the diapers as she raced around the store. Her heart hammered. She felt nauseous. She had never been so afraid in all her life.

"What's wrong, Mami?" she heard him ask as she tore out of the store and looked up and down the street like a mad woman.

Her knees damn near gave out beneath her as panic set in.

Julius stormed into Caress's apartment feeling strangled by fear. Kendrick walked up to him. "Damn, man. You must've flown from New York," he said.

"Any news yet?" he asked, his throat tight.

"No, not yet. Come on man. Sit down before you fall down."

Julius allowed Kendrick to lead him to a chair by the front window. He saw Caress talking to a police detective with Tamara close at her side.

"How could this happen?" he asked again, trying to make sense of his son being snatched right under Caress's nose.

He felt like he was being kicked by twelve mules in the gut and nuts. He looked over at Caress again but then looked away.

"The police want to talk to you too," Kendrick told him.

Julius nodded as if it all made sense. But it didn't. None of it did.

He thought about his son out there with a stranger. Or worse.

He closed his eyes and lowered his head in prayer for Justin's safe return.

The mood of the apartment was somber and as dark as the approaching nightfall. Caress sat unmoving on the sofa with one of Justin's blankets clutched to her chest. She was numb and filled with all of the what-ifs and the guilt and the regrets. It was a horrible, horrible nightmare and she wished someone would pinch her and wake her up.

Caress looked up as Tamara lightly patted her thigh and handed her a cup of coffee. She shook her head in refusal and allowed herself to get lost in the numbness.

The Newark Police Department had nearly taken over the block, particularly the corner store. They were canvassing the neighborhood for any possible witnesses and had already called in the missing persons division of the FBI.

Someone had stolen her baby, and though Caress felt like her mind was slipping and sending her close to the edge of insanity, she knew she had to fight and hold on.

But what if she never saw her beautiful Justin again?

* * *

"Rock a bye baby on the treetop . . ."

Her thin hands pulled the baby out of his carrier and onto her lap where she sat on the floor of the sparsely furnished apartment. He cooed up at her and she smiled back, feeling love for him fill her like a hot meal.

"You're all mine now," she told him in an eerily soft voice, rocking her frame back and forth as she continued to sing to him softly.

Tamara eyed Julius and Caress in concern as she stood by Kendrick's side in the kitchen. "They haven't hardly said a word to each other," Tamara whispered to him.

Kendrick also eyed Caress forlorn and lost within herself on the couch while Julius stoically sat far across the room from her.

It didn't bode well.

Not well at all.

"This is Sara Martin reporting here from Santos Bodega where a three month old baby was kidnapped today . . ."

"Humph."

Julius grabbed the remote and turned the television off with a click.

Caress's swollen and red eyes shifted from the television to him. "You blame me, don't you?" she asked in a quiet and ominous voice as she looked at him across the dimly lit room.

Julius didn't look at her as he fixed his gaze out the window instead. "It's not the time for that, Caress," was his hardened reply.

Her eyes blazed and her face twisted in anger as she roughly sat her bottom on the edge of the sofa to point her finger accusingly at herself. "You think I don't know it's my fault, Mr. High and Mighty Julius Jones? And now I have to sit here with your ass playing holier than thou and not talking to me? You think I need your . . . your . . . shit right now?" she roared, spit flying from her mouth as tears raced down her cheeks.

Tamara stood up and moved in the center of their line of vision. "Don't do this. You need each other more than ever right now," she warned them.

Julius leaned to the right to look past Tamara to lock eyes with Caress. "My son needed his mother to keep him safe," he said coldly.

"Julius!" Tamara said sharply in reprimand.

For an instant, pain filled Caress's eyes. Sharp, piercing, tumultuous pain. Quickly she masked the extra hurt his words caused. "Get out! Get out! GET OUT! GET OUT!" Caress screamed at the top of her lungs as she beat her fists down on the top of her knees.

There was no denying the regret on Julius's face as he rose to his feet.

Caress began reaching for the what-nots on her coffee table and throwing them at him. An angel crashed against the wall before Tamara snatched her arm down.

Kendrick jumped to his feet. "Enough!" he roared, in a rare show of anger that made everyone pause.

The figurine she held dropped to the floor before Caress flopped down to the sofa, covering her face with her hands.

Julius rammed his hands into his pockets with his jaw clenching and unclenching as he paced.

Kendrick eyed them both. "This right here is a family and we all need to stick together."

Caress sat back on the sofa and pulled her feet underneath her as she almost blindly reached out for Justin's blanket. She pressed her face into the softness and got lost in his scent. "Oh God, where is my baby?" she wailed as pain and despair weighed her down.

Her pitiful cries echoed in the still silence of the room.

Julius turned away from Caress. He wanted to comfort her but he refrained. Something held him back.

"I'll be back," he said, feeling his own frustration and helplessness claim him as he strode out of the apartment and jogged down the stairs.

"Julius!"

He paused on the stairs and looked up at Kendrick exiting Caress's apartment. "Don't go, man. I know you're hurting just like she is, but if you leave right now—especially like this—you're gonna break something you might not be able to fix."

Julius released a heavy breath as Kendrick continued down the stairs toward him. "I wish I could say I wasn't mad at her but I am. She shoulda been watching him."

"I'm not in your shoes so I can only guess at how you feel, but you know Caress would never do anything to hurt Justin."

"How in the hell could she not see someone pick up a big ass carrier and walk away with our son?" Pain twisted Julius's face at the mention of his missing baby. He turned and pounded his fist against the wall as he pressed his forehead to it. He regretted lashing out at her but in truth all he could think of was the absolute worst, and those thoughts made him feel like he wanted to get as far away from Caress as he could.

Caress welcomed the darkness and quiet of her bedroom. She had feigned being sleepy to be left alone, but now the loneliness was frightening.

Guilt plagued her enough—wondering whether Justin

was warm, safe, fed, and loved—and Julius's distance and coldness weighed her down even more.

If only she hadn't stopped at that store.

If only she had watched Justin constantly.

If only . . .

If only . . .

If only . . .

Her stomach growled in hunger, but Caress pushed it aside. She couldn't eat not knowing if her baby was hungry as well. It had been hours since he was snatched.

Caress looked over her shoulder as the bedroom door slowly opened. She knew from the silhouette that it was Julius. "What do you want?" she asked, her voice as lifeless and listless as she felt.

He leaned against the wall by the door, still covered by darkness. "The FBI just left. They needed photos of the baby," he told her.

Caress just turned and faced the wall, saying nothing.

"Caress—"

"Don't, Julius, just don't."

He stood there a while longer before turning and quietly leaving the room without another word.

She sat with her back pressed to the corner as she eyed the baby sitting crying in his car seat. The smell of his soiled diaper filled the air along with his cries.

She had tried everything she could think of to stop him from crying and nothing worked.

She pulled her knees to her chest and pressed her hands to her ears as she squeezed her eyes shut as tightly as she could. She just wanted the crying to stop.

* * *

Julius nursed the glass of cognac he was sipping while Kendrick mainly twisted his glass around on the table. It was nearly two in the morning and no one in the apartment was asleep. Tamara was in the bedroom with Caress while Kendrick and Julius were in the living room.

"Thanks for being here with us," Julius told him.

"We're family, man, and we wouldn't want to be anywhere else when my little godson comes home."

"If he . . . if something—"

Kendrick shook his head. "Don't even think that way."

Julius nodded his head even though the thoughts remained.

"I just can't believe no one saw anything," Julius said in frustration.

"The person must have run out of the store and right into a car," Kendrick theorized.

A high-pitched scream pierced the air.

Julius and Kendrick both took off to the bedroom.

Tamara was sitting on the side of the bed rocking Caress in her arms. She looked over her shoulder at them. "She woke up screaming," she mouthed to them, motioning for Julius to come forward.

He shared a brief look with Kendrick before moving ahead to sit down on the bed on the other side of Caress. He put his arm around her, attempting to pull her into his chest but Caress whipped her head around and glared at him.

The look in her eyes pained him and he knew his earlier accusation had caused this reaction.

"Julius, just go home."

"Caress, we need to talk."

Tamara motioned to Kendrick, and the two of them left quietly, leaving Julius and Caress alone.

"Julius, please . . . please just go home," she stressed, the anger gone. "Please."

Their eyes locked.

Hers were filled with pain and anger.

His were filled with regret.

"I'm sorry, Caress. This is a horrible situation—"

"That I caused," she said accusingly. "Right."

His eyes shifted from hers just slightly but it was enough for his real feelings to be revealed.

Caress laughed bitterly. "You know sometimes you've made me feel like I'm not good enough for you but I really don't need you making me feel like I'm a bad mother."

Julius dropped his head. "I never said you were a bad mother."

"Whatever, Julius. Just get out my face right now," she told him, lying down across the bed to clutch one of the pillows to her chest.

Julius rose to his feet and stood there looking down at her before he turned and left the room.

Tamara and Kendrick rose to their feet as Julius strode into the living room and grabbed his jacket and keys. "I'm out," he told them before heading for the door.

"No, Julius," Tamara wailed dramatically.

He paused with his hand on the doorknob. "I'm not staying somewhere I'm not wanted," he told them before walking out the door,

Kendrick grabbed his jacket from the chair. "I'm going with him. He doesn't need to be alone either."

Minutes slipped into hours and those hours became the break of a new day. Caress hadn't slept. She felt and looked haggard. She pushed the breakfast of eggs and bacon Tamara made around on her plate with her fork. She had no intention of eating it but wasn't in the mood for Tamara constantly urging her to eat something.

How could she when all she heard was her baby crying out for her?

Emotions during the hours since Justin went missing had run the gamut and with the rise of the sun, Caress was angry.

At herself.

At Julius.

At whomever took her baby.

At the world.

"Hey, what's going on up the street?" Tamara hollered from the living room.

Rising from her chair, Caress walked over to stand next to Tamara at the front window of the apartment. With deadened eyes she saw several FBI agents with weapons drawn going into the apartment building on the corner.

Caress's face filled with confusion.

Boom. Boom. Boom.

"FBI! Open up!"

The loud bamming jarred her from her sleep on the matted carpet. She jumped up in fear, her eyes darting to the baby who awakened and began to cry loudly at the noise.

She screamed out as the front door burst open, and her frightened eyes went straight to the barrels of the guns pointed at her. She closed her eyes to block everything: the strangers going room to room searching the sparsely furnished apartment, the baby's cries easing as he was lifted from the car seat, the soft voice of the woman asking where her parents were.

Why couldn't they all just leave her and her baby alone?

* * *

Caress tore down the stairs and raced up the street. Feet bare, hair flying, clothes disheveled, eyes nearly swollen shut from a night filled with tears. She couldn't care less.

She heard Tamara calling and running behind her but Caress didn't stop.

She was just reaching the apartment building when the black female agent who interviewed her yesterday walked down the stairs with Justin in her arms. She felt weak with relief as she cried out. Her baby.

As the agent placed him in her open arms, she barely registered the agents placing little Luretha in the back of one of their cars.

Chapter Seventeen

Caress couldn't take her eyes off of him. She almost felt like if she blinked he would disappear in an instant. She never wanted to go through that type of ordeal again. She just thanked God he was returned to her safely if a bit neglected.

Caress had been right about Luretha's sad life but never had she imagined their worlds would collide so disastrously. According to the FBI agents, Luretha was molested by a male family member last year. That had led to her getting pregnant, but the baby was stillborn. Her infatuation with baby Justin was a desire to replace the baby she lost. The baby she thought would give her the love she couldn't get from a drug addict mother and missing father. In fact Luretha's mother hadn't been home in several days, which had enabled the child to hide Justin. It was his constant cries that alerted the neighbors that a baby was in the apartment with her.

"Welcome, home, Justin," she whispered down to him as she lovingly massaged his back as he gave in to his slumber. He was examined and released by the hospital. He was freshly bathed, fed, and back home safely. He deserved a good nap. And so did she. Now that he was home she felt the fatigue of the last twenty-four hours settling down on her.

The bedroom door opened and Julius walked in, looking nothing like himself with his disheveled clothing and unkempt beard. Her initial reaction was to run to him, but she remembered the bridge he built between them and just wrapped her arms around herself instead.

What would all of this mean for them now?

He barely acknowledged her as he walked over to the bassinet, bent down, and picked Justin up into his arms.

"Julius, I just put him down for a nap," Caress protested, reaching for the baby who only snuggled down deeper in the crook of his father's arm.

Julius frowned. "Caress, I would like to hold my son," he told her defensively.

She squeezed her hands shut and placed them at her side as she fought the urge to take Justin from him. She watched carefully as he sat down on the edge of the bed and just held Justin and watched him.

"This all could have turned out worse," he said, using the side of his finger to stroke Justin's plump cheek.

Caress remained silent.

Julius looked over at her. "You're exhausted. Why don't you take a nap? I'll watch him."

Caress immediately shook her head in refusal. "I'm fine," she assured him.

They fell silent. Words that shouldn't have been said and even more that needed to be said hung in the air between them.

"I'm sorry, Caress. I was angry and afraid, and I lashed out at you," he said, shifting on the bed to look over at her.

Caress said nothing at all, holding her feelings in. *What's the use?*

"We need to talk about this, Caress," he insisted.

She laughed bitterly, but still said nothing in response to him.

"Caress, I've given you my apology. You know I love you—"

"Oh, I do?" she scoffed.

Julius closed his eyes and took a deep breath. "Don't do this, Caress. What we have is too special."

"I thought so. I thought so," she told him, moving to stand by the window. "You know what? Julius. I'm not even hurt or pissed that you blamed me for Justin getting snatched away from me. Hell, I blamed myself. But I needed you yesterday. I needed you to suck up whatever you were feeling and comfort me and let me comfort you. We should have been there for each other and you failed me. For me, that is very telling. Actions speak louder than three lousy ass words, Julius."

He rose and set Justin back inside his bassinet. "So what are you saying? We're through?"

Caress knew he was hurting just like she was but in that moment forgiveness was not a part of her vocabulary. Right, wrong, or indifferent. *It is what it is.*

"The ball is in your court, Caress," he said, walking over to stand beside her.

She held her body stiff as he pressed a kiss to her forehead. "I love you," he told her huskily.

Caress just shifted past him to go and stand beside Justin's bassinet.

For what seemed the thousandth time, he walked out of the bedroom without saying anything else.

Caress awakened with a start. She looked around the room and felt panicked. When she finally gave in to the fatigue, she had laid Justin on the bed beside her with her hand on his back—her only assurance that she would be awakened if anything happened to him.

She dashed out of the bed and flew out of the room. Relief flooded over her to see Tamara bouncing Justin on her knee. Caress was still visibly trembling when she walked over to them.

"You're up already?" Tamara asked, frowning as Caress pulled Justin from her grasp. "I used my spare key to get in. Are you okay?"

Caress planted kisses on Justin. "I'm fine," she snapped.

Tamara sat back on the sofa and watched her friend. "Julius said he was over here earlier."

Caress just shrugged as she smiled down at her son.

"Are you two okay?" she asked.

"I'm fine," Caress insisted.

"Yes, but are you and Julius okay?"

Caress sighed. "Let it go, Tam," she insisted.

She felt Tamara's eyes on her but Caress focused on changing Justin's diaper.

"Caress, don't let a terrible event ruin your life," Tamara advised her in a soft voice.

"What do you mean?"

"Your son was kidnapped by a sad little girl. That doesn't make you a bad mother, and you don't have to become super mom to prove that to anyone. You can't be all things to Justin. That's impossible."

Caress ignored everything Tamara just said. Justin was *her* son.

Julius listened to the phone ring endlessly before he hung up. He leaned back in his chair and tilted his head to look up at the ceiling. He was beginning to give up hope of Caress forgiving him. Days went by and she never called him. Whenever he called she didn't answer.

He hadn't seen his son and he missed him.

He missed her too.

He picked up the phone again and dialed Tamara's number at work.

"Tamara Lawson."

"What's up, Tamara?"

"Hi, Julius, you are just the man I need to talk to."

He reached for the glass paperweight on his desk. "Yeah I needed to holler at you too."

"Me first?" she asked.

Julius smiled. "Of course," he said in a tone like there was no option really.

"Okay, Caress is straight tripping. She has not gone back to work, she's paying for his day care even though the baby doesn't go. She will not let him out of her eyesight. Hell, I offered to babysit and she looked at me like I had a dragon flying out my damn nose."

Julius's eyes were troubled. "I don't know how much help I can be. I haven't spoken to her and I haven't seen my son, Tamara. Which for me is the biggest problem out of this."

"Well, I can understand her fears but she can't live this way forever. It's not healthy."

Julius nodded as he focused his eyes on the photo of Caress breastfeeding Justin. "I don't know what to say," he admitted. "Hell, I called you for help, remember? I don't want to push her, but I have every right to see my son, Tamara."

"Yes, I know you do. It's just so hard to know the right way to handle any of this."

Julius glanced at his watch. "I'm going over there," he said rising to his feet. "I want my woman and my son back."

"Just tread lightly, Julius," Tamara cautioned.

"Talk to you soon."

Dwayne was off for the day, so Julius locked the studio up securely before he hopped in his SUV and headed to Newark.

As he steered through the streets he tried to make sense of how quickly the good thing between him and Caress had come to an end.

Surely she wasn't ready to end things forever? And if so, how would that affect everything else?

Yes, he had been angry at Caress for Justin's abduction but he wasn't ready to say good-bye to a relationship with her. To never wake up with her in his arms? To never make love to her again? To never feel the way he did when she smiled at him or touched him?

He was in no way ready to deal with seeing her with another man or feeling like a sideline parent because her new man—or even husband one day—had stepped into Julius's rightful role as father.

They had to work this out.

Nothing else made much sense.

Julius parked his Rover in front of Caress's building, hopping out to walk up the stairs. He started to use the key she gave him, but refrained and knocked instead.

"Who is it?"

"Julius," he said, leaning against the wall with his hands in his pockets.

There was a long pause and he thought she wasn't going to open the door . . . but she did.

Caress left the door open and walked back to the living room. As she sat down on the sofa, Julius eyed how good she looked in the white sports tank and pants she wore. He closed the door behind him. "Where's the baby?" he asked.

"Right here in his bassinet."

Julius removed the shades he wore as he leaned on the

edge of the sofa. "I've been trying to call you, Caress," he said.

She reached in the clothes hamper by her foot and began folding the clothes in it. "I've been busy."

"Does Justin need anything?" he asked, trying to avoid the annoyance he felt growing.

Caress dropped the blanket she held and looked up at him. "No, no thank you."

Julius frowned. "So you're going to stay mad at me?" he asked.

"I'm not mad, Julius."

"So if you're not mad then what are you?" he asked, rising to his feet.

"Done."

He was taken aback. "And that means what?"

"Do we have to do this right now?" Caress asked.

"Hell yeah," Julius insisted. "I need to know where we stand. I have that right, Caress. This isn't just your life."

Caress went back to folding clothes, and Julius had to fight the urge to toss the entire basket and its contents out the window. Instead he stepped in front of her, grabbed her arms, and pulled her to her feet before him. "So you don't love me anymore?" he asked huskily as his eyes raced over her face to land on her mouth.

He lowered his head to hers and he didn't miss that her mouth parted a bit as he did. "Damn, I miss you, Caress," he moaned, pressing his lips to hers.

For a second she gave in, but then she roughly jerked back from his embrace and put distance between them. "Julius, I just need space right now and you need to respect that," she said, walking around to the other side of the couch.

Julius turned his head to look at her. "So you're just going to hide out from the world because something horrible happened? Something horrible that we all survived," he added.

Caress's eyes went to Justin.

"You think you can watch him forever. You're never going back to work? You're never going to take him back to the day care center? No one can watch him but you? Make sense, Caress?" he snapped in frustration as he watched her.

"I didn't say that," she snapped back. "I just want to enjoy a week home with my baby. Is that so wrong?"

Julius forced himself to count to ten. "If you try to keep secluded and away from the world. Yes, Caress, yes that would make you dead wrong."

"A few days ago I didn't know if he was dead or alive. For hours I sat in this apartment imagining the worst."

"So did I, Caress," he asserted with a long hard stare. "I love him just as much as you do. I was just as scared as you but you can't shelter him and escape from the world in this damn apartment!"

"Yes, but I carried him," she flung at him angrily, snatching up her shirt to show him her C-section scar. "I got cut giving birth to him. Not you."

Julius looked at her like she was crazy. "Don't disrespect or belittle my position as his father, Caress. Don't pull that shit with me 'cause I'm not the one."

Her eyes flashed as she worked her shirt back down around her waist. "And what the hell does that mean?" she asked, coming around the sofa to stand in front of him.

Julius hated that things were at this point. He felt like he tried. What more could he do?

"It means this, Caress," he began as he locked his eyes on her with the utmost serious expression. "If you want your space that's fine, but that only goes for me and you. I will not become a damn shadow in my child's life to suit your paranoia. If we're over that's fine, but I will not be shut out of my child's life. You have the wrong man for that shit. I want visitation rights and I'll pay you child support."

"Keep your money, Julius Jones," she told him coldly.

"No, I will not because I have every right to see my son, and I will see him, and I will help take care of him."

"Or?"

Julius looked at Caress for a long time. "You're the same woman who promised me no drama. Who said this was a team? Who wanted more of a father for her child than she had?" he asked, raising his hands to applaud. "Good performance, Caress."

He turned and pressed a kiss to the back of Justin's head before he turned to go. "Don't try to keep me from my son, Caress," he warned, before walking out the door closing it forcefully behind him.

Caress felt like all the energy she had left her after Julius stormed out of the apartment. She slumped down onto the chair, hating the emotional wreck she had become as a result of this entire ordeal.

How could she make them understand the fear that clutched at her throat like a rabid dog whenever Justin was out of her eyesight? How could she explain that she tried to leave him at the day care but had barely made it out the door before she turned and went back to get him. Could she get through to them that she could only go at the pace her psyche was letting her? And right now, fear of another psycho, wacko, and disturbed little girl stealing her child had her messed up. Yes, she knew it, but the only way she knew to get over it was one day at a time.

Caress dropped back against the couch as she thought of Julius. Did she love him? Of course. Love didn't fade that quickly, but she had to learn to forgive him for not being there after Justin was snatched.

To her, his love didn't measure up to hers.

Oh, he cared about her. He loved having sex with her. They hung out and shared interesting conversations with their differing views. But when the chips were down, he showed his true character to her and that scared her.

He bailed on her just like that. What type of love was that?

Love him? She adored him.

Miss him? She craved him late in the night as her lonely bed mocked her.

Take him back? That she wasn't so sure about.

Caress tried to wipe away the stress she felt around her eyes. She needed a mental vacation big time. If Julius, Tamara, and the rest of the world didn't leave her alone to figure things out on her own time she would wind up in a crazy hospital somewhere.

She had just turned the television to *The View*, hoping she could stomach whatever bull Elisabeth Hasselbeck was spouting so that she could get a good laugh from the rest of the panel, when someone knocked at her door. Frowning, she rose and moved to the door to peer out the peephole.

Her mouth dropped open in shock to see a scary-looking woman with ashen lips and yellowed eyes standing there. "Who is it?" she asked through the door.

"You don't know me, but I'm Luretha's mother, Kinnia. Can I talk to you please?" she called back through the wood.

Caress had to swallow back her anger and keep from pulling the door open to snatch her in and wear her behind out for her role in turning her daughter into an emotional and psychological mess. This woman was just as much to blame as Luretha as far as Caress was concerned.

"I don't have anything to say to you," Caress told her, already walking back to the sofa. "Stay the hell away from me. Straight up."

"Please help my baby. You don't understand what she's been through. Please," the woman begged through the door.

The FBI had filled Caress in on Luretha's story and it truly was a heart-tugger but what the hell did this woman think Caress could or would do?

Jumping to her feet, Caress strode to the door and yanked it open. "You have no right coming to my house, and let this be the last time. Your daughter stole my son and left him in shit with no milk all damn night while you were out tricking for your habit."

The woman's stench reached Caress, and she prayed it didn't seep into her apartment.

"She lost her own baby—"

"And why was your daughter pregnant?" Caress asked.

That caught her off guard. "Huh?"

"You heard me."

"My baby was molested," she screamed with indignation as tears filled her eyes.

"And where were you when that went down?" Caress asked, cutting her no shorts.

"You don't know nothing about me."

"Except what I see," Caress countered. "And I don't just mean that you use drugs. You're running from life by getting high. Probably got your own battle scars from life. Memories you can't handle, right?"

The woman's yellow eyes dropped from hers.

"Why don't you help your daughter and yourself by getting your act together. Don't come and ask me to do more for you and her than you are. You feel me?"

Caress stepped back inside the apartment and closed her door securely. She didn't move from her door until she heard the woman walk down the stairs and out the door. Caress moved to the window and watched Kinnia head straight up the street with her head hung low looking beat down by the world. Sometimes the truth hurt.

Chapter Eighteen

"Caress, this is Julius. Call me."

There was a long pause.

"Caress, he's my son, and you have to learn to trust me to take care of him. You're not being fair."

Another pause.

"Call me."

Beep.

Caress chewed the gloss from her lips as she deleted Julius's latest voice mail message from her cell phone. Any guilt she felt over the clear remorse in his voice she pushed aside as she set the cell phone back down on the top of her desk.

She never said Julius couldn't see their son, she just wasn't prepared to let Justin spend every other weekend with him the way he wanted. How could she easily agree to give up two weekends a month? And why would Julius ask her to?

Now that their relationship had fizzled their only communication was about Justin, and most times they couldn't seem to agree on anything. She couldn't deny that everything was much simpler when they were a couple. Julius had left most of the hands-on decisions to her. Now that they had gone their separate ways he was a lot more opinionated about everything, and she could admit she was a lot more defensive.

Going back to work was the hardest thing Caress had ever done. Every day it got a little easier walking away from Justin and not feeling like he wouldn't be there when she returned, but she still had those fears nagging at her. The reality was she had to work. She knew she drove the day care crazy calling twice a day to check on him, but she did whatever she had to in order to make it through the day.

She was still adjusting back to normalcy. Why couldn't Julius understand that?

Her cell phone vibrated again and Caress picked up the phone. She sighed at the caller ID. Why was Julius working her nerve?

She turned to the wall and cupped her mouth after she flipped the phone open. "Hello."

"Caress, did you get my message?" he asked.

"Yes, Julius."

The line went quiet before he released a heavy breath. "Listen, it's time for us to sit down and come to some firm visitation plans concerning our son, Caress. Can I come over to your apartment tonight?"

Although the husky tone of his voice asking that question was not intended to titillate her . . . it did. Damn him.

Pushing aside the sharp pang of desire she felt for him, Caress dropped her head in her hands. "Can't we talk about this later?" she asked rubbing her eyes.

"Yes. Tonight. At your apartment."

"Not tonight, Julius," she insisted, not sure if she could take being alone with him in her small apartment.

"You said that before and here we are on week two and I have barely seen my son, Caress. I'm trying to respect your privacy and your space but you're pushing it."

"No, *you're* pushing it, Julius," she flung back, lowering her voice as a coworker passed her desk and gave her a curious look.

"Why? Because I want to see my son outside of when and where you say?"

"I only ask that we wait for overnight visits until he's older, Julius," she snapped because she felt like he was misconstruing her words and actions.

"How long are you going to punish me?" he asked.

"The better question is how long are you going to punish me, Julius?" she countered with a hint of sadness and honesty in her voice.

"I just want to see my son on a regular basis. I want him to know me just as well as he knows you."

Caress slammed her hand down on the top of her desk. "Damn, Julius, you wanted me to have a damn abortion when you found out about him!"

Caress gasped and covered her mouth with her hand as soon as the words left her mouth. She closed her eyes wishing she could rewind time and take them back. She had no doubts that Julius loved Justin just as much as she did.

"Low blow, Caress. Low damn blow."

Yes, yes it was, and she was ashamed of herself for even going there. "Julius, I—"

The line disconnected.

That night Caress was up late, long after she put Justin to bed. The apartment was dimly lit. Not even much of the normal street noise echoed from outside—probably because of the steady rain. Freshly bathed and dressed in a long cotton nightgown she folded her petite frame onto the couch and pulled the throw from the back of the chair over her feet and legs.

Sleep eluded her a lot these days because in her slumber she gave in to emotions and desires that she doggedly fought during her awake hours. In truth, she always had a nagging fear that Julius's love wasn't as strong as hers, and his coldness toward her after Justin's kidnapping had awakened all those fears. Even if she wasn't willing to risk her heart and lay it out there for him to destroy, it didn't change the fact that she still loved him.

Using the remote, Caress turned on the radio, and soon the sounds of Lauryn Hill mixed with the rain pelting against the window and on the streets outside.

As Lauryn sang from her soul, Caress let herself think of Julius. She let herself imagine things the way they used to be. The problem wasn't the past. It was the future she worried about.

She shifted to her side. It reminded her of the night Julius had teased and fondled her here on the couch as they watched *National Geographic* on TV—his choice of course. His teasing had turned into him hitching her gown up to her hips, lifting her legs high, and then entering her from behind to fill her completely.

Too bad sex wasn't the most important component of a relationship because when it came to that they had no disagreement. No misunderstandings. Not one single, solitary problem.

Caress had a lot on her mind. Not just the ensuing drama with Julius—which she planned to correct with an apology, but the constant nagging about her father. She let her eyes focus on her precious framed photograph. More and more she was considering getting off her butt and looking for him, instead of trying to capture some connection through a faded photograph.

Did she have brothers and sisters?

Did he know she existed?

Did he care?

More and more as she raised her own child, her mind turned to her own lineage. Especially with the holidays nearing. Even with her son and her friends, Caress felt so alone in the world sometimes. No one could say family wasn't important.

During one of their late nights lying with their bodies entwined in the middle of the bed, Julius had even encouraged her to try and find her father. And she missed the times they would just talk, reminiscing on growing up in Newark, the eighties' fashions and music, the difference between gangs back then and now. Anything. Everything.

A rainy night like tonight? She knew they would have been snuggled up somewhere together.

Sighing, she pushed aside all her worries and closed her eyes, allowing herself to get lost in the sultry sounds of Lauryn Hill and the pouring rain.

Julius turned over onto his back and crossed his forearm over his closed eyes. The sound of thunder echoed as the rain pelted against his bedroom windows. It was a damn shame for a man to be in bed alone, naked as the day he was born, without a woman to snuggle up to.

A night like tonight he and Caress would have made sure to spend together. Making love to a sexy woman as thunder roared and lightning flashed, barely illuminating her body as she was made love to? It would be the best sex ever.

He still couldn't believe Caress had thrown away everything they had shared. He thought they had been happy together, yet now there was this baby mama drama about seeing Justin. Julius actually thought Caress wouldn't bring that drama to him.

But he had thought a lot of things about Caress and been wrong.

As badly as he missed her.

As badly as he wished she was here riding him in that exquisitely showy way of hers.

As badly as he still loved her.

Maybe it was good that it was over before it even really began.

His focus now was on his son. First and foremost.

Tamara spooned closer to Kendrick as she watched the rain splatter against the window. Kendrick's snores resounded loudly in her ear but she had long since learned to ignore them. Plus, her thoughts were filled with Caress and Julius.

She loved them both. They both were her best friends. More and more she was feeling like she was getting drawn into the middle—and for the first time it was not a place she wanted to be.

Kendrick told her they were grown and able to make their own decisions without her constant mothering. Maybe he was right. If things got any worse before they got better she would hate to have to choose between them.

And she could see both sides. True, Caress had lessened her overprotectiveness about Justin in terms of her returning to work and taking him to day care, but Tamara couldn't remember the last she had babysat her godson. Having your child snatched had to be a horrific experience with plenty of residual effects and Tamara understood that, but that didn't excuse the fact that Caress was indeed going overboard—something Tamara hadn't had the nerve to tell her.

And yes, Julius had made a bad move during Justin's kidnapping—something Tamara had chided him about.

Sighing, Tamara turned over on the bed and faced her husband. She reached up to caress his face as love for him flooded her heart. Thank God, everything with them was beyond good. No unnecessary drama. No misunderstandings. Just love. All love.

Caress slammed on her brakes so hard her body slid forward and she hit her chest against the steering wheel. It stung a bit but that wasn't going to stop her. Nothing could.

She left her car and marched across the pavement to step onto the freight elevator leading up to Julius's studio. She paced the length of the large metal contraption as she waited for it to grind to a stop. She could hardly wait to get her eyes—and maybe her hands—on him.

The doors opened and she whirled to step off of it. "Hi, Caress," Dwayne said, his face changing from pleasure to outright curiosity at the stormy expression on her face.

She barely spared him a wave as she kept it moving toward Julius's office. Whipping the leather curtain back like a lightweight cape, Caress flung it from her as she walked up to Julius's desk. "Are you that mad at me because I broke up with you?" she blazed in a hard and cold voice that barely covered the pain and betrayal she felt as she slammed the court papers down into the middle of his take-out lunch.

Julius rolled back in his chair to avoid the reddish sauce of his food from splashing on the ivory knit sweater he wore. "This has nothing to do with you and me, Caress," he told her as he used a napkin to clean the sticky spots from the top of his desk.

"When I talked to your sneaky behind yesterday you didn't say a damn thing about suing me for partial custody, Julius. Not one damn word," she said in a bitter voice with angry eyes as she slammed her hand on the top of his desk.

Julius's eyes shifted past her. "Dwayne, you can head on home," he called out to his nosy assistant.

"Are you sure because I wanted to . . . to . . . uh . . . uhm . . . dust my desk?"

Julius shot him a hard look and just pointed to the elevator.

Caress crossed her arms over her chest as she paced the length of his office, causing her black wool pants to bunch a bit between her thick thighs. She was mad enough to strip and fight Julius like she used to do during girl fights back in the day.

"I've been asking you to sit down with me—grown man to grown woman—and work out what's best for our son," Julius said, removing the court papers from his food before he threw the container in the trash at the end of his desk.

"And I asked you to just wait until he was older, Julius," she shot back with her eyes blazing, "But no, it's your way or no way, right? You're a goddamn hypocrite, Julius."

"And you believe Justin is yours and I have no say. You won't even cash the damn checks I send for child support because you think that lets you run the show."

Caress threw her hands up in the air. "This ain't a show. It's our child."

Julius jumped to his feet. "Damn right. *Our* child, Caress. And I am not going to sit back and be relegated to a footnote in my child's life to suit you or any other damn woman. I don't understand why you of all people don't want the same thing for your child."

"You go to hell, Julius," she told him coldly as she refused to let a tear fall in his presence. "What kind of man tries to take an arm baby from its mother? Huh? Huh? A selfish one who is mad because the candy store is *closed*."

Julius flung his hand at her dismissively. "Caress,

please. You better be careful not to fall off the pedestal you put yourself on."

Caress fell silent—speechless—as she eyed him with her hands on her hips. "Let me get this straight," she said in a soft voice that was still filled with anger and the pain of what she saw as the ultimate betrayal. "I'm a neglectful mother you can't even trust to raise your child and now—according to you—I'm some troll who thinks too highly of herself?"

"Stop putting words in my mouth, Caress," he told her dismissively before he dropped back down in his seat.

Caress snatched up the court papers. "These are proof positive that I made the right choice to leave your ass alone."

Julius nodded his head as he looked up at her. "Considering the type of woman I see you are now, I thank you. Believe me."

That hurt like a dagger to her chest, but she covered it well. "If it's war you want, Julius, then that's not a problem, player."

Julius waved his hand at her. "Call me or come back when you want to sit down like a grown woman, Caress."

"Sit down for what, Julius? Huh? You're trying to take my child from me."

Julius forcefully slammed his hands on the top of his desk as he jumped back up to his feet. "Caress, I am not trying to take him from you," he roared, before he turned and walked away from her. "We're not getting anywhere with this, Caress. Please just leave."

"You started this," she told him, turning to leave.

"Correction, I'm finishing this," he flung back at her.

Caress ignored him as she kept it moving out of the studio. Once she was in the security of her car she dropped her head to the steering wheel and cried.

* * *

"Can you believe she came in accusing me of trying to take Justin from her when all I've been asking for is the right to see my son?"

Tamara picked up the cup of hot chocolate and sipped deeply as she diverted her eyes from Julius.

"You know what? Black women are such hypocrites," he said with emphasis as he threw his hands up in the air.

"Really?" Tamara asked, as she crossed her legs.

"Yes!" Julius sat forward to cross his arms on top of the small table in the donut shop on Broad and Market. "You have a man begging to step up to be a father and she is pushing me away. Now if I threw her on the street when she was pregnant and let her lay up in the hospital alone and then walked away from my responsibility it would give her something to tell Maury Povich about."

Tamara took another sip of her cocoa because she was really trying to keep her neck and nose clean of this feud between her two best friends. She hoped they would be able to handle this, but alas the courts were now involved and Tamara knew she would be getting a call from Caress just like the one she got from Julius an hour ago.

With an internal sigh, she placed a neutral look on her face and let Julius get it all off his chest.

"He is so petty, Tamara!"

Tamara nodded sympathetically at Caress before she purposefully placed her face in the soft crook of Justin's neck.

"How dare he sue me for partial custody, Tamara? What the hell is Julius thinking? And to think for one hot second last night, with all that rain, I started to tell him to come on over and get a little bit. Humph. He can forgetaboutit."

Tamara stood Justin up on his legs and bounced him as he smiled at her like he should be in commercials. He was so completely oblivious to the ensuing drama between his parents. She wished she could say the same.

As Caress continued to pace and insult Julius, Tamara was seriously regretting her role in getting the two of them together.

Seriously.

Chapter Nineteen

One month later . . .

Caress sat at her living room window watching the snow
fall. Fall and then winter had always been her favorite time
of the year. The coldness kept the streets free of most loiterers, and under the blanket of the crisp snow the urban land-
scape was almost majestic.

She was just fighting the urge to raise the window and
scoop some of the snow into her hand when her doorbell
rang. Pushing aside the rare show of child-like frivolity,
Caress felt nerves attack her stomach as she moved over to
open the front door.

She had been dreading this moment since last week when
the family court judge awarded Julius liberal visitation
rights. It was a temporary order until their child custody case
in a couple of months. Things were so bad between them that
they mutually insisted that Tamara, Kendrick, or Dwayne do
the picking up and dropping off of Justin so that they didn't
have to deal with one another.

Caress smiled at Tamara and Kendrick as they stomped
the fresh snow from their feet before entering the apartment.
"Hey, y'all."

"What's up? The baby's ready because we really want to get out of this snow," Tamara said, not bothering to remove her winter white wool coat and fitted cap.

Caress nodded as she moved over to start putting Justin into his puffy snowsuit. Her son smiled up at her and she bent over to press a kiss beside his mouth. "I'm gonna miss you, little boy," she said to him softly.

Kendrick lightly touched her shoulder and Caress pushed away her misgivings. Not that it mattered anyway. Okay, she couldn't stand Julius right now but she knew he would never intentionally hurt their son.

"You are coming to our dinner party next week?" Tamara asked as she picked Justin's bursting-at-the-seams baby bag.

"Will *he* be there?" she asked, maneuvering Justin's cap down onto his head.

Caress didn't miss the look Tamara and Kendrick exchanged.

"Does it matter?" Tamara asked, sounding tired and aggravated.

Caress gave her friend a sidelong glance as she rose to her feet with Justin in her arms. He absolutely hated the confines of his snowsuit. "I don't want to be in his company any more than he wants to be in mine."

Tamara took Justin out of Caress's hand as Kendrick grabbed his car seat before heading to the door.

"I'll tell you like I told him. You're invited and I expect to see you there, Caress." Tamara headed for the open door, but she turned on the heel of her boots. "And don't spend all weekend worrying about Justin. You know he will be just fine with Julius."

Yes, yes she did. She nodded and turned away, not wanting to witness them walking out the door. This was the longest she would ever be separated from her baby. With a sigh, she set out to make herself busy with anything to take her mind off being apart.

Caress scrubbed her bathroom.

She cleaned out her fridge.

Dusted her entire apartment.

Mopped her kitchen floor.

She was just making a fresh pot of hot chocolate to enjoy while she watched TV when there was a knock at her front door. After wiping her hands on a dish towel, she went to the door and looked out the peephole.

It was her new neighbor from upstairs, Ahmad Pittons.

Caress had found the rather tall and rather handsome man to be polite and helpful since he moved in two weeks ago. She stepped back and opened the door with a friendly smile. "Hi, Ahmad," she greeted him as she tilted her head up to adjust to his six-foot-five-inch frame.

"Just wanted you to know I put down some salt around your car while I was doing mine," he told her in that deep voice of his.

Surprised and pleased, Caress reached out and lightly touched his wrist. "Thank you so much."

"No problem."

And with one final wave he walked away and continued up the flight of stairs to his third-floor apartment. A real gentleman. No wiggling for an invite inside her apartment . . . or in her bed. No making her feel like she owed him something.

Caress closed her door and locked it. She liked Ahmad and not just because of his physical appeal but because his chivalry reminded her of Julius.

Or at least the Julius she thought she knew and loved.

The days of Julius playing man of the house were over and Caress had to admit that Ahmad came in handy—and all without one advance made.

Finishing up preparing her hot chocolate, Caress filled a

cup that was big enough to be a small bowl, and then settled down to veg out on television, pretending that the best parts of her life weren't at Julius's.

"Thanks, Tamara," Julius said, his words framed by cold air as he hurried to throw the baby bag over his arm as he held a blanket-covered Justin in his car seat.

"You didn't have to come downstairs," Tamara called out the window from the passenger seat of the car as Kendrick rushed back inside the heated interior.

"I'm good," he hollered over his shoulder as he made his way to his front door.

"Don't forget the party," Tamara hollered out the window into the light snowfall as they drove up the street.

Julius didn't bother answering as he hurried inside his home.

Excited to finally spend time with his son, Julius rushed into the living room already cozy and warm from the lit fireplace. He unbundled him from the confining snowsuit. "Whaddup, son?" he joked as he stretched his arms to hold Justin high above him in the air.

Justin, who had to be the most even-tempered baby he knew, laughed with an open mouth causing one long drool of saliva to land on his chin. Julius just laughed. "I love you, little man," he told him with complete honesty.

Caress hated his guts, but Julius was proud of himself for stepping up and fighting for a better relationship with his son.

He was just sorry he had to lose Caress in the process.

Tamara had had enough.

She was beginning to feel like a rope being tugged from

both ends by her friends. They couldn't—wouldn't—even communicate without her. Both complained to her about the other. Both wanted her to take sides. Wanted her to choose.

Well enough was enough.

Tamara watched as Caress strutted into Pages Restaurant on Halsey Street downtown. She looked good in the dark denim jeans she wore with ankle boots and a short leather jacket. Tamara just smiled at the way Caress was completely oblivious to the stares and second looks she received from the men she passed.

"Hey, girl." Caress unzipped her coat before sliding into the booth seat across from her. "How's my baby?"

"Why don't you call Julius yourself and ask him?" Tamara suggested as she played with the straw in her cup of fruit juice.

Caress frowned. "I'm *not* calling that fool," she snapped.

"And why not Caress?" Tamara asked patiently.

"After what he did to me?"

"What exactly did he do to you?"

Caress sat back and eyed Tamara for a long time before she finally spoke. "So you're on your boy's side, then?" she asked with a tinge of anger in her voice.

Tamara did not back down from Caress's long and hard stare. "So you're going to burn another perfectly good relationship because you'd rather feel right?" she asked.

Caress frowned. "Excuse me, Oprah?"

"No, I'm your friend . . . and I'm Julius's friend," Tamara banged her finger against the top of the table as she spoke. "And I am fed up with both of you. Seriously."

The anger dissipated from Caress's face. "What did I do?" she asked, obviously surprised by Tamara's anger, like she was the only one entitled to the emotion.

"Threw away a perfectly good man," Tamara began, ticking her points off on fingers. "And treated him like he didn't have just as many rights concerning Justin and you do, and then got mad because he stood up *like a man* and demanded those rights, Caress."

Caress's eyes widened more and more with each reprimand. "Well damn, Tamara, say what you really feel."

Tamara softened her face as she reached across the table to playfully swat Caress's hand. "Somebody needed to say it, and don't worry I got some words for your baby daddy too."

"Like what?"

Tamara eyed her. "Those words are for his ears."

Caress drummed her fingertips atop the table. "Julius started this whole mess," she insisted.

"Caress, do you want to be right or do you want to be happy?" Tamara asked. "Say what you want, but you two are no happier with this semi-war than you are apart. You two are miserable because you're fighting so hard not to get along. I mean, really, two grown people who can't accomplish the simple task of dropping their son off at each other's house. Are you two kidding me?"

Caress shifted her eyes away from the truth of Tamara's words.

"Do you really hate Julius that much, Caress?" Tamara asked softly.

"I never said that I hated him."

"Do you still love him?"

"No," Caress said quickly. Too quickly.

"What*ever*." Tamara rose from the booth. "My point today is not about matchmaking. My point is to look out for my godson because the foolishness has to stop. You both were—are—wrong in this and Justin deserves better than two stubborn, horny fools trying to win. In the end, Justin is losing *big* time. It's time to put Justin first."

Tamara walked to the buffet spread to fix her plate, leaving Caress to marinade on that.

Lady O has nothing on me.

Julius was completely stunned as he watched Tamara bend down to blow air bubbles against Justin's smooth and round brown belly. She did that in between telling him that he was wrong for suing Caress. "So I should let her dictate when and where I see my son?" he asked, as he leveled his eyes on her.

"No, but you could have let her know you were hiring a lawyer before he slapped court papers down her throat. Or you could have been a little more patient with a woman whose child was kidnapped. Or you could have checked yourself before you blamed her for the kidnapping."

"So I'm wrong and she's right?" he asked in disbelief.

Tamara looked over her shoulder at Julius. "No, you're both wrong, and you're both so busy claiming you can't stand each other because you know you want to lay each other. Keep it funky right now, Julius. Okay?"

Julius opened his mouth to protest but Tamara held up her hand. "I'm not concerned anymore with making you nuts realize what you're throwing away. I'm on strike from Hell Date. My point is to pull myself out of the mix before you two have me bald-headed from stress and unnecessary drama."

Julius shifted his position in the club chair. "What does that mean exactly?"

"I'm telling you like I told your baby mama—"

Julius winced. "She is not my baby mama. She's the mother of my child."

Tamara rolled her eyes. "Anyway, I'm out of it. If you two need to communicate with each other about Justin then please do that. Call each other. Don't call me. I will no longer play taxi, transporting him between the two of you. I'm out. Done. Finished. Finito. Stick a fork in me because—"

Julius held up his hand. "I get your point," he told her dryly.

"Good."

Caress was tired of being cooped up in her apartment. It made her miss Justin more and not even a marathon of Celebreality shows on VH1 could erase Tamara's words from her mind. Her apartment was as clean as she was going to get it, and she was sick of snacking.

Hell, she was even sick of her own company and her inability to occupy her time without Justin, without work . . . and without a boyfriend. "I need a life," she muttered aloud.

Since Julius had Justin every other weekend—for now at least—she would have more time on her hands . . . whether she wanted it or not. "Asshole," she muttered at the thought of her ex.

Do you really hate Julius that much, Caress?

She frowned. "Aw, shut up, Tamara," she said aloud at the memory of her friend's words as she grabbed her coat from the rack and walked out the door.

Before she reached the bottom of the stairs she had slid the cap from her pocket down over her head and ears, wrapped the scarf around her neck and mouth, and shoved her hands into knit gloves. She could feel the biting winter winds as soon as she stepped outside.

Several of the neighborhood children were outside enjoying the snow. Caress walked down the salt-covered steps and saw two girls whom she didn't recognize in bright coats trying their best to build a snowman in front of the apartment building.

"Hello," Caress said to the girls who looked about ten.

"Hi," they said cheerfully in unison, obviously oblivious to the cold.

"Aren't they cute?"

Caress turned and smiled at Ahmad walking down the stairs. "Your daughters?" she asked, digging her face down deeper beneath her scarf.

Ahmad made a face like that idea was impossible. "They're my nieces. They're spending the night with their favorite Uncle Ahmad."

"You're our *only* Uncle!" they exclaimed in unison, like they were used to playing that game with him.

Ahmad just chuckled.

"We're making a snowman."

"And then we're going to the movies."

"And then to get pizza."

Caress's eyes widened as they talked in rapid-fire succession. "Wow, you ladies are keeping your Uncle Ahmad very busy," she said squatting down to scoop up a handful of the brilliantly white snow.

"Yup," they said in unison.

Caress thought they reminded her of Jordan and Mia's twins Aliya and Amina. Although those girls were in their teens, Caress bet they had been just as adorable as these two.

Ahmad squatted down beside them and started shoveling snow into a bucket Caress just noticed he was carrying. "Wanna help?" he offered, looking over at Caress with a smile.

"Sure," Caress said, accepting the miniature toy shovel one of the girls handed her.

Soon the winds and the softly falling snowflakes took second to the fun Caress had with Ahmad and his nieces. Their pitiful snowman sat lopsided atop the little hill in front of the apartment. A soft ball of snow accidentally thrown at her led to a snowball fight that really took Caress back to her days growing up in this city.

She ducked to avoid a clump of snow Ahmad flung at her and countered with one of her own, laughing as it hit Ahmad square in the face, dissolving into snow dust as it did.

"Ah hah, Uncle Ahmad," one of the twins teased.

Caress's eyes widened as Ahmad came rushing at her. She squealed and took off around her snow-covered car.

"Run, Miss Coleman," the girls yelled, jumping up and down excitedly.

Ahmad was tall and one of his steps equaled two of hers so he caught up with her easily, wrapping one arm around her waist as he scooped up snow.

"I hate to interrupt."

Laughing they both looked over their shoulders.

Caress's eyes widened and her laughter faded as she eyed Julius standing there with Justin in his arms. She broke free of Ahmad's loose hold and made her way through the calf-high snow to them. "Look at my baby!" she exclaimed, ignoring the disapproving look on Julius's handsome face.

"I can bring him back later if you're busy," he said sarcastically as he handed their son over to her.

Caress looked up at him, hating that she was so aware of how good he looked in the charcoal-fitted cap and leather pea coat. "I'm never too busy for my son, Julius," she snapped, just low enough for his ears only.

"Humph."

Caress eyed him strangely before turning away from him. "Ahmad, I'm going to head in, but thanks so much for a fun time y'all," she told them genuinely.

The girls waved good-bye before going back to their play.

Ahmad bent down to smile at Justin. "Hey, man," he said, laughing when Justin led out a healthy belch and then smiled.

Caress gave him one last smile, aware of Julius's stares, as she headed up the stairs and into the apartment building. She was surprised when he followed her inside, but she refrained from arguing with him in front of her neighbors. She couldn't help but be aware that her behind was almost directly in line with his face as they climbed the stairs. When they reached her apartment door, she turned. "Thank you for dropping him off," she said coolly, avoiding looking at him as she reached for Justin's baby bag. Good-bye."

"Is that your new man?" he asked.

Caress frowned, finally leveling her eyes up on him. "*That's* none of your business."

"Humph."

Caress released a heavy breath. "Julius, I'm sick of arguing with you—"

At the sound of the downstairs door opening Caress swallowed the rest of her words. Moments later the twins preceded Ahmad up the stairs. She smiled at them as she switched Justin to her other hip and watched them pass by to climb the stairs to the third level.

Caress turned her eyes on Julius as soon as she heard his apartment door open and close behind them. "You've dropped off our son and I got your check in the mail yesterday—which I will be cashing. What else do we have to talk about?"

"So Big Foot lives upstairs?" he asked. "You two make one helluva pair."

Caress held up her hand as Justin began to whine. "Jealousy ain't a good look for you, Mr. Jones," she told him sarcastically, before turning to put her key in the lock to open her door.

"Jealousy?" he balked. "I'm just interested in what men you have around my son."

Caress looked over her shoulder to roll her eyes at him

before she walked into her apartment. "Negro, puh-leeze," she drawled, attempting to close the door but Julius stepped inside behind her.

"I have every right to know who is around my son."

Caress sat down on the sofa and worked to get Justin out of the snowsuit and ignore Julius. "How is mama's baby?" she cooed to him as he continued to cry.

Julius opened the baby bag he was still holding and pulled out a bottle, striding with it to the kitchen.

Caress quickly removed Justin's jeans and unsnapped his onesie to change his diaper. She was relieved to see and smell that he was fresh. Julius obviously had changed him regularly and bathed him well. *But of course, what else would a neat freak like him do?*

She was sitting a still-crying Justin up on her lap when Julius handed her the slightly warmed bottle. She eyed him briefly before taking it from him. Their hands touched momentarily, and she jerked away from the sparks she felt. "Thanks," she mumbled, before giving it to Justin whose tears instantly dried up as he sucked away.

"Teamwork works, Caress," Julius said, coming around to remove his hat as he sat on the edge of the chair. "We used to be in this together."

Caress closed her eyes against a pang of hurt and regret. "Yes, until you accused me of being a bad mother and sued me for custody," she countered, ignoring the sound of Tamara's voice echoing: *Do you want to be right or do you want to be happy?*

"And I can hold it against you for keeping me away from my son . . . but I want us to get along. Let's both admit we made mistakes and move on."

Caress took the bottle from Justin's still-puckered mouth as he fell asleep. She said nothing as she rose and walked into her bedroom and laid him down in his bassinet. She dropped down to the edge of the bed and leaned in close to lightly rub circles and pats on his back lovingly.

"So are you and your boy from upstairs . . ."

Caress looked up to find Julius leaning in the doorway. It reminded her of the many days he would stand there and just quietly watch as she put Justin to sleep. Good times. Before the kidnapping.

Do you still love him, Caress?

She really wanted Tamara out of her head.

"The same way you're jealous and we're not even together, don't you think he would mind you're being here?" she asked, looking for a diversion from her thoughts and her feelings as she rose to leave the room.

Julius reached out and lightly touched her waist as she attempted to pass him. She looked up at him. "What are you gathering evidence for the custody battle?" she asked sarcastically, still fighting the undeniable pull she felt toward him.

Julius's face immediately closed up as he released her. "You really don't think much of me, do you?" he asked, his fresh and cool breath fanning down against her face.

"Just like you don't think much of me," Caress countered.

Julius laughed as his eyes dropped down to her mouth. "I don't think much of you? I love you, Caress."

Her heart pulsed crazily and slammed against her chest at that, but she just shook her head and walked away from him with a wave of her hand.

"Why are you doing this to us?" he called behind her.

Caress whirled in the center of the living room to look at him. "Why is everything my damn fault?" she asked as she frowned.

"How was your weekend, Caress?" he asked out of the blue.

That threw her off. "Why?"

"How was it?" he asked again as he walked up to her.

"What's your point, Julius?"

"You and Justin made it through him being at my house all weekend. He's fed. He's clean. He's happy. He's well taken care of," he told her. "You can say what you want, Caress, but you've damn near been on a vigil since he was returned to us. The break *had* to do you some good."

Caress shrugged. "Okay, fine. Yes, Julius, but I missed my son."

He smiled at her as he applauded. "I only had him one weekend and I'm tired as hell," he admitted with a big toothy smile.

Caress's heart tugged.

Julius stepped closer to her and extended his hand. "Even though we can't seem to work out you and me, I'm willing to cease this war for the sake of our son."

Caress eyed his hand warily. "What exactly does that mean?" she asked, crossing her arms over her chest.

"I just want to be able to see my son, Caress, and if we can work this out between us then we don't need the courts in our business." Julius reached out and tugged the ends of her hair. "You have to trust me."

"I do trust you . . . with Justin," she added.

"But you don't think I love you?" Julius asked, incredulous.

Caress bit her bottom lip but stopped when those intense eyes dropped to watch the innocent habit of hers. "Not enough. No, I don't," she told him honestly.

Justin let his hand fall to his side. "I never cheated on you. I never mistreated you. I never put my hands on you. I did all the romantic things women read about in books. I begged you to move back in with me. I put it down in the bedroom each and every time. And I'm a damn good father to our son."

"I never denied that."

"I've done the work, and I've said the words. Why in the hell do you think I don't love you enough?" he asked, obviously exasperated.

Caress felt that crazy energy between them slowly building and she stepped back from Julius. From it.

"You think Shaq will love you more than me?" he asked huskily, stepping close to her.

"He is not my man, Julius," she stressed, running her hands through her hair.

"Do you want him to be?"

Caress shook her head.

Julius looked at her. "Seeing his hands on you messed me up, Caress," he admitted.

Caress foolishly let her eyes meet his and suddenly she felt like she was drowning in the black depths.

"It made me realize that I love your crazy ass, Caress. And you know what? You love me too." Julius placed his hands on her hips and pulled her body close to his. "Don't you?" he whispered to her huskily as he lowered his delicious mouth close to hers. "Huh? Don't you?"

"You scare me, Julius. This scares me," she admitted aloud to herself for the first time.

"It scares me too. I have never felt like this before, Caress."

She swallowed over a lump in her throat. "I have never loved someone as much as I love you and that is saying a lot because I cosigned for a car for my last man."

Julius frowned comically. "His credit was worse than yours?" he joked.

Caress swatted his arm. "Shut up."

"Listen," Julius said, regaining his seriousness as he brought his hands up to massage her neck as he stared into her eyes. "Love is about taking chances, Caress. I'd rather take the risk than continue on without you in my life. These last two months have been . . . different without you. You are worth the risk, Caress."

He pressed kisses to her open mouth and Caress raised up on her toes to get closer to the pleasure of it all. So many emotions gripped her . . . but it all felt like it was happening too fast and too soon. So many words and hurtful actions had passed for this head first fall back into a relationship.

Caress allowed herself one last passionate kiss that was everything: arousing, dizzying, shattering, and numbing; before she broke the kiss and stepped out of his heated embrace searching for space and clarity before that familiar chemistry between them overcame reason and good judgment.

Caress held up both her hands as he stepped closer to her again. "I need to think. I need time. I . . . please, Julius. Give me a minute to breathe."

Julius closed his eyes and Caress could feel his frustration and see his clear erection. "Come on, Caress, why are you making this so hard?"

Trying to lighten the mood, Caress dropped her eyes down to the bulge straining against the front of his pants. "Very hard I see," she said with an arch of her brow and tongue in cheek.

Julius blessed her with a smile but his eyes remained serious. "We've lost two months, Caress. Let's work this out. It's worth it."

She remained silent as she nibbled on the tip of her thumbnail and looked at him. He nodded and reached out to stroke her cheek softly before turning and leaving the apartment.

Chapter Twenty

Julius walked into Don's Diner, the bustling eatery on Nye Avenue in Irvington. The spot was just as crowded as any other Saturday morning but he immediately spotted Kendrick sitting at the counter waiting for him. "Thanks for coming, man," he greeted his friend as he removed his black suede overcoat and leather gloves before he took a seat on a stool.

Kendrick wiped his mouth with a napkin before giving Julius a pound. "No problem. No problem. So what's up?"

Julius ordered his favorite breakfast of corned beef hash, scrambled eggs and cheese, and home fries before swerving a little to face Kendrick. "I need some advice about Caress."

Kendrick laughed a little as he picked up his fork to shovel a heap of his grits, eggs, and bacon into his mouth. "Stubborn huh?"

Julius just shook his head. "It's been a week since I came at her about getting back together and still nothing."

"I got a stubborn one at home. You know that."

"But the problem is before last week I was resolved to leave her alone. Love or no love, I was done. Finished. Finito. Stick me with a fork I'm—"

Kendrick eyed him. "You been hanging around my wife too much."

Julius laughed, giving the waitress a smile as she set his cup of coffee before him. "Anyway, man, seeing Caress all laughing and hugged up with that dude shook me up. I was ready to beat that Negro's ass and then it hits me: This is my woman. Mine."

Kendrick nodded and continued to eat.

"I want my woman back, man," Julius stated with clear intent in his eyes. "I want things back like before."

"Or better," Kendrick added around a deep sip of his own brew.

Julius looked at him curiously. "Huh?"

"The next level man. Step up," Kendrick said simply.

"I asked her to move in with me already."

"Like free milk, huh?" Kendrick leveled his eyes on Julius over the rim of the cup.

"First off, I can't even get her to get back together with me and you want me to propose?" Julius balked.

"I didn't say propose but have you even *thought* about marrying Caress one day?"

Julius was glad when the waitress set his food before him because the truth was he hadn't thought about it.

"I didn't think so," Kendrick said, signaling for a refill of his cup. "If you can't figure out what you want from the relationship in your head and in your heart then how can you expect that of Caress . . . or any other woman for that matter?"

Marriage? Julius said to himself. *Mini-vans. Joint bank accounts. Completely and totally together spiritually, physically . . . and legally?* Julius picked up his fork. "Marriage is a whole 'nother level," he said out loud, pushing his eggs around with his fork.

"Sure is." Kendrick let out a little belch as he placed his

elbow on the counter by his now empty plate. "You're so quick to call her your woman and get jealous over some other man, but you never thought about marriage . . . even five years down the line or something? Humph. The way to truly make a woman yours is as old as time, brotha. You better recognize it."

Julius let out a long and extremely heavy breath as he pushed his plate away.

Caress eyed the finance papers for a long time as she sat in one of the small and cramped cubicles in the rear of the car lot. It was more than just her signature on paper. It was three and half years of car payments and full insurance coverage.

Two new bills.

But it also meant a reliable ride. No more riding around with her fingers, toes, and eyes crossed that her little hooptie didn't poop out on her and Justin.

"Miss Coleman."

Caress looked up at the elderly white man sitting across from her.

"Everything okay?" he asked, looking like his too small shirt had him locked in a bear hug.

Caress reached down for her locket and opened it to look down at the picture of her and her baby. Willing to take on the extra burdens for him alone, she closed the locket, picked up the pen, and quickly signed her name next to all the spots marked for her with an *X*.

Nearly two hours later Caress left behind her hooptie as a trade-in and pulled out of the car lot on Route 22 in Union in her silver Honda Civic. She was proud of herself. It was an early Christmas present for her and her son.

Caress was blasting her worn out copy of Lauryn Hill's

CD when her cell phone vibrated from where she had it sitting between her thighs. She quickly checked the caller ID, thinking—and hoping—it was Julius. It wasn't. Pushing aside her disappointment that Julius's daily phone calls were noticeably absent today, Caress flipped the phone open. "Hey, Tam-Tam," she said, turning the CD player down and then pressing the button to put the cell on speakerphone. "How's Justin?"

"Right here looking in my face and tearing up this bottle with his greedy self."

Caress smiled. Just about the only time he cried was if he was hungry or sitting in poop. "I should be there in about twenty minutes," she told her, slowing down in traffic.

"Did you get the car?"

"Yup."

"Good. I'm proud of you, and you needed it. You have to treat yourself sometimes for working hard."

"Thanks." Caress set the phone down on the console and steered with both hands as she came up on a winding section of the road. "Uhm . . . have you guys heard from Julius today?"

"Not me, and Kendrick's not here so I don't know if he did."

Caress chewed the gloss from her full bottom lip.

"Ready to get back with your boo?" Tamara teased.

"It's just weird he hasn't called at all today, that's all."

"Girl, you don't know what you want," Tamara said. "Just yesterday you was saying him calling you twice a day wasn't exactly giving you space."

Caress remained silent in the face of truth.

"Do you know what you want, Caress?"

"No, I don't," she answered with honesty. "Hey, Tamara, I'll talk to you when I get there."

"All right."

Caress picked up the phone to snap it closed before she pulled her car into the parking lot of a supermarket.

Had Julius given up?

Had he changed his mind?

Had someone new caught his attention?

Was he tired of her waiting for some huge sign that they had a real future?

Caress let her head fall back against the headrest as she twisted and turned her cell phone in her hand. She flipped it open to call him but then flipped it back closed again.

She had asked for time. Maybe he just needed some of his own.

Or maybe he regretted last Sunday—the thought only increased her reservations.

Releasing a heavy breath, she drove her car back into the heavy Saturday afternoon traffic resolved not to let figuring out what Julius was up to now get her down.

"I've missed you, Caress. Tell me what I have to do to make you mine."

She sighed as Julius pressed a row of sweet kisses to her neck, each one more delicious than the last. "I will always be yours," she promised as she easily spread her shapely legs and welcomed his hardness into her warmth with a sharp hiss of pleasure.

"Julius, Julius, Julius," she sighed in reply to each delicious thrust.

"Julius . . . Julius—"

Brrrnnggg.

Caress's eyes popped open as she lay in the middle of her bed with her sheets tangled with her limbs and her mouth still open from moaning his name out loud. Even with the brutal December winds raging outside she felt like her body was on fire.

Brrrnnngg.

"Not again," she sighed as she wiped the sweat from her brow and her cleavage with a trembling hand.

Night after night after night her dreams were filled with Julius. It seemed the more she faced her internal battle of what to do with their relationship the more her frustration was transforming into pure lust at night.

Brrrnnngg.

Rubbing her eyes, Caress rolled over in the darkness and grabbed her cordless phone. "Hello?"

"Congratulations on your new car."

Caress's eyes opened in surprise at the sound of Julius's masculine tones coming through the phone line. Goose bumps raced down her arms as she sat up in the middle of the bed. "Thanks."

"You got *all* your money's worth out the other one," he joked.

Caress laughed low in her throat, mindful of Justin sleeping in his bassinet. She settled back down in the bed finding comfort on her piled-high pillows.

"I just called to check on Justin and to see if I could pick him up Friday instead of Saturday?"

Caress's face filled with disappointment. "Oh . . . okay. Sure. Yeah. No problem," she said, wanting to smack herself upside the head at how flustered she sounded.

"Well, I'll let you get back to sleep," he said.

Caress's eyebrows drew in close as she tried to ignore that her feelings were hurt by his obvious distance. "Okay, see you Friday then."

"Good night, Caress."

"Good—"

The sound of the dial tone cut her off. Her mouth dropped open as she stared at the phone in disbelief.

The following week seemed to drag by for Caress. Friday just wouldn't come fast enough for her. And she was ready for TGIF because she had something up her sleeves for Julius Jones. His sporadic and brief calls centered around Justin had continued.

Was he just playing with her head and heart a couple of weeks ago?

Was it a ploy to get some baby mama bed play?

What happened to all that love and all the worthy risks?

"Baby, your mama is going to show your daddy just what he's missing," Caress said to Justin as he sat in his motorized swing playing with one of his many colorful rattles.

Studying her reflection in the mirror, she twisted and turned this way and that. Her hair was a riot of curls, her make-up heavier than normal and her long sleeve tee and jeans tighter than usual.

"Humph."

She was spraying every possible heated spot on her body with perfume when there was a knock at her door. "Show time, Justin," she called over to her baby, who focused on drooling over his toy as she slipped her feet into three-inch gold heels.

Walking carefully so that she wouldn't trip, Caress made her way to the door. She almost stumbled as her ankle turned in, but she held her hands out to steady herself. "Get it together, Caress," she warned herself, straightening her spine and making her way to the door without incident.

She pulled the door open with a smile that faded at the

sight of Ahmad. "Hey," she said, sounding as unenthusiastic as she felt.

"Wow, you look different," he said, taking her all in.

Caress held up her hand and eyed him with an I'm-not-in-the-mood look. "Cool your jets, playboy, I got enough man drama," she drawled, stepping out of her heels to kick them away from her.

"No, cool *your* jets, playgirl, because I got enough man drama of my own," he countered.

It took just a moment for that to register with Caress, but once she got it her mouth shaped into an *O*. "Uhm, okay. All right. I got it," she said, thinking he was so different from Dwayne. So very different. She had no idea this man was gay.

For a sec she thought about hooking him up with Dwayne, but wasn't it wrong to assume they would get along when the only thing they seemed to have in common was their sexual preference?

Ahmad smiled like he was used to her reaction from others. "Anyway, I just wanted to ask you to watch my apartment this weekend while I'm out of town."

"Sure. No problem," she told him, crossing one ankle behind her leg. "And have fun."

He turned with a brief wave but then turned back. "I'm gay, but I know a woman trying to bait a man. So you have fun this weekend too."

Caress arched her eyebrow. "Actually I'm trying to make one see what he's missing and not what he's getting—cause he ain't getting it."

Ahmad shook his head. "And I thought men played games."

He laughed as he jogged up the stairs.

Caress stepped back inside her apartment and closed the door. She was headed back to her bedroom for a pair of shoes with a lower heel when she heard the front door to the building slam closed. She hurried across the living room floor, almost slipping, trying to rush back into her heels. Forcing herself to take deep and steadying breaths to calm down, Caress walked to the door slowly just as there was a knock at the door.

"Who is it?" she called out barely able to hear herself over her pounding heartbeat.

"Julius."

Caress opened the door wide and stepped back to let him in. She frowned behind his back when he barely gave her a second glance. *What . . . the . . . hell?*

"I'll go get the baby," she said, praying she didn't fall flat on her face as she walked back to her bedroom.

She kicked off those shoes as soon as she was out of his sight. "Your daddy's going to wind up with one of these shoes down his throat and the other one up his butt," she muttered as she freed him from the swing and grabbed his snowsuit.

When she walked back into the living room with Justin in one arm and his baby bag in the other, she was surprised to see Julius standing by the door.

His nonchalant face shaped into a smile as he took Justin out of her arms. "There's Daddy's boy," he exclaimed animatedly.

Justin squealed in response.

"I'm going to head out then," Julius said, turning to open the door with his free hand.

"Julius!" Caress snapped in disbelief.

He turned and looked at her in confusion. "Huh?"

Caress fought the urge to pop him or stomp her foot in full Karina-diva mode. "You know what? Nothing. Never mind. Enjoy your weekend."

"Okay. Cool. See you Sunday," he said before walking out the door.

Caress grabbed the door and then slammed it forcefully. "I am seriously . . . *seriously* through with Julius Jones!"

Julius chuckled as he pressed a kiss to Justin's face. "I got your mama right where I want her," he said, laughing as he made his way down the stairs and out of her apartment building.

"I'm not really hungry, Tamara," Caress said the next night from her seat in the back of Mia's Tahoe as the car turned into the parking lot of Mahogany's.

"Well, tough because this is ladies' night and we are going to eat and drink and be merry."

Mia just shot her an encouraging wink as they climbed out of the SUV. The ladies all gathered their coats around them to block the cold as they hurried inside.

Caress was so busy taking off her coat that she didn't even notice until she looked up that all eyes were on her. She immediately felt self-conscious and looked down to make sure she wasn't having a Janet Jackson boob moment in her fitted Apple Bottoms' denim dress.

"Girl, come on," Tamara said, reaching for her hand to pull her forward through the crowd which was splitting like the Red Sea for them.

What is going on? she wondered as they reached the front of the club.

Suddenly Julius, who was dressed to the nines in a *baaad* tuxedo and holding Justin who was similarly dressed, stepped forward into the center of the crowd.

Caress felt the eyes on her as Tamara and Mia nudged her forward into the center with Julius and Justin.

Julius smiled at her before reaching for her hand and pulling her close. "Hi stranger," he teased as he massaged the small of her back.

"Julius. What is going on?" she asked, forcing a smile.

Kendrick stepped forward and handed Julius a cordless mic, slapping his friend on the back before retreating.

Julius cleared his throat and raised the mic to his mouth as Justin reached out and opened his closed palms for Caress. "He wants to get to his mommy just like me," Julius joked, drawing laughter from the crowd.

Caress hid her surprise at that remark as she reached up to appease Justin by playing with his pudgy little hands.

"So a little over a year ago a nosy little friend of mine—"

"Hey!" Tamara cried out with a playful pout.

The crowd laughed again but Caress had missed it and looked at Julius and now her eyes were locked with his. There was something in the depths that let her know that this was a serious matter.

"So Caress here—and this is the beautiful Caress for those who don't know her—and I came here for that date. I don't think either one of us was looking for love or happily ever after and for sure not our son here nine months later."

More soft laughter.

"But that night was special for me, and I think it was special for her too." Julius pointed the mic toward her mouth. "Was it special for you, baby?"

Caress pulled back a bit thinking the mic was ridiculously phallic. "Yes, it was," she said huskily with honesty.

"We had the food, the music, and this connection that maybe we both took a little too lightly?" he asked working the mic back and forth between them as they spoke.

Caress nodded as she continued to stare at Julius. And only Julius.

"So I think Mahogany's will always be special to us."

"Definitely," Caress stressed, feeling some major excitement creeping up on her.

Julius looked at her for a long time like he wanted to get his words just right. "Lord knows we didn't have anything in common, but somehow we clicked. It worked. And we've had our ups and downs but in the end we both know that what we have together is way bigger than anything we'll ever have apart."

Caress felt completely breathless as she listened to his words, looked into his eyes, and felt his emotions.

"A good friend told me that there is only one way to truly claim someone as your woman and he was right. So I thank him for that advice."

"You're welcome," Kendrick said behind a cough.

Julius motioned for Tamara, and she stepped right up to take a squirming Justin into her arms.

As if on cue that same jazzy rendition of "*I'm Going Down*" began to play softly as Julius bent down on one knee, taking Caress's trembling hand back in his. She smiled at the realization that he was trembling too.

"So I wanted to prove to you, Caress, that I do love you. I am so in love with you, and there is one way to truly make you mine. And what better spot than right here where it all began, on this very dance floor, to ask you to please do me the honor of becoming my wife?" he asked, holding a glittering diamond solitaire in his hand.

At this point Caress hardly knew how her legs supported her, so she lowered herself to her knees before him—equal with him—and breathlessly, with all the love she had for him, answered, "Yes."

The crowd erupted in applause and sighs as Julius

noisily dropped the mic and lifted his hands to cup her face, kissing her with all the passion and promise he could muster.

Caress didn't think—in fact she knew she never had been made love to before tonight. Julius had made a bold move to commit and devote himself to her, but the way he relished, adored, and stimulated her body let her know he was making yet another statement.

Time was endless.

Pleasure unbound.

Love blissfully infinite.

As his strong, muscled arms held her body tightly— almost until she couldn't breathe—Caress laid back against the lushness of the hotel suite's bed and enjoyed the hard and slow push of each of his delicious thrusts. Every circular wind of his narrow hips pressed his rod against her walls as he blessed her from shoulder to shoulder with loving kisses and hot words that blew against her heated skin.

She knew she was wanted.

Caress tilted her chin up and licked her lips as she brought her hands up to hold his face. Her tongue flickered out to hotly trace the outline of his lips. She felt him shiver from his head to his toes and even deep within her. Their eyes locked as his tongue darted out to stroke hers. They moaned as Caress suckled his tongue sensuously, deep into her own mouth. She felt his rod stiffen as he continued to stroke her deeply.

She knew she was desired.

As his thrusts deepened with intensity until she felt like he truly wanted them to be merged as one, Julius leaned up enough to look down into her sex-glazed eyes with clear intent to please. She gasped. He thrust. She moaned. He thrust again. She sighed. And he thrust again. A mind blowing cycle that left her panting and breathless, working hard, but energized all at once.

She knew she was irresistible.

Caress brought her hands up to wrap around his neck as she brought her legs up to tightly wrap around his waist. Moving in sync with one another to their own primal rhythm they felt as if it was the most natural thing in the world. They stroked the fires within each other at a slow and sensuous pace. The chemistry that neither could fight from the very beginning built around them as they clung to each other tightly in sweet anticipation of their oncoming climaxes. No words were spoken. None were needed.

She knew she was loved.

Epilogue

Life was beyond good.

Caress looked away from the minister and up at Julius. She smiled beneath her shoulder-length veil to find his eyes already on her as they stood framed by candlelight at the altar. He squeezed her hands and she squeezed back.

I really love this man, she thought, unable to believe how blessed and happy she felt for having him in her life.

Even as they spoke their vows of love, commitment, and devotion, and pledged their vows, Caress blossomed in the midst of not only Julius's love but that of her family and her friends.

Julius had taken the lead and hired a private detective to locate her father. Unfortunately they hadn't been successful so far, but she had faith and she loved Julius all the more for even trying to fulfill her dreams.

"May I present to you Mr. and Mrs. Julius Jones."

Caress and Julius ended their passionate first kiss as a married couple to the thunderous applause of the wedding goers. They smiled as they turned to face everyone. Mia released Justin, and he came waddling up to his parents for Julius to scoop his tuxedo-clad body up into his arms.

Just as the pianist began to play and the soloist belted out an upbeat rendition of *"You're All I Need"* by Marvin Gaye and Tammi Terrell, Caress wrapped her arm around Julius's as they strutted down the aisle and into their future together.

Dear Readers,

For those readers of mine since the early days I know you're glad to enjoy catching up with Jordan and Mia Banks from *Three Times a Lady*. Nice surprise, huh? Well, there will be a *Three Times a Lady* sequel coming soon. The older kids are *finally* old enough to have their own stories and it is on my list of things to do.

Now, back to Julius and Caress. This story will forever be special to me because my mother loved the concept of it from the moment I called her on the phone and told her all about it. Well, sadly she's gone on and will never be able to see if I did the story justice. This was the hardest book I have ever written because it is the first one I did without the love, support, and sometimes guidance from my mother. I think she would love it because I definitely get my realness from her. I know she was here guiding me in spirit and I hope you enjoyed the book as much as I think she would have.

I love my readers so much, and I just want to thank you all for the continued love and support over the years. You all are blessings to me. For real.

Best 2 U All,
N.

Want more?
Turn the page for a preview of
Niobia's hottest novels!
Available now wherever books are sold!

Heated

Prologue

Holtsville, SC

Careful not to alert anyone to his presence, he moved in the darkness across the wild and grassy field with speed. He was nervous that he would be caught before his mission was complete. Like thunder and drums all rolled into one, his heart pounded in his chest. Sweat dampened his shirt, making it cling to his shoulders and back.

A sudden noise echoed from the surrounding darkness. He caught his breath and held it as nerves caused his bladder to fill. He quickly dropped down, pressing his stomach and knees to the cool earth surrounded by weeds and grass that was nearly three to four feet tall.

Holding his breath . . . he waited. Listening. Scared of being caught.

He heard nothing but the normal night sounds of the

country: owls hooting, frogs singing their tunes, crickets busy scratching their legs.

Warily, he rose and moved ahead.

When the barn—already worn and torn from age and shameful neglect—came into view, he paused. For a second he looked up at the massive structure framed by the full moonlight.

It was almost majestic.

Swallowing any regret, he dashed inside.

He emerged moments later and ran as quickly as he could away from it. His feet thudded against the earth, his chest heaved with pain from his exertion.

He dared turning around only when he was cloaked by the trees—trees that welcomed and hid him.

The flames engulfing the barn were reflected in his ebony eyes.

Chapter One

Atlanta, Georgia

"Say cheese, Dr. King."

Bianca smiled as instructed, posing with her glass star-shaped Woman of the Year award from *Modern Women* magazine held in front of her. She tried not to grimace as the flash went off several times in rapid succession.

"Absolutely beautiful, Bianca."

Her smile stiffened. She knew without shifting her eyes from the camera that it was Armand Toussaint.

"Thanks, Dr. King and congrats again," the male photographer said, moving back into the Imperial Ballroom of the Marriott Marquis Hotel to take further photos of the social event.

Bianca took a deep breath as she slid her circle-shaped beaded purse under her arm. She had just stepped into the hall outside the ballroom for a small reprieve from the room of people there to honor her with yet another accomplishment in her career as an equine veterinarian.

She considered Armand's appearance an intrusion.

"Hello, Armand," she said, not even sounding like she meant it.

"*Une belle femme ne doit pas être seule*," he said, his French accent very heavy as he told her she was too beautiful to be alone.

Armand had lived around the world and spoke seven languages, but when he was really trying to put his mack down he always reverted to French—a language he knew Bianca spoke fluently.

Bianca sighed. "I thank you for the compliment on my beauty, but I also thank you for respecting my desire to be alone," she countered with ease. She knew it would take more bluntness to send the amorous admirer truly on his way.

It's not like he wasn't appealing to the eye—the man was tall and gorgeous like a young Sidney Poitier—and Bianca even found his conversation quite amusing—when he wasn't trying to seduce her out of her La Perla panties . . . and there was a certain allure to a tall man with skin like dark chocolate with a French accent. The man was just insufferable because he was aware of his attributes and he couldn't fathom that there was a woman in existence who didn't want him.

Bianca certainly didn't.

She usually ran into Armand at the many charity and social events they attended in Atlanta. They both served on several of the same boards, advisory councils, and minority organizations. On every occasion—whether with a date or not—Armand let Bianca know that he had a personal cure for her "supposed" loneliness blues.

Was Bianca lonely?

She fixed her hazel eyes on the rogue and saw his eyes shift to her left. Bianca turned to see what drew his attention and her eyes fell on a curvaceous woman in a strapless dress that defied gravity. She turned her gaze back to him and he smiled at her in a charming—and apologetic—fashion.

Not *that* lonely.

She firmly believed his penis had more miles on it than two hundred laps around the Indianapolis Speedway. Even though he loved to tell Bianca that he was quite skilled in making a woman come at least ten times in one session of lovemaking, Bianca was more than willing to pass.

"No one should be alone on such a beautiful night as tonight, *mon doux*," he said in a husky voice, stepping closer to her.

Bianca stepped back. "I'm sure you'll find . . . *something* to get into," she told him wryly.

"Bianca—"

Her cell phone rang from inside her purse. "Excuse me, Armand," she told him, pulling it out to answer. "Dr. King speaking."

"This is Travis out at the Clover Ranch."

"Yes, hello Travis."

"We got a mare about to foal. We've been monitoring her and she was doing good with the rolling to position the foal, but for the last five minute she's actin' awful funny for normal foaling, you know?"

Bianca nodded. "Has her water broke?"

"No, ma'am."

"I'm about twenty good minutes from the ranch, but I'm on my way."

"Thank God," Travis sighed.

Bianca bit back a smile before she ended the call.

Armand came to stand beside her, lightly touching her bare elbow. "Everything okay, Bianca?"

"I have to go. Please make my apologies to everyone."

"But—"

"Goodbye, Armand."

Bianca flew out of the ballroom, not even waiting for the elevator as she took to the grand staircase. She was quite a site with her shoulder-length pressed hair flying behind her and the slinky skirt of her mocha sequined Roberto Cavali dress in her hands as she hitched it up around her knees to run straight down the center of the staircase.

Very Scarlet O'Hara–like.

She wasn't aware or caring of the dramatic sight she made, though. She just wanted to get to the ranch and it was a good fifteen miles just outside of Atlanta in Sandy Springs.

Thank God I keep a change of clothes in my trunk.

She was soon accepting the keys to her silver convertible Volvo C70. She lowered the automatic roof as she sped away from the hotel.

"Home sweet home."

The sun was just beginning to rise when Bianca dragged herself into the foyer of her elegant three thousand square foot home in an affluent gated community in a suburb of Atlanta. She flung her dress over the banister and carried her award into her study. She came to a stop before her massive cherry desk and took in the full wall of shelves behind it. Every accomplishment of her adult life was chronicled. There were more awards and accolades than she could count. She didn't even know if she could make room for her latest achievement.

Reflective, she walked to the far end of the study and slowly began to review all of the statues in various shapes, sizes, and materials. Some meant more to her than others, and those she touched briefly with a hint of a smile.

For anyone on the outside looking in at her life it was seemingly ideal.

She started her own veterinary practice at twenty-seven

from her savings. Just three short years later her workload nearly doubled and she brought on two additional vets. She was now thirty-two, and her equine clinic was one of the top such facilities in the Southeast.

Not bad for a little black girl from Holtsville, South Carolina.

Bianca came to a stop before the 8 × 11 photograph in the center of the wall of awards and certifications. It was a picture of a tall and distinguished man standing beside a little girl and woman atop a horse. They were all smiling and obviously happy.

My eighth birthday, Bianca thought.

Her parents had just surprised her with her very first pony, Star. Even though she had had plenty of access to ponies living on a successful horse ranch Star had been special because Star was hers alone.

The photo was one of the few that she treasured.

A reminder of better times.

The little girl in that picture didn't have a clue that her mother would die seven years later and her stable world would never be the same again.

Bianca set her award on the shelf with the photo as her eyes fell on the handsome man. Her father. Her daddy. Once her hero.

She hadn't seen him or the ranch in fifteen years.

When her mother died Bianca thought her world would end. Her one saving grace had been her close relationship with her father. She knew they would help each other through the loss.

But that hadn't happened.

Her father shut down completely. He isolated himself in his bedroom for days at a time, only to emerge reeking of alcohol. The ranch felt his neglect, right along with Bianca. That hurt.

It was far too much weight for a fifteen year old to bear. Between going to school—and maintaining her grades—and trying to take over running the farm, she would sometimes wake up and find her father sprawled out by the door drunk as a skunk.

She barely had time to grieve her mother's passing because she began cleaning up her father's messes. She became really good at it. She became just as good at hiding her anger and disappointment.

Until the day her father brought home Trishon Haddock—a woman twenty years his junior—and proclaimed that at forty he was getting married.

That's when Bianca—soft, agreeable, and passive—welcomed that part of her personality that let her hit the roof. It hadn't been little Bianca struggling to make sense of her world. She was seventeen-year-old Bianca, senior in high school, and running a horse ranch—and she was *pissed*.

Even though she told her father that he was being a fool for marrying a woman with the reputation around town of a harlot; even though she told him he was disrespecting her and her Mama by bringing another woman into their house; even though she refused to be nice as he requested . . . she never once told him that it hurt her that he made time in his life for a wife when he hadn't made time for his daughter.

That she held on to, protected, shielded.

As she stood at her second-story bedroom window and looked down at the wedding she refused to attend, Bianca made the decision to leave her father in the chaos he created. Bianca rescinded her decision to attend a local university. The further she got away, the better.

She left for college in Georgia that summer and hadn't been back since.

Bianca turned away from the photo, but her memories—very painful recollections—remained. Her relationship with her father was barely visible. They spoke on the phone sporadically and went through motions.

Pathetic as hell, she thought.

Releasing a heavy breath, Bianca strolled out of the study and headed toward the rear of the house to her kitchen. She was ready to fall into her bed and sleep away the hours, but she had appointments at the clinic, so rest would have to wait.

Bianca hoped some of her "kick-ass" iced coffee would get her going again.

Soon the slow drip-drip of the coffee maker seemed to be the only sound in the house. Most considered that quiet to be peaceful, restful, and precious. To Bianca it was the sound of living alone, which she refused to equate to being lonely. Sometimes, however, she thought that the sound of children laughing and a husband showering to prepare for his workday would be . . . peaceful, restful, and precious.

With her last date being more than two months ago perhaps the line between alone and lonely was thinning to the width of a strand of hair.

"Maybe I need a dog," she muttered, pouring a large cup of coffee that she sweetened and lightened considerably before pouring it over a tall cup of crushed ice.

Bianca took a deep sip. "Liquid crack," she sighed.

She was strolling out of the kitchen when there was a knock at her kitchen door. She smiled at the sight of her nearest neighbor and friend, Mimi Cooley, peering through the glass of the door.

"Let me in, Sweetie, before people think I'm a Peeping Tom, okay," Mimi said in that odd voice of hers that was a blend of nasal whining and Southern belle haughtiness.

Mimi was an ex–child star of the popular Seventies sitcom, *Just the Two of Us*. At thirteen, the show was canceled and, unfortunately, her acting career ended. Her family moved from Hollywood back to Atlanta and tried to give Mimi as normal a life as possible.

But normalcy and Mimi didn't go in the same sentence.

She married the first of her seven husbands at eighteen—men who were wealthy and a tad bit older than Mimi. At fifty she now lived off syndication from the show and the hundreds of television commercials she did during her childhood career. She never got used to the idea of a nine to five job, and spent her days shopping and drinking Long Island iced teas—without showing one indication of being drunk or even tipsy.

Regardless of the time of day, Mimi was always dressed to the nines: heels and skirts, slacks and spectator pumps, and not a pair of jeans to be seen. Her make-up was always in place, and her hair was perfectly coiffed—and religiously died jet black—like she was the second coming of Diahann Carroll's character on *Dynasty*.

Mimi was one of a kind, and Bianca loved the diva to death.

"Hi, Mimi."

She breezed in with a cloud of Chanel No. 5 and turquoise silk. "I thought I was going to have to retire and collect Social Security before you let me in, darling."

"How can I help you, Mimi . . . *dah-ling*?"

"Well, a shot of brandy wouldn't hurt a bit, Sweetie," Mimi said, moving across the kitchen to set her purse on the center island.

"For 8 A.M. coffee sounds like a better bet," Bianca countered.

"Some barkeep you make. All that advice without the actual, huh, what . . . liquor, that's right, Sweetie."

"Nothing but coffee 'round here," Bianca said, taking a deep sip of her iced brew. "Want a cup?"

Mimi rolled her elaborately made-up eyes—she was so

dramatic. "Sweetie, I'd rather be buried in a Wal-Mart, okay," she said with a shiver.

Bianca doubted Mimi had even seen the inside of a Wal-Mart, or even knew where to find one. She frowned as she watched Mimi open her purse and extract a silver monogrammed flask.

"Bianca, a lady is always, huh, what . . . prepared, that's right," she said, before taking a small swig. "Now, I usually have the cul de sac all to myself this time of day. Whatcha doing home, Sweetie?"

"A mare foaled last night."

Mimi wiped the corners of her mouth with her index finger and politely placed the flask back in her purse. "Honey, I'm waiting for the English translation, okay, right."

Bianca smiled as she folded her arms over her chest and leaned back against the marble counter. "I delivered a horse's baby," she explained patiently, ready for the drama. Mimi didn't fail her one bit.

She made a comical face of pain as she pressed her knees together.

Mimi didn't have any children. Bianca didn't know if it was by choice or not.

Deciding to egg her on Bianca said, "Pulling the foal out with chains by its legs wasn't the hard part—"

Mimi shivered and crossed her slender legs.

"Now sticking my arm inside the horse's vagina to turn the foal—"

Mimi pretended to gag. "T.M.I., Doc. T . . . M . . . I."

Bianca flung her head back and laughed, unable to stop the hoglike snort that always came with her laughter. T.M.I. was Mimi's acronym, for "too much information."

"I don't know what's worse, Sweetie. The image of your arm up a horse's ass or that laugh, Sweetie. You need to, huh, what . . . work on it, that's right."

"Shut up, Mimi," Bianca said with a deadpan expression. "At least I'm not known for the oh-so-clever sitcom saying "You and me makes we."

Mimi looked off into the distance—something she did whenever she was discussing the sitcom. "Oh, yes. A better time. And it kept me from being lined up to swallow the scent of horse ass, Sweetie."

Bianca had to laugh at that one. "Listen, this is fun, but some people got a job, Mimi."

She rose, sticking her purse under her arm. "Alright, Sweetie, I'm going. I have a save the children or feed the whales breakfast thingy."

"Isn't it Save the Whales and Feed the Children?"

Mimi just waved her hand before moving to the kitchen door. "As long as they can cash the check, they don't care what I call it."

Bianca shook her head.

Mimi opened the door and paused, turning to look at Bianca. "Listen, Sweetie, is what they say about a male horse's . . . uhm, well, you know . . . jingy-thingy. Is that . . . is that true, Sweetie?"

Very tongue in cheek, Bianca answered, "Big as my arm," with a meaningful stare.

Mimi sighed as she patted her perfectly coiffed French roll and leaned a little against the door with a soft smile.

"Mimi?" Bianca said to nudge the woman out of her reverie.

"Just made me think of Vincent, my third husband, Sweetie. Now it's so hard to say *he* was good for nothing."

With nothing to say about *that*, Bianca started walking out the kitchen. "Goodbye, Mimi," she called over her shoulder.

"Toodles, Sweetie."

The door closed behind her.

Bianca climbed the spiral wrought iron staircase to the second level of her home. As she strolled into her master suite she looked at her watch. It was 9:30 A.M. Just enough time to shower, change, and head to her clinic for a 10:30 A.M. appointment. Her next appointment after that was at 1 P.M., and she was hoping to visit Mr. Sandman as much as she could before then.

Bianca removed the scrubs she kept in her car for emergency vet calls like last night. Dressed only in the beautiful lace thong she originally put on under her evening gown, Bianca took another deep sip of her drink as she moved over to her night table to check her messages. She had a service answer work-related calls and she'd already checked those messages during her drive from Sandy Springs.

"Hi, this is Bianca. Do what you need to do."

Beep.

Bianca studied her reflection in the oval mirror in the corner, twisting and turning to see if any new cellulite had moved onto her thighs.

"Bunny . . . uh, I mean Bianca—"

She paused at the sound of her father's gravely and distinctive voice. The thought that the days of him calling her by the childhood pet name were gone pained her.

"Call me when you get a chance."

Bianca lowered her hands from examining the pertness of her breasts—and wondering when a man would touch, tease, and taste them again—to reach out for the cordless phone sitting on its base.

Beep.

"Bianca—"

Her hand paused just above the phone and her face became confused at hearing her father's voice . . . again.

"Never mind."

The line went dead.

Beep.

Snatching up the phone she quickly dialed her father's number.

"King Ranch."

"Daddy, this is Bianca. Is something wrong?" she asked.

He remained quiet—and that was more telling than anything he could have said.

"Daddy?" she asked with more firmness in her voice—like she was the parent and he was the child. Bianca pressed the phone closer to her face. "What is it?"

"I need your help. You gotta come home, Bianca."

Hot Like Fire

Prologue

"¿Me das este baile?"

Garcelle Santos looked over her bare shoulder at the tall and handsome dark-skinned man requesting a dance at the wedding reception of Kahron Strong and his new bride, Bianca. The man was Bianca Strong's friend from Atlanta. Armand Touissant.

There was no denying the interest in his eyes, but Garcelle was looking for nothing more than someone to dance and maybe laugh with. She smiled as she placed her hand in his and let him twirl her rather dramatically onto the center of the dance floor. She actually flung her head back and laughed as he pulled her body to his while Syleena Johnson's "I Am Your Woman" played.

"You are one of the most beautiful women I've ever seen in my life," he whispered in her ear, with his hand at the small of her back.

"Thank you," was all that Garcelle said. She hoped that was the end of the talking.

But he continued with his compliments, even trying to press Garcelle's body closer to his. She stepped back from him, with a chastising smile. As they two-stepped, she looked over his broad shoulder with her beautiful, doe-shaped eyes. All of Holtsville was in attendance. Some faces she recognized, and others she didn't.

Kahron and Bianca were dancing together in a playful and sexy way. There was no denying the love and passion. *The fire burns between them so strongly,* Garcelle thought, wishing them well as Armand guided their bodies into a series of turns.

Bianca's father, Hank, was dancing with that whacky Mimi. They made an odd pair: he was so tall and broad, while she was so petite and crazy as hell. Garcelle just shook her head at that pairing.

Kaeden and Kaleb, two of Kahron's brothers, stood at the bar watching a pretty, dark-skinned beauty saunter by. Kaleb said something, and both men looked absolutely wolfish before they laughed. The Strong men really were strikingly handsome, particularly when all four of the brothers were together. Somehow each of them made having prematurely grey hair the sexiest thing ever.

But one was missing. The mean and sullen one.

Feeling mischievous, Garcelle swung her head to the left and then to the right. *How like him not to enjoy the festivities.* When Armand again sent their bodies into a series of turns that drew the attention of the crowd, Garcelle caught a glimpse of silver curls and broad shoulders over in the rear of the reception tent. *Alone.* She whipped her head around and looked at him, only to find that his intense stare was already locked on her. Her heart raced madly.

He had once angered her when he accused her of

stealing. That day they had insulted each other like children, and now they barely spoke to one another. But she couldn't deny that of all the sexy Strong brothers, he was the most divine. And the thought of his eyes on her made her *muy caliente*.

The music changed to an up-tempo song, and Garcelle broke free of Armand's hold, grabbed the full skirts of her crimson dress, and began dancing the salsa all alone. Soon the dance floor cleared, and she was left alone to give in to the passion and electricity of the dance. But she noticed no one. No one but Kade.

Her eyes were locked on him. Even when she spun, she would stop so that she was facing him, and their eyes would lock once more. With each of her spins, she found he was moving closer and closer to the edge of the dance floor.

Garcelle enjoyed the warmth of his eyes as she handled the footwork with ease. The crowd applauded her. She moved her body like a snake when need be. She gyrated her hips like she was working a hoola hoop. She danced like her life was dependent on it.

She danced for him, and even though he stood there, with his hands in his pants pocket, his face the same brooding and unchanging mask, she knew he had not missed one bit of it.

When the music came to an end, Garcelle spun her body across the dance floor until she came to a dramatic stop before him, with her flared skirt floating in the air before it slowly drifted down around her shapely legs. Everyone applauded her, but Garcelle's eyes were locked on Kade's. Pure electricity ran through her body.

Even as she moved away from him, casting one last look at him over her shoulder, Garcelle knew that in that one moment, *everything* between them had changed.

Chapter One

Two Months Later

As soon as the alarm clock sounded and woke him from his sleep, Kade Strong rolled out of bed. No snoozing. No lounging. No adjusting to being awake. No sitting on the side of the bed until he got out of that half asleep–half awake zone. Just up and at 'em. It was time for a hard day's work, and he didn't mind it one bit.

Five years ago, when his father decided to semi-retire from running the daily operation of the ranch, he turned it over to Kade, his oldest son. And Kade had been profoundly touched that his father had entrusted him with Strong Ranch. Kade had always worked the ranch along with his brothers, but now he initiated new ideas and made it his business to take the ranch into the future. So he went from paid manager of the farm to part owner. He never wanted to fail his father or ruin a highly successful business. So if continued success meant working right along with their forty ranch hands from dawn to dusk, then Kade was more than willing to do it. Besides, he always had been a hands-on type of man. Sitting in an office, making sure he didn't get dirt under his nails, wasn't his thing.

Nude, he strode into the adjoining bath of his bedroom and relieved himself, with a long sigh. After flushing the commode, he stretched before he started the shower. He looked down at the sink. One washcloth. One towel. One toothbrush. One rinse cup. One of everything in his life. Constant reminders that he was alone now.

It had been close to three years since his wife, Reema, had passed away. Years that seemed like forever without her.

That's why he hated to be in bed alone. A pillow to hold at night was a poor substitute for spooning his wife. Holding her. Smelling the scent of her hair and her neck. Teasing her nipples in the last moments before he dozed off. Her hand reaching back to lightly rest on his thigh. Their innocent embrace suddenly turning to hot caresses and the most passionate lovemaking ever. The unique scent of their sex. Intimacy. Affection. Love.

Sighing, he stepped inside the shower, pulling the curtain closed as the steam surrounded his body. As he began to lather his washcloth, his elbow slammed against the tiled wall. He winced and swore. The dimensions of the bathtub left a lot to be desired for a man of his size. Six foot five and 225 pounds, Kade was solid and strong. Trying to shower— or God help him—bathe in a bathroom fit for someone under six feet was more injurious to his body than working the ranch.

For a second, as he dragged the soapy cloth across his ridged abdomen, he thought of the master suite at his own house. Reema had made sure everything had been custom built to fit him. The high ceilings. The extra long bed. The oversized Jacuzzi tub. The tiled shower big enough for him to spin in.

The night before Reema died had been his last night in

that house. He hadn't been back since. He hadn't wanted to return.

Kade finished his shower and rushed to get dressed in one of the nearly thirty Dickies uniforms in the closet. As soon as he pulled on his Tims, he left the room and walked across the hall to look in on his seven-year-old daughter, Kadina. Even though he knew she was sleeping, because of the predawn hour, every workday he liked to look in on her before he went out to work the ranch.

She was the only thing that had kept him sane in the first few months after Reema's death. He had had to at least pretend to be strong for his child. Strong. Humph, sometimes he had found it so hard to live up to his name.

Kade shut her bedroom door and jogged down the stairs. The scent of coffee hit him before he even reached the bottom step. Ever since he was a little boy, his mother had gotten up with his father, made him a cup of coffee, and fixed his breakfast before he left to work the ranch every day. Thirty years later, the tradition lived on.

At the sight of his parents, Kade came to a halt just before stepping into the kitchen. His father, Kael, was sliding his hand under his mother's knee-length gown. It was not exactly the warm family scene Kade wanted to be a part of.

Kade backtracked and headed down the hall to the front door. As badly as he craved his morning cup of coffee, he wanted to respect his parents' privacy. He lived with them, and he didn't want to be an intrusion.

Kade jogged down the stairs and climbed into his Ford Expedition. Although he had every intention of heading toward the rear of the ranch, he followed an instinct and, instead, steered his vehicle down the winding road leading to the main highway, in the direction of Summerville, South Carolina. His heart raced a bit as he eventually made the turn off of Highway 17. His grip on the wheel tightened. His body jostled as he drove down the dirt road, swerving around crater-sized potholes.

Set back in the center of three acres of land was *the* house. His house. He climbed out of the SUV, with his eyes fixed on the two-level brick structure of over three thousand square feet. With the Strong Ranch hands keeping up the maintenance of the land as he requested, it appeared to be a warm home awaiting the return of the family, but that house had not been a home for years.

Kade slid his large hands into the pockets of his navy Dickies pants. The silver curls of his prematurely gray hair glistened in the rising sun. Memories unfolded before him like a movie, causing a soft smile to play at his supple lips.

Kade climbed the steps, with his keys in hand, but the front door swung open before he reached the top step. He was surrounded by the sweet and subtle scent of his wife's perfume just before she leaned her tall, full, and curvaceous figure against the door frame, with a welcoming smile filled with the love he knew she had for him.

He paused for a second at the top step as his love—that deep, lasting, one-of-a-kind love—filled his chest. Reema was his wife, his friend, his lover, the mother of his child, the keeper of his secrets, and the believer in his dreams. He couldn't imagine his life without her.

"Hey, you," he greeted her as his smile broadened and his bottomless dimples deepened. It was their first night in their new home. The first of many more to come.

Reema flung her braids over her shoulders as she stepped forward to press her hands against his broad chest and her lips to his. "Welcome home, baby," she said softly against his mouth.

Their eyes locked as Kade pressed his hands against her hips and deepened the kiss.

"Kadina's upstairs napping. Dinner's in the oven keeping warm. . . ."

Kade grinned wolfishly as he bent slightly to swing her ample, curvaceous body up into his strong arms with well-practiced ease. He stepped inside the house and used his foot to kick the front door closed behind them.

The image faded, and Kade swallowed a lump in his throat. He literally shook away the sadness as a tear raced down his cheek. He released a heavy breath and wiped his face.

He leaned back against the SUV and looked up. Everything was calm and serene. He used to love this time of the day. Every morning, before he left their home, Reema would rise with him, just like his mother did for his father. She would fix breakfast, and they would sit on the patio outside the kitchen and watch the sun rise.

It had been so long since he'd let himself enjoy something so simple yet so beautiful. He missed this. He missed a lot of things. His wife. His home. His bed. His privacy. His life.

Kahron Strong sped up Highway 17, heading back from Charleston. He had just made a run to Lowe's for supplies and was anxious to get back to his ranch. Cattle that he purchased at the livestock auction last week were being delivered today, and he was anxious not to miss it. His masculine hands drummed the steering wheel as he listened to "Don't Matter" by Akon, playing on his satellite radio. He was singing along off-key as he looked out at the stretches of emerald green trees and grass lining the highway.

He smiled as he thought of his wife, Bianca. She was a tall, fair-skinned beauty with luscious lips he could suckle forever. She was everything he never knew he wanted. *Everything*.

The wide screen of his BlackBerry lit up where it sat on the passenger seat of his truck. He quickly turned down the volume of the radio and reached for it. His heart skipped a beat.

"Hey, you," he said, his voice filled with warmth, pleasure, and love.

"Hey, you," Bianca said in return, her voice husky with sleep and emotion. "I wanted to see you before you left the house this morning."

"I didn't want to wake you, since you got in so late last night," he said, placing his signature rimless aviator shades atop his silver faded head as he steered the vehicle easily with one hand.

"And *because* I came in so late, I had something I wanted to *give you* this morning."

Kahron's smile broadened at the obvious sexy intent in his wife's voice. He loved and adored the woman. His woman.

When he first saw Bianca King driving her flashy convertible as her riot of curls blew in the wind, he never imagined the mysterious woman would later become the love of his life. She was the one person that knew him better than anyone else.

His eyes shifted to the digital clock on the dash. "I'll be home in ten minutes."

"I'll be waiting."

Kahron felt anticipation fill him as he ended the call and propelled the vehicle forward. Bianca was not only an equine veterinarian servicing the local farms in the area, but also co-owner and operator of King Equine Services, and her time had been stretched thin lately. They had to make time for each other. Since they were used to making love once daily—if not more—they had some making up to do for the last few weeks of their marriage.

Kahron's head swung toward Kade's house as he passed it. He did a double take before quickly pulling his SUV off the paved road and slamming on his brakes. Dirt and pebbles flew up around him. Quickly, he checked for traffic in his mirror before he did an illegal U-turn. He squinted his eyes as he turned left onto the unpaved road leading to Kade's home.

His heart literally ached to see his older brother obviously struggling to enter the house. It was well known that Kade had not been at the house since the night before his wife passed. Kahron wanted to go to him, help him through such an obvious big step in his life, but another part of him knew Kade wanted to do it alone.

Kahron released a heavy and expectant breath as his brother's tall frame finally disappeared through the front door. He snatched up his BlackBerry and quickly dialed the number even as he climbed out of the SUV. "Hey, I need everyone to get over to Kade's ASAP."

Kade was lost in memories he had pushed away and protected from his grief. As he drifted slowly through the house, each room shook some buried emotion from him. Each brought some seemingly insignificant moment in time to the forefront.

He paused in each room as his life played out before him like a movie. Late nights in the den, cuddled with Reema on the couch, watching movies. Coming home late from work and sitting in the nursery to just hold Kadina as she slept. Waking up every morning to that poster-sized photo of them smiling on their wedding day.

His emotions ran the gamut and left him shaky.

In his bedroom, Kade sunk down at the foot of the bed and looked up at the photo as he locked his fingers between his knees. He felt spent. He felt weak. Drained. Depleted. Lost. Incomplete. But for the first time in years, he also felt hope, peace, and confidence that he was ready for the future. As one lone tear raced down his cheek, he stood and walked out of the house, knowing it was time to move on with life.

Kade paused as he stepped out onto the porch. Surprise filled his handsome face, and he quickly wiped the moisture from high cheekbones. His deep-set eyes took in each compassion-filled face of his family as they stood at the base of the steps. His parents, Kael and Lisha Strong. Kaleb, Kaeden, Kaitlyn, and Kahron and Bianca. Somehow he wasn't at all surprised to see them there. Not at all.

"You okay, son?" Kael called out in that deep baritone voice of his as he hugged his wife close to his side.

Kade nodded as he descended the few steps into their midst. "I'm good. In fact, I'm better than I've been in a long time."

Kaitlyn stepped forward and wrapped her arm around his waist. "What's going on?" she asked, bumping her hip against his side.

He lifted his hand to muss her short crop of dyed jet-black hair. "I've decided that Kadina and I are going to move back into the house," he told them, playfully looking down at his palm for dye before he wiped his hand on his pants leg. The brothers all loved teasing their baby sister about dyeing the grey out of her hair.

Kaitlyn just gave him a saucy eye roll.

Even as his brothers all stepped forward to either hug

him close or clap him soundly on the back, and his sister and sister-in-law kissed his cheek, he saw the immediate concern on his mother's face. Kade moved through the small group and pulled her into a tight embrace.

He smiled at the way her head barely reached his chest. "We'll be fine, Ma," he assured her as she squeezed him tightly.

"Did we say or do something?" she asked, tilting her head back to look up at him. "You know how much I love having Kadina and you around the house."

"It's just time. That's all," replied Kade. "That's the *only* reason."

Her eyes searched his for a few moments before she hugged him one last time and nodded her head in understanding. Then she stepped back from him.

Kaeden stepped forward to playfully punch Kade's arm. "My big brother just wants to get back to normal, right?"

Kade nodded. "Right," he agreed. "Now I want to say . . . especially while you're all here," Kade continued, giving each of his brothers a long and meaningful stare. "I'm not ready for this to become a bachelor pad, with women coming in and out of here quicker than cars at a drive-thru window."

Each of the brothers nodded in understanding, and Kade hoped they truly did understand. His eyes took in that comfortable and loving way Bianca massaged his brother's back, and he glanced away. He hated to admit to the jealousy he felt about their intimacy.

"Well, who's gonna help you with Kadina?" Lisha asked. "Getting her ready for school when you're already up and at the ranch. Her hair. Her meals."

Bianca pulled a rubber band from the back pocket of her jeans and gathered her hair into a ponytail. "I agree,

Kade. You're going to need help. So much of your time is wrapped up in the ranch."

Kade held up his hand before his mother could even let the offer flow from her lips. "Thanks, Ma, but no thanks. Dad has just about retired, and it's time you do the same. You two should buy that camper and travel, the way you always said you would."

"He can hire a nanny," Kaeden offered.

"Oh God, and wind up on the six o'clock news, with all the weirdos in the world today?" Lisha retorted.

"Yes, make me have to catch a case, Kade," Kaitlyn added.

"I'm not saying go find any jackrabbit on the street," Kaeden countered. "There are many reputable agencies that thoroughly screen their employees."

"Oh, like the Catholic Church?" Kaitlyn flung back.

Kade released a heavy breath as nearly his entire family began a full-blown debate on the pros and cons of hiring a nanny. He loved his family. He cherished them, but . . . they could be overwhelming at times.

He slid his hands into the pockets of his Dickies and shook his head a bit as he looked heavenward and licked his lips.

"I have just the solution for you, brother-in-law," said Bianca.

Kade lowered his eyes and then looked into Bianca's smiling face. "Give it to me, sister-in-law."

"Garcelle," she said simply, with a subtle lift of her rounded shoulders.

"Garcelle?" asked Kade.

"Garcelle," she said again, with finality.

Kade squinted his eyes as he thought of Garcelle.

Having worked the last couple of years as Kahron and Bianca's part-time cook and housekeeper, Garcelle Santos had already proven herself to be trustworthy and loyal. She was the daughter of Kahron's foreman—someone else who had proven to be a valuable asset to his brother's business. And although Kade had treated the woman with suspicion and some disdain during their first meeting, he had come to see just how very wrong he was.

Kadina already loved Garcelle. Everyone did. She was more of a family friend than an employee. She was perfect for Kadina.

Kade nodded. "Garcelle," he stated, with equal finality.

"Good," Bianca agreed, with a wink, before turning and walking back to the rest of the family.

Garcelle. Yes, she is just what I need, thought Kade.

The seemingly innocent thought startled him. He shook his head as if to clear it. *I mean she's just what Kadina needs,* he corrected himself before stepping forward to rejoin his family.

Live And Learn

Prologue

Ladies

"Check *this* bitch out."

Three more pairs of eyes in varying shades of brown immediately darted like bullets to the feet of their unknowing victim. The woman sashayed by their table in the crowded nightclub with her head held high, unaware of their catty criticism and disdainful looks.

"Pay-*less*," the four friends sang in mocking unison, distaste obvious on their faces as they thought of the national shoe store specializing in low-end footwear. It was one chain of stores they wouldn't dare frequent.

When it came to fashion, they searched for only the best labels: Gucci, Prada, Roberto Cavalli, Armani, and Dolce & Gabbana—just to name drop a few. Fresh hairdos and nails were weekly necessities. And when it came to the men who flittered in and out of their lives with the longevity of a lit match, only those who could afford their taste got a second look: celebrities, athletes, and wealthy warriors of the streets who had blown up like a keg of TNT. *Unless* he had that "turn your straight roots nappy" kind of sex that the women enjoyed. But those sex-you-down brothas didn't get any of their real time—just late night calls to supply them with a nut, if their more financially set man at the moment couldn't do the job.

Alizé, Moët, "Dom" Perignon and Cristal—a.k.a. Monica Winters, Latoya James, Keesha Lands, and Danielle Johnson, respectively—were four childhood friends. They were sisters without the blood lineage with plenty of lessons to learn.

Chapter One

"Whassup y'all?
I'm Alizé."

I'm anything but a morning person, especially *this* particular morning. Rah's king-sized water bed felt too damn good, and my body felt hella bad. A late night of drinking, partying, and then having sex until three in the morning will do that to you.

Last night my girls and I all met up at Lex's apartment—that's Dom's boyfriend—to celebrate his twenty-fifth birthday. Whoo! We got so tore up off Henny—ahem, Hennessey—that I didn't want to see any more liquor for a minute. I could feel the effects of it all up and through my body. Trust.

There was no way I was ready to face the world yet, but I had a ten o'clock class.

Trying like hell not to wake my man up, I eased up the arm he had over my waist. I couldn't do nothing but roll my eyes when he stirred in his sleep and tried to hold me tighter. Rah and I were cool. We were basically happy with each other, but when I wasn't in the mood to fuck, I just wasn't—in—the—mood—to—fuck. Too bad I couldn't get *his* ass to understand that.

"Rah, I gotta get up. Move."

He shifted closer to me and pressed what I hoped was a piss hard against my bare ass. "Where you goin'?" he asked, his voice full of sleep and his morning breath reaching me like a slap in the face. His hand rose to tease my nipple as he started kissing my shoulder.

Now I was wishing like hell that I'd gone home to my mom's and not spent the night at his apartment. My own mother wasn't *this* aggravating, and she was Mrs. Persistence with an extra large, extra tall, big and bold-ass capital *P*. My daddy swears it's one of the main reasons they got divorced. I couldn't front on my father; my mother could be hell to reckon with.

But let me repeat, when I wasn't in the mood to fuck, there wasn't shit *anybody* could do to get me in the mood.

I shifted his hand from my breast, but he just moved it down to lift my leg up to play in my moistness. "Rah, I gotta go to class. Let me up."

I was a senior at Seton Hall University in South Orange, NJ, majoring in business finance. I loved money and all of the nice things it bought, so my major was an easy choice for me. Oh, trust, I'm a sistah with a plan when it comes to my career. I will graduate this May and then take full benefit of my two-month summer internship at one of the top investment firms in the country. Then in the fall it will be back to the grind at ole SHU to work on the all-important MBA—Master of Business Administration to some and More Banking of Assets to me.

I'm headed to the top of the corporate ladder with my MBA in one hand and my Gucci briefcase in the other as

I take no prisoners and accept no shorts. I'm *going* to be part of the next wave of African-American women bursting through the glass ceiling. My name *will* be on *Fortune* magazine's Fifty Most Powerful Black Executives. *Black Enterprise* magazine will do a spotlight on me and my rise to the top. I ain't playing.

One thing I know about myself: if I set a goal I will reach it. Anyone not with my program can either ride with me or get run the fuck over. Period.

"Skip class."

See, *that* ain't part of my program.

"Roll over, baby," he moaned against my neck as his hand rose again to claim my breast. Neither my body, mind, nor spirit was in the mood.

See, money is power, and right now Rah was thinking— whether he said it or not—that he was the money man in the relationship, so he could get this pussy whenever he wanted.

He thought wrong.

I turned on my back and looked up into his fine face with "the look"—a mix of faked sadness and regret that gets 'em every time. Trust. "Baby, I wish I had time, but I'm running late and I have a big test today that I can't miss," I lied with ease. "You know I get sleepy after sex."

Rah pulled me atop him and slapped my ass with a quick kiss to my cheek. "Get goin' 'fore I change my mind."

I felt like a prisoner who got a "get out of jail free" card. I didn't hesitate to roll out of bed and dash into the bathroom.

I literally jumped back at my reflection in the mirror. I looked like a cross between Don King and a raccoon with my thick shoulder-length hair all tangled and sticking up over my head. There were telling circles under my red-rimmed eyes that didn't look good at all against my bronzed cinnamon complexion. Drool was dried on my face.

Too much partying. Too much drinking. Too much damn fun. And it showed big-time.

After a long hot shower, a facial, a few eye drops, and getting rid of the tangles in my hair with a ventilated brush, I felt a *little* better. I could only shake my head at the condition of my hair. Even though I'd just been for my weekly appointment to the hairdresser yesterday, I would be on my cell at nine sharp making an appointment for later today. There's no way I'm sporting a dang-on ponytail all weekend.

Looking and dressing my best was important to me. See, my girls and I always made sure we stepped out of the house with our shit together from our hairdos to our Jimmy Choo shoes. This was a must.

All through high school and our entrance into early adulthood we were the popular ones. Other girls either hated us or wanted to be one of us. We kept our hair in the latest styles, and our gear was always the trend. We wore nothing but designer fashions: from the stonewashed Guess jeans and Timberlands of the nineties to Prada and Manolos in the new millennium.

Ever since our freshman year at University High there were always just the four of us. We looked out for one another. We had each other's backs. There's an unbreakable trust between us built on ten years of friendship and sisterhood.

There's Latoya, Keesha, and Danielle, a.k.a. Moët, "Dom" Perignon, and Cristal. Dom came up with the nicknames one day back in 2000 while we were eating lunch in the caf. She got the idea from the late and great rapper Biggie Smalls' 1994 classic "Juicy." Those nicknames made us even more popular, and they've stuck ever since.

Six years later, although no one was really popping Dom as much, and Jay-Z had called for a boycott of

Cristal because some bigwig had dissed hip-hop, we kept those names.

Oh, me? I'm Monica, but everyone *except* my parents calls me Alizé. No, I don't have a fancy champagne name like everyone else, but that's cool. Just like the drink, I'm the sweetest of the bunch anyway.

I didn't leave the bathroom until I wrapped a towel around my body because there was no need to tempt fate. I was too happy to open the door and find the bedroom empty. I heard him in the kitchen.

Good. He loved to catch me fresh from the shower or a bath and eat me out.

I grabbed my overnight bag and pulled out some fresh undergarments to hurry into. My cell phone rang. As I sprayed on the only perfume I wear—Happy, by Clinique— I picked my phone up and flipped it open, forgetting the mandatory check of my caller ID.

"Hey," I said in a little singsong fashion—my usual greeting.

"Whaddup, baby girl."

I felt my face wrinkle into a nasty frown as I recognized my ex's voice. I couldn't stand the sight, smell, or sound of Malik's sorry ass. This knucklehead tried to holler at Cristal behind my back.

That was a definite no-no.

Being the home girl Cristal was, she told me all about it . . . *after* she slapped the hell out of him.

But that wasn't the first time Cris and I didn't let a boy cause drama between us.

It was 1999. Freshman year of high school. New school. New faces. New rules. New cliques.

And since I was the only one from my elementary

school to get accepted into University High, that meant new friends, but I had no worries.

I was looking good in the latest Parasuco gear. My bob was laid out, and my gold jewelry was in place. My pocketbook and bookbag were Gucci. My parents were *real* good to me. Being the only child had its benefits.

All eyes were on me as soon as I walked into my homeroom. The various conversations buzzing around the room lulled. A few of the boys whistled or shot me their "let me holla at you" smile. I went right into spin control and threw on a smile like I had the world in the palm of my hand. A few people smiled in return. A couple of girls immediately bent together, and I felt like they were talking about me.

There was an empty seat next to a tall, slender girl with skin the color of shortbread cookies. She was busy flirting back with a slender dark-skinned kid with long, asymmetrical braids and a big Kool–Aid smile. I made my way past the rows of students in chairs with attached desks, speaking to every last person I made eye contact with.

"Whassup," I said to Shortbread and Braids as I set my things on the long bookshelf behind us.

Braids looked at me from the tip of my fresh white Nikes to my eyes, not missing anything in between. There was no denying the interested look in his deep-set hazel eyes as he turned in his chair to face me and turn his back to Shortbread. "Better yet, shorty, how *you* doin'?"

I saw the disappointment on Shortbread's face, and even though he was as fine as Tyrese, I wasn't looking for drama this early in the school year. "I'll be doin' even better when you go back in her face and out of mine."

His pretty-boy face fell, and I knew lover boy was shocked that all his deliciousness rolled off my back like water.

Shortbread laughed, holding her hand over her mouth. "No need him turning this way again," she said with attitude.

"Oh, so both y'all gone play me?" he asked, straight white and even teeth flashing.

We both looked at him like "Negro, please."

He sucked his teeth, waved his hand, and turned to a dark-skinned cutie sitting in front of him.

Shortbread and I looked at each other, gave each other some dap, and then laughed at how we shut down his wanna-be playa ass.

"I'm Monica."

"Danielle."

We've been inseparable ever since, and we've always been loyal to each other.

Too bad Malik's dumb ass didn't know that.

"What you want?" I snapped, my eyes flashing as I focused my attention back on him. "No! As a matter of fact, who gives a shit?"

I slammed the phone closed, immediately dismissing that clown. True, his money had been good and he had been free-giving with it, but bump that, I don't need a no-good Negro trying to pay me with one of my girls. When it comes to shit like that, I'm like Aretha: give me my R-E-S-P-E-C-T, understand?

Besides, I've moved on to bigger and better things. Malik didn't have nothing on Rah.

Once a big-time drug dealer, Rah had pooled his money and bought businesses that let him get out of the game before the game got him.

Okay, Malik can throw down a thousand times better in bed, but R-E-S-P-E-C-T, remember?

It's not like I ever loved Malik or even Rah for that matter. Shit, I've never been in love and that's fine by me. Love's nothing but a bunch of bullshit. What I wanted from men, I got: money, nights out on the town, shopping sprees, and companionship when I wanted it.

True, Cristal was always hounding me about my need for "thug love," but I liked me a roughneck. Timbs and "wifebeaters" turned me on more than suits and ties. A hard brotha with that swagger and an "I don't give a fuck" attitude made me wet while those whitewashed brothas (from the same corporate world I yearned to be a part of) made me laugh.

I can't explain it. I just liked what I liked.

Rah walked into the bedroom naked as the day he was born and smoking a blunt as thick as three fingers. I was glad my ass was already dressed.

A little shopping excursion would be good, but putting up with him and his minute-man sex wasn't on my agenda for the day.

He held the blunt between his straight and even teeth as he climbed back into bed. "What time you get out of class?"

"I have classes all day and my dance class tonight. Did you need something?"

"Naw, I'm straight. I'll be at the new store all day," he said, reaching for the remote to turn on the sixty-one-inch flat screen on the wall.

"Wish me luck on my test," I said, moving to the bedroom door.

"Good luck." He exhaled a thick silver cloud from his pursed lips. "Love you, baby girl."

"And I love you, too," I said without pause.

Another lie. Maybe the biggest of them all.

Show And Tell

Prologue

Ladies

2000

The four teenage girls walked through the double doors of University High's cafeteria like they owned the school. They knew without looking that all eyes were on them. Hating them and hating on them. They were used to it and maybe even thrived on it a bit. Popularity. Envy. High school fame.

Even as they settled at "their" table and began munching on the sandwiches they purchased from the store up the street—of course the cafeteria food was a no-no— people watched them. Wanted to be them. Wanted to be with them. But it was just the four.

Friends since freshman year, they weren't looking to

enlarge their clique. It was them and only them. One for all and all for one. Even though they all were as different as night and day, they clicked. They had each other's backs. They knew their friendship would last past their high school years.

"Did y'all see the new Biggie video last night?" Keesha Lands asked, in the Tommy Hilfiger tank she wore with tight-fitting jeans. Her gold herringbone chain and bamboo earrings gleamed against her smooth dark skin and seemed to glisten in her cat-shaped eyes.

"Not me," Latoya James said, looking prim and proper as always in her white collared shirt and ankle-length navy blue skirt with her shoulder-length hair pulled back into a tight ponytail that seemed to make her caramel complexion stretch.

Danielle Johnson rolled her deep-set eyes heavenward as she applied pale pink lip gloss that perfectly matched her fair complexion and pretty features. "My new foster family let their sickening sons watch *Nickelodeon* last night," she said, putting the gloss into her Esprit purse before taking a bite of food. She made sure not to spill a drop on her dark denim dress.

"Well, I'm an only child and my parents ain't churchy, so you know I was right there in front of the TV," Monica Winters said, flipping her thick shoulder-length jet black hair over her shoulder as she flashed them a sassy smile on her cinnamon face. She did a little dance in her seat and winked at Keesha.

Keesha started rapping the words to "Juicy" and the girls all joined in with her. Even Latoya knew the words, although her parents ran a secular music-free zone. Ever since pulling the shy church girl into their fold, the girls were sure to bring Latoya up to speed on everything fun and fly.

They all laughed and gave each other high fives after they finished.

"Well, I've decided to call myself Dom," Keesha stated with confidence.

"Dom?" the other girls all asked in unison.

"Yup, Dom as in Dom Perignon," she explained with attitude. She pointed to Latoya. "You're Moët . . . Danielle, you're Cristal—"

"What about me?" Monica asked, feeling left out.

"I don't know any more champagnes," Keesha said with a helpless shrug. "But Biggie's always talking about Alizé. I heard it's a real sweet drink with liquor in it."

"Then that's me to a tee," Monica said with satisfaction.

The four girls all raised their cans of soda and toasted their new names.

Chapter One

Cristal

"Hello, this is Cristal again. I have my mind on money and money on my mind."

2008

Okay. Let me explain how I feel in my man's arms—*if* it is at all explainable. I feel secure. Loved. Cherished. Pampered. Needed. Perhaps most important of all . . . I feel wanted. Growing up as a foster kid and not knowing if my parents were dead, alive, or indifferent, feeling wanted is important as hell to me.

I am Cristal, or Danielle Johnson, and my man is Mohammed Ahmed. He is tall, handsome, and strong with cocoa-scented dreads that reach to his waist. He is everything I ever needed and nothing that I ever wanted.

Just *try* to make me leave him.

"Danielle," he whispers in my ear with that sexy Jamaican lilt.

I shiver as he presses his warm naked body above mine. My legs spread with ease as I wrap them around his waist. His body and the bed sandwich me. The feel of his hard dick against my belly makes me anxious. Ready. Waiting.

As he bends his strong muscled back to lower his mouth—that delicious and skillful mouth—to my breast, he circles his tongue around my nipple. Clockwise. Counterclockwise. He uses his strong hips to prod the tip of his dick between my lips. We both gasp hotly. He circles his hips, pressing his hardness against my walls. Clockwise. Counterclockwise.

Jesus.

These moments in his arms and his bed are worth it all. Worth every damn thing I gave up for him. For this. Each stroke delivers my point home.

The money.

Pop.

The fame.

Pop-pop.

The fancy houses and cars.

Pop-pop-pop.

The glamorous life.

Pop-pop-pop-pop.

Mrs. Sahad Linx.

Pop-pop-pop-pop-pop-pop-pop.

All of it. Gone.

We are in tune with one another. United. Joined. He knows he is making me cum and that makes his dick harder than jail time. And that makes me cum even harder until I am panting. Sweating. Clutching him with my pussy walls and my limbs as he strokes harder and faster inside of me.

"Yes," I cry out as he leans up a bit to look down at me with those silky brown eyes I love.

His sweat drips down onto my titties as each of his

pumps makes them bounce up and down. "Dick good ain't it?" he asks roughly as his face gets intense. "Huh? Huh?"

"Yes, baby, yes," I whisper as I reach up to caress his handsome face with my quivering hands.

His head whips to the right to capture my fingers in his mouth. He sucks them deeply as he slows down his strokes to a lethal grind that brings the base of that dick against my clit.

Damn. Goddamn. Damn. Damn.

"Watch this, Miss Danielle," he says thickly around my fingers.

I already know what time it is.

His entire body freezes as he looks hotly down into my eyes. I feel the jolt of his dick against my clit as he fills me with his cum. He smiles as he licks my fingers like the freak that he is. Each pluck of my clit pushes me further over the edge until I am working my hips up and down off the bed to pull downward on *my* dick. His mouth forms a circle as he closes his eyes and pushes down deeper into me.

I reach up to snatch off the leather strap holding his hair and his dreads surround our heads like a curtain. "Who the best? Huh? Who?" I whisper up to him.

"Danielle . . . Danielle . . . Danielle," he chants as I drain that dick until it is empty.

With one final kiss to my lips, he rolls over onto his back and then pulls my weak body to his side. I gladly snuggle my face against his chest and take a deep breath of his scent like I can absorb it into me. With his free arm, he reaches over to turn off the lamp.

"Damn, that was good," he whispers into the darkness before he slaps my butt cheek playfully.

"I aim to please," I whisper back with a smile.

He laughs a little but soon his snores fill the air.

Damn, I love him.

* * *

"Good morning, Miss Danielle."

I open my eyes and stretch. There he is just as constant as time looking down at me as he lays on his side on the bed. Okay, I love him but I do not do morning breath, Okay? All right.

I pull the thin sheet up over my nose. "Good morning."

Mohammed just laughs at me before he flings back the covers and rolls out of bed. "You have time for breakfast?" he asks over his broad shoulder.

I hardly hear him. I am too busy letting my eyes skim over the hard details of his back and buttocks. "No, I did not bring a change of clothes," I finally answer once he turns fully to look at me.

Mohammed reaches down to open a drawer. "What do we have here?" he says mockingly. "An empty drawer. What should we fill it with? Any suggestions, Danielle?"

I give him a sarcastic smile. First a drawer and then some of the closet and then pack up all your things and move in. Nothing doing. The last time I lived with a man he threw me out of his penthouse apartment. Well, he caught me cheating (ahem, *with* Mohammed) but that did not excuse the fact that if I had not kept my apartment for my friends, Dom and Moët, to live in, then my pretty high-yellow behind would have been homeless. To make matters worse, he kept mostly everything he ever bought me, even down to my lacy La Perla underwear.

No. I am nicely settled back in my beautiful apartment in The Top in Livingston. I have my best friends to help me keep up the hefty rent. Sure, I had to get used to the lack of quiet or privacy but it is *mine* and no one can throw me out.

Plus . . . Mohammed's house left *a lot* to be desired.

"One day, baby. One day," I promise as I roll out of bed.

I look at him and I know from the look on his face that he did not believe me. Truth. He is smart not to. I begin to climb back in the Gap charcoal gray turtleneck and pencil skirt I wore to our dinner date to IHOP last night. I wish I had a pair of sneakers to throw on instead of my suede high-heeled boots. As soon as I pull on my black leather trench, I walk over to where Mohammed is lounging across the foot of the bed watching a recap of some football game.

"Enjoy your day off," I tell him as I bend down to snuggle his cheek.

Mohammed is the repair man at The Top. My friends, Dom, Alizé, and Moët, still cannot believe I am with him. Not when my life used to be about men who helped keep me from my life of robbing Peter to pay Paul. Athletes. Celebrities. Wealthy businessmen. I had been on the hunt to be the ultimate celebrity wife. My ex-fiancé Sahad Linx is the CEO of Platinum Records. His money, his fame, and his lifestyle had almost been mine. I let it slip through my fingers like sand so that my hands were free to grab Mohammed.

He reaches across to lightly touch my face and I get chills. Fuck the money and the fame. I got love and lots of it.

"See you later?" he asks in that Jamaican accent that has the power to make me wet.

"Yes," I whisper against his lips.

Walking out of that bedroom and leaving my man in the bed naked, willing, and with his dick rising is almost as hard as he is. I try not to judge his house as I grab my hobo from the kitchen table. I can fit half of Mohammed's entire three-bedroom house inside my living room. It is furnished just like the bachelor he is. Mismatched this. Tore-up that. Wal-Mart this. Target that. Mohammed likes to say his house has character. Whatever.

I look inside my Gucci purse (a purchase from my more glamorous days) for my keys and my hand rubs across my "bible." Forgetting the keys, I pick up the address book. Inside is each and every man I have ever dated or slept with. For each man there is a brief bio and a photo, if I had one. I used dollar signs to rate how free giving they were with their money, and stars to rate how good they were in bed. The more dollar signs and stars the better.

But this book isn't me anymore. Since I have been with Mohammed I have not made an entry. I have not called one number. I have good friends. A good man. A good life.

I am happy. I am.

Then why do I still have it?

Ignoring the answer to that million-dollar question, I shove the address book down deep in my bag. I finally close my fingers around the keys before I rush out of the house.

More of the Hottest
African-American Fiction from
Dafina Books